M000284874

By Sharon Skinner

In Case You Didn't Hear Me the First Time

*The Nelig Stones**
*Mirabella and the Faded Phantom**

Also from brickcavebooks.com

* Forthcoming

THE HEALER'S LEGACY

Sharon Skinner

Renee –

Joyful journeys!

Sharon

SFCC 2014

Brick Cave Media Books, Mesa

Cover Illustration by Thitipon Dicruen [xric7].

Brick Cave Media
brickcavebooks.com
2012

To all the amazing, supportive women in my life.
Thank you.

Acknowledgments

I would be remiss in not personally thanking those individuals who helped to make this book a reality. Thank you to Anne Lind, my friend and one of the most amazing editors I know, for her willingness to read and reread my work and always help me make it better. Thank you to Diane Tuccillo, for her unflagging belief in my writing, and for the amazing hikes that got me out and away from the computer. Thanks most especially to my mother, Joan Katz, for reading the (really) early drafts and for her amazing support through the years.

I am so grateful to know you all.

CHAPTER ONE

Kira tasted blood. She ran her tongue along the inside of her swollen mouth and winced. The cut on her lip had reopened. Shifting in her saddle to ease the pain that burned through her body, she glanced at the men who rode beside her. They were tough and strong, battle-hardened soldiers, two of Toril's fiercest fighters. "Escorts," he'd called them. Kira knew only too well what they really were.

The other four men were younger and less experienced. Kira didn't know them well, but the thin rider behind her seemed uneasy. Reins grasped tight, back rigid, he wasn't much more than a boy, his light beard not yet grown in. He'd been among her escort for several weeks, but unlike the other men, surprise and concern had flitted across his face when she'd limped out of her tent that morning, her face swollen and fresh bruises darkening against her pale skin.

They plodded along beneath the thick canopy of beech and oak, while high above, glittering scales flashed among the dark leaves. *Take care, Vaith! Stay hidden.* Kira averted her eyes from the small winged reptile perched overhead and forced herself to stare forward.

The late summer heat thickened about the riders as they emerged from the shade of the forest. Faded wildflowers bordered the dusty track, and Kira squinted her eyes against the sun's sudden glare. The cottage stood

1

alone at the near end of the wide vale, just as she remembered. Its weathered walls had cracked, and the thatched roof with its bare patches showed the wear and tear of the past year's harsh seasons. The shallow creek still ran out of the forest, passing within yards of the lonely house before hastening along its course toward a distant lake, but the water of the narrow rivulet barely reached halfway up its banks, and the reeds beside it were yellow and withered.

The yard in front of the cottage was also withered. The plot of herbs that had once grown bright and green, now a barren space of dirt spotted with weeds. A tangle of discarded objects lay piled beside the house, a broken loom, some faded rags and an assortment of cracked pots. Bits and pieces of things no longer useful. The sorrowful state of the house and yard plunged a dagger of guilt into her. Things had changed a great deal since she had lived here with Heresta, helping with the gardening and housekeeping chores.

Kira had changed, too. But returning here, seeing this place again, made her realize she was, in many ways, still the young girl who had trotted along beside Heresta, carrying bundles of herbs and looking with wonder at the seemingly simple roots and leaves that harbored so many amazing properties inside them. She wondered how much her sudden leave taking had changed Heresta. Her hands shook. Could she truly face her old mentor, now? What words could mend the breach she had created between them?

She took a calming breath to steady her nerves and strained to sit up straight. Her gray horse, Trad, stepped lightly, as if to avoid jarring his bruised passenger, but the men ignored her discomfort. Most of them avoided looking at her, not because seeing her battered face bothered them, but because they feared the violence Toril might inflict on them should they show too much interest in his woman.

Out of the corners of her eyes, Kira studied two men who rode beside her. She was tall, but both men were each at least a head taller than she, broad shouldered and muscular. Dagger, on her right, had taken his name from a badly healed knife wound that left a scar that ran the full length of the left side of his face. He sat astride his horse, rigid, and scowling as if he believed that the task of guarding Toril's woman was beneath him. Or perhaps, Kira considered, like her he would rather be any place else.

The black-haired man on her left, whom she knew as Rasten, rode lazily, reins looped over the pommel. He glanced over and caught her looking at him. An evil-looking smirk crossed his face before she turned her eyes away. Rasten had a reputation for being merciless on the battlefield, and Kira could well believe it.

The men halted their horses a short distance from the cottage as Kira rode on into the dusty dooryard. She dismounted, easing her aching muscles out of the saddle, and smiled to herself. Every one of the waiting men was frightened of this place. The fools believed the death of a healer to be a bad omen.

Omens and superstitions! Kira struggled to keep herself from laughing at them. It was true that some healers had more skills than simple herb lore. Some, like Heresta, had the gift of seeing, through dreams and visions, into the future. But most were simply trained to heal, using the gifts that nature supplied. Yet, many people still feared them.

Heresta had often told her that one of the greatest weaknesses of all men and women was fear, especially of the unknown. Once, when she was still a child, Kira had asked her mentor why the healers would allow the superstitions and legends about them to stay alive if they weren't true.

Heresta had answered with shrug. "Are not the healers' skills highly valued by a warlord and his army, kitten? Do not healers tend the wounded and mend them so they may fight again? And if you were a warlord, would you not kill your enemy's healers if you did not have a reason to fear harming them?" Kira had marveled, knowing she had been given the gift of a great secret, one she would keep and take with her when the time finally came for her to return to the wheel of life.

Kira's leather boots raised puffs of dust from the dry earth as she led Trad to a grassy area beside the stream. She stroked his neck, whispering into his ear that he should graze and wait. Glancing back, Kira saw Dagger's eyes narrow, a sneer creasing his face. Kira knew the men watched her suspiciously, that they believed her ability with animals to be some sort of healer's magic. Yet, not one of them ever questioned why Toril had not died of slow poison or suffered an evil curse for his treatment of her. Ignorance. Worse: ignorance without question. Let them think what they would.

She dropped her reins and strode across the yard, rapped on the door and waited. No sound came from inside, so she pushed open the door. The leather hinges had been recently oiled and the door swung inward without a squeak. So, at least someone has been helping to care for a few of Heresta's needs, Kira thought, and she blessed the unknown benefactor. She stood for a moment in the doorway, hesitating. She told herself she was simply allowing her eyes to adjust to the dim light inside before stepping into the gloom, but it was more than that. A full year had passed since her sixteenth birthday and the last time she and Heresta had spoken. Their last quarrel had ended abruptly when Kira had cursed Heresta for a bitter old woman with no room for love in her heart and slammed out of the hut. Kira knew her words were lies when she spat them at Heresta, knew they were malicious and meant to inflict pain, but she couldn't stop herself. And once spoken, she'd been too stubborn, too ashamed, to take them back. She drew in a halting breath and squared her shoulders, then stepped inside, letting the door swing shut behind her.

Kira inhaled the familiar scent of roots and herbs. Nothing seemed to have changed since she'd left. Even the mess, she thought ruefully. Many hours of her youth had been spent straightening up after the brilliant, but disorganized, healer.

Plain furnishings and clutter filled the single room. A still form lay on the bed against the far wall. Kira's breath fluttered in her throat as she crossed to the narrow pallet.

Heresta had grown thin, her cheeks sunken with age and illness. Her chest rose and fell in shallow breaths. When she'd sent word, asking for Kira to come to her, Toril had raged at the idea. But even as powerful a warlord as he, would not dare risk the punishment his superstition imagined by denying the final wish of a dying healer. He'd allowed Kira to come, but not alone. And not before he'd given her a sample of what would happen if she tried to leave him again. Last night's beating was nothing to his uncontrolled brutality after her last escape. Her freedom had been brief and had cost her dearly. Kira shrank from the memory.

Outside the healer's hut, Toril's men waited for her to say good-bye to the dying woman, the woman who had raised her and trained her as an apprentice in the healing arts. They would be impatient to leave, fearful of being present at the time when a healer's spirit left the body. Foolish fear based on superstition and misunderstanding of what was a natural turn on the wheel, Kira thought. *Let them worry.* Heresta had been like a mother to Kira after her parents were killed. She wouldn't leave before the old healer had departed on her journey to the wheel. In the meantime, she would do all she could to ease and comfort her for what time remained.

She tiptoed about the room, pulling bits of dried herbs from the bundles that hung from the rafters and walls—sweet balm, maythen, skullcap, willow bark, battree flowers, lammint. She rolled the leaves and stems back and forth between the palms of her hands to release their oils. Then she tied the herbs in a clean piece of cloth and dropped them into the small iron pot on the hearth. She stirred the embers in the fireplace and added kindling, ladled fresh water into the pot and hung it on the blackened metal hook over the fire. The smell of soothing herbs filled the room as the mixture warmed and began to steam.

She leaned over to dip out some of the sweet-scented liquid, pouring it into a worn wooden bowl to cool. Turning back, she saw Heresta's eyelids flutter, then open, and the corners of her mouth turned up in a weak smile. "I knew you would come, kitten," she said. She used her pet name for Kira, as if they'd never been apart, as if Kira had never flung harsh words at her and stormed out of the door. Kira hung her head, remembering how she'd been so blinded by her love for Toril that she'd refused to listen to the voice of reason. Love? But how could she have loved anyone who could become so cruel? No, she thought, it couldn't have been love. But then, what else could have driven her to behave the way she had?

Kira's eyes stung, but tears refused to come. "Hello, old raven," she whispered. She raised her head to survey the thin woman lying before her.

"You see," Heresta said, "some things are not forgotten so easily. Some things do not change." Her voice was weak, but there was a teasing lilt to her words.

Kira wondered how it was that Heresta could act as if nothing had happened. The old healer made it seem as if they had never argued, as if they'd only been apart for days, not the full four quadrants of a year. Kira shook her head. "Nor do some people, nor their habits," she managed to tease back as her gaze swept the untidy room.

Heresta started to laugh, but her breath was ragged and her laughter became a body-jarring cough. The cough came from deep inside, and Kira heard in it the sound of the fluid that filled the healer's lungs, slowly drowning her. Kira felt a tightness grasp her chest. She waited for the coughing to stop, then offered the herbal brew. The old woman nodded assent and Kira helped her raise her head so she could sip from the proffered bowl. Afterward, Heresta lay back on the bed, sighing as the herbs eased her pain.

Kira set the bowl down onto the table before pulling a low stool over to sit beside the bed. Heresta's eyes glittered in the firelight, shining as they had when she'd taught Kira the secrets of herbs and healing.

"Forgive me, old raven. I should never have left you." Kira's throat constricted.

"Would you have stayed here always? Never to leave?"

Kira's hand shook as she clasped the old woman's bony fingers. "Perhaps not. But I was wrong to leave the way I did. You were right. I saw only what I wanted to see. I let my desire blind me to the truth."

"As is the way with youth and love." Heresta's wispy hair, floating on the pillow about her face, caught the firelight and glowed like a silver aura. "The truth is often hard, and less desirable than our dreams. But it is not for me to forgive you. It is you who need to forgive yourself, child. You who have been unjustly punished for your choice." She gave Kira a knowing look. "My eyes are still as strong as ever. These shadows cannot hide his brutality. And I know that the pain goes deeper than the flesh. Tell me, why do you stay?"

Kira turned away, her shame bringing the blood to her cheeks. "I've tried to leave," she whispered. After a moment she turned back to Heresta and, keeping her voice low though she knew the men outside couldn't possibly hear, added, "It was a mistake I paid for. Now, I'm never alone. His men are always near, keeping watch. They're waiting outside to take me back. My *escorts*." She clenched her jaw shut.

Heresta brushed Kira's cheek with fragile fingers. "There will be an opportunity for you soon. I have foreseen it." She struggled to sit up and the coughing began again, wracking her frail body. Kira reached down to comfort her, raising her up and holding her gently until the coughing subsided. The old healer's bones were like brittle sticks beneath the thin layer of flesh. Heresta wheezed and tried to speak again, trembling with the effort. Kira laid her gently back on the bed. "There is little time left. I have something to give you," she continued, her eyes sparkling.

"Don't speak, old raven. Rest. Rest and breathe," she urged, emotion and fear making her voice throaty to her own ears.

"Too late, kitten. Too late. I return to the wheel. But there is one last thing I must do." She pushed herself up with her elbows and tried to rise once again.

"What is it?" Kira asked, ready to fulfill any request Heresta might make of her.

Heresta gasped for air, reaching a frail hand toward the far wall. "The jug." Her strength spent, Heresta fell back onto the bed panting.

Kira brushed Heresta's hair from her face, recalling the many times Heresta had done so for her, and a sob forced itself from her lips.

Heresta's gaze burned and her finger flicked toward the wall. Kira forced herself to look where she pointed. Along the wall a wide shelf stood crowded with bottles and jars. At one end stood a misshapen clay jug. She glanced back at Heresta.

The old woman gripped the edge of the pallet and nodded.

"You still have it? You kept it?" Kira couldn't suppress a smile as she recalled the day she'd made the jug. Molding the clay, smoothing the sides and cutting into the bottom to create a hollow storage space where she could hide her treasures. She'd still been a child, thinking that she could save the things she valued merely by hiding them from others.

"Yes. I—saved it—for you. Bring it—here," Heresta gestured to Kira with a frail hand.

Kira fetched the bottle and brought it to the bedside.

"Open it," the healer told her between labored breaths.

Kira moved her hands over the underside of the jug and put pressure on one edge, forcing the opposite side of the bottom to drop down. She grasped the edge with her fingers and pulled, gently slipping the false bottom out of the jug, and spilled the contents out onto the table.

Heresta watched intently as, one by one, Kira picked up the items from the table, fingering them. A child's treasures, they had remained where she'd hidden them, when she'd run off with Toril against Heresta's wishes, she hadn't taken the jug. At sixteen, she had reasoned she no longer had need of a child's keepsakes. Now, looking at these treasures, she felt small again. She held up the tiny piece of ash crystal with its smooth sides and mirrored surface. She'd found it in the rubble of a small landslide that had tumbled rocks and debris into the Kerstig River near the farm where she and her parents had lived. One by one she held up the six glass beads, each a different shape and color, that she'd traded for at the traveling market. The last item, a small copper comb, had been a gift from her father.

9

"Inside," Heresta wheezed out the word with a small gurgle. She pointed to the jug. "Something more."

Kira picked up the jug and felt inside the opening on its underside until she found something flat and hard. Pushing gently, she urged the item out of its hiding place. It dropped onto the table with a metallic clink, spinning on its edge before falling over with a clatter. It was a small gold medallion not much larger than a half-coptec coin. A twisted woven-looking design was etched into its center. She picked it up and turned it over. The other side had what appeared to be writing on it, but the letters were foreign to her.

"It is from your mother's people," Heresta rasped. "She asked me to keep it for her when you were just a babe. She—would have wanted you—to have it."

"My mother's people?"

"Yes, kitten. Her people came from over the Zendel Mountains, from beyond the Faersent Sea." Heresta's breath still came in gasps and the words she spoke were faint, but their meaning was strong enough to sting.

"That can't be," Kira said. "My mother's people were from Skybel. That's where she met my father, when he'd gone to the great market with Uncle Zhak. The folk from across the Faersent Sea are all strange creatures with monstrous powers—" She stopped short as she realized what she'd just said. No. It wasn't possible. If the stories of these people were true . . . She fingered the coin.

"Think, kitten. Do you truly believe the tales spun by those who fear to learn what lies beyond the next hill? Have you forgotten all that I taught you?"

Kira's eyes opened wide. Could it be true? Was this kinship the root of her strange gift?

"Heresta, why didn't you tell me before?" She glanced from the medallion to Heresta's pale face. Sadness filled the old healer's eyes.

10

The medallion felt warm in her hand. Kira traced the twisting design with her finger, recalling how beautiful her mother had been. A tall pale woman with unusual green eyes and flaming red hair. The same hair and eyes that Kira had inherited. Was that where she had gotten her powers? From her mother? From her mother's people? Was she really related to the strange folk who inhabited the shores across the Faersent Sea?

A raspy wheeze came from Heresta and the healer's eyelids fluttered. The last of her energy was escaping. The powers that gave and took life were calling her spirit out of her body.

"Don't leave me," Kira cried out softly.

Dropping to her knees beside the bed, she grabbed Heresta by the shoulders. If only she could find a way to drain the fluid from her lungs, she could save her. But Kira knew there was nothing she could do. Heresta had been right. The old woman had known the time of her leaving had come, and Kira felt her pass away, beyond the reach of the living. Kira collapsed in a heap. Wrapping her arms about herself and squeezing tight, she tried to contain her grief. She wanted to howl out her pain, but she dare not.

Instead, she bowed her head over the old healer, and spoke a blessing for her spirit's journey. She wanted to arrange the body, to perform the ritual burning, but Toril had made it clear before they rode out that morning that once the old woman was dead, Kira should be returned to him in haste. Nothing would motivate the men outside to disobey their warlord's orders. She held out her shaking arms and made a circle in the air, the sign of the Wheel Goddess, Troka, she who brought life and death.

Through the cracks in the old door, Kira could see that night was falling, darkness and shadows creeping near. Little time left, Heresta had said. How had she been so sure of the time of her passing? Had she had a vision, or was it another of the old woman's riddles? Kira didn't want to leave her like this. And she didn't want to go back to Toril.

She pushed away the thought of what Toril would do to her if she tried once more to leave, and once more failed. But if she didn't try, she would remain trapped, living in constant fear that he would turn on her at any moment for nothing more than a perceived slight. She had no reason to believe the beatings would ever stop. No reason to believe he would ever become the man she once thought him to be. The man she believed she had fallen in love with.

Firelight streaked the room as a log collapsed and fell into ash. I must escape him, she thought, and it must be now. Heresta had been right, there was little time left. But perhaps a little was all Kira needed.

She grabbed the medallion off the table, hesitated a moment, then scooped up the other trinkets as well, tucking them into the small leather pouch at her waist. She searched the room and found a sturdy piece of cloth in the pile of fabric strips Heresta had used for bandages and cleaning. She gathered up some dried fruit, a water skin, a flint and a steel knife, then wrapped them in the cloth. With a long piece of leather cord, she tied the bundle and stuck it under her shirt at the back of her waist, pulling the shirt back down under her belt. It wasn't much, but she couldn't risk taking more. The men would suspect something if she tried to leave the cottage carrying a bundle of food and clothing.

She pulled on the dried herbs that hung from the rafters, yanking them down and piling them onto the hearth in front of the fire. Then she took the oil jug from the shelf and doused the herbs with fuel, emptying the last of the jug's contents onto the floor and walls. She silently prayed Heresta would forgive her for not performing the full ritual. *But at least I can give you into the cleansing fire.* She grabbed a taper and lit it. For a moment she hesitated, gazing at the body of Heresta lying in repose on the narrow bed.

"Thank you, old raven," she whispered, and touched the burning taper to the dried herbs. "Thank you for this opportunity. For your last gift of love."

A choking sob erupted from her throat, as the oil and debris caught and flared. Flames rose and smoke filled the room. Kira ran out of the door, grabbed Trad's reins and pulled him away from the hut. Choking on the smoke and her own fear at being caught out, she yelled, "Fire and evil! Fire and evil! The wretched old woman is working a spell. She's trying to defeat the wheel." She pulled at Trad's reins, slapped his flank to hurry him, and ran with him away from the cottage. "We must quench the flames before she is consumed or she will take us all with her wickedness!"

The terror in her voice must have convinced the men. Every one of them leapt up, pulling their horses back toward the trees and looping their reins over low-hanging branches before running back to the burning hut.

They fought with a ferocious energy to douse the fire. She could almost smell their superstitious fear over the bitter smoke. Dagger beat at the flames with green branches from nearby trees, while Rasten used the remains of discarded pottery to haul water from the shallow stream. The blaze spread quickly, engulfing the little cottage within minutes, but still the men continued their fight.

The soldiers struggled against the growing heat and flames, and Kira slipped back toward the forest. As she passed the horses, she eyed the sword that hung from the pommel of Rasten's saddle. She hated the tools of war, hated the way Toril had forced her to learn their uses, but a part of her longed for something with which to defend herself. Heresta's voice reminded her there was little time. She dared not stop for the blade. The small knife would have to serve.

The moment she reached the cover of the trees, she flung herself onto Trad's back. She turned only once to stare at the tortured flames that writhed toward the darkening sky. Wrenching her eyes away, she whispered a final prayer of thanks to Heresta and Goddess Troka, then turned Trad's head toward the trees and slid into the shadows of the night.

CHAPTER TWO

Kira urged Trad forward, heading deeper into the woods. It wouldn't take long for the men to notice she was gone. When they did, they would come after her. If she could make it back to the main forest road, she should be able to take one of the small side trails that led into the woods. A dark gloom had already descended on the dense forest. If she could reach one of those less-used paths, she would have the entire night to put some distance between herself and her pursuers.

Too soon, she heard the change in the cries of the men. Their yells, no longer those of encouragement, became bellowed curses. Kira peered ahead, straining to catch sight of the main road. Trad's hooves beat a loud tattoo against the hard dirt, but she could hear the noise of pursuit rising in the distance.

The sound of the pursuing horses grew to a low thunder as she and Trad burst onto the main road. She leaned low over Trad's neck as the big horse veered right and lengthened his stride. The shouting of the men grew louder. Their curses carried through the woods, echoing between the trees.

Kira urged Trad to quicken his pace. They had to put more distance between them and Toril's men. At the sound of hooves behind her, she glanced back. Through the deepening shadows she saw movement. One of the men charged onto the main road, his horse a dark shadow moving beneath him. An arrow whizzed past, low and to the left. She sucked in her breath and hunched down in the saddle, squeezing tightly with her knees as Trad's speed increased.

She cringed. The consequences of her flight loomed over her, a mountainous shadow of fear and doubt. The arrow wasn't intended for her. It had been aimed at Trad. Toril's men were trained archers. If not for the darkness, the arrow would have struck deep. The next shot would be better placed. The only chance for escape lay among the trees. She glanced from side to side, scanning the edges of the road for a path that would take them off the main road and into the enfolding darkness of the forest.

A break appeared on her right. Hardly more than an animal track, it angled down and away from the road. She reined Trad around. He spun on his heels and leaped down the slope, carrying her between the massive trees, hulking trunks growing close together. Coarse bark scraped her legs as she passed between them.

Trad drove on.

Darkness folded in on them. Kira sat up and peered ahead. The openings between the trees were nearly impossible to see. A dark shadow loomed before her and she ducked as they passed beneath a low branch that narrowly missed her head. She crouched lower, gripping Trad's mane in her fist.

They forged deeper into the forest and their pace slowed. The underbrush thickened into a tangle of bramble that clawed at Trad's feet and legs. Kira realized abruptly that the trail had disappeared. She peered back they way they had come, but in the darkness couldn't distinguish between tree and shadow. She could still hear the shouts of the men and the falling of their horses' hooves in the distance, but she could no longer see where the path intersected the road. No more arrows flew. Nothing stirred nearby.

She pulled Trad to a halt, slipped from the saddle and, with wary steps, drew him along behind her, guiding him farther into the woods, away from the road. Kira moved with as much stealth as possible, fighting the impulse to run. The woods darkened until she could see only a few inches ahead. One arm outstretched before her, she edged forward, making sure there was room enough for Trad before moving on.

They stopped behind the trunk of a massive tree. A mild breeze fluttered the leaves overhead and the scent of mossy oak surrounded her. Trad's breathing was still heavy from the hard run. She placed a calming hand on his nose and whispered soothing words. His ears twitched as Toril's men crashed through the underbrush, cursing and blasting threats at her. Flickers of light appeared in the distance, threading through the trees. The men had made torches. Kira shuddered and buried her face in Trad's mane. Had those torches been ripped from the ruin of Heresta's cottage? The distant lights bobbed and flittered like spirits in the night.

One of the twitching flames weaved toward them. Kira stood as still as the trees beside her. Dry branches cracked and snapped as the soldier pushed his way through the trees. Brush and leaves crunched under heavy boots. The bitter torch smoke wafted nearer.

Her stomach clenched. She eased her hand inside her shirt. Her fingertips touched the bundle of items at her back and she inched it around to get at the knife. It wasn't much of a weapon, but there was nothing else. The glowing torch drew nearer. Silently, she drew the knife from the bundle, every muscle poised for action. Trad shivered beside her.

A loud crack rang out, followed by an angry curse. The light fluttered as the torch whipped from side to side. Another string of curses followed the thud of a boot against a tree trunk.

Kira stood frozen in the shadows. The man was close. The torchlight stretched out before him, reaching for her. Pale illumination crept across the ground toward the toes of her boots. Closer. Something hissed in the nearby darkness. The man swung his torch toward the sound and Kira tensed. Her heart galloped against her ribs. The hiss turned to a fierce growl that rose on the night air.

The soldier gasped, whipping his torch from side to side. The flame crackled and sputtered. He tried to back away, tripped and fell. The growl came again, low and menacing. The man jumped to his feet and crashed back toward the trail, heading away from the frightening sound. Away from Kira.

The torch's flame receded and the familiar touch of Kelmir's feline mind pushed aside her fear. She let herself breathe and opened her senses. Her mind flowed out, seeking in the dark for Vaith's fluttering presence.

It had been months since Toril had allowed Kira out alone, and she had not been able to be with her beloved companions in all that time. They'd always remained as near to her as possible, while staying far enough away to keep from being discovered. She'd had to use all her strength and force of will to keep them from coming to her and revealing themselves. She'd needed them to stay away. Needed them to be safe. Now they were with her and her spirit leaped.

Kelmir was close now; she could feel the pulse of his blood and his pounding heart, matching the rhythm of her own. He came quickly and silently, padding on his great feet. His dark fur, a mottled red and brown in sunlight, was a black mantle beneath the trees, and he moved like a shadow to sidle up beside her and rub against her, licking her hand with his rough tongue.

Vaith perched on a branch overhead and they waited and watched. Without the moon, Kira had no way of telling how much time passed. She leaned against Trad, one hand kneading Kelmir's thick fur. Soon, the deep night filled the forest. The voices of the men grew quiet and muffled, replaced by the chirrup and buzz of insects.

Kira let go her breath in a rushing sigh and tucked the knife into her belt. Without a sound, Kelmir stepped in front of Trad to lead the way through the thickening forest. Trad nickered low in recognition of the big feline, and Kelmir rumbled a throaty growl in return. Kira reached out a hand, stroking the horse's mane, willing him to remain quiet.

A rush of leathery wings circled above her and she raised her left arm up level with her shoulder. Vaith folded his wings and landed, gripping Kira's wide leather wrist guard. Using his wings to balance himself, he sidestepped up her arm to perch on her shoulder, careful not to tear through the sleeve of her shirt with his sharp claws. Then he wrapped his long tapered tail around her neck. She felt the coolness of his scaly skin across the back of her neck, the tip of his tail twitching just below her right ear. The little wyvern peered nervously about, swiveling his tiny dragonish head to listen for the sounds of pursuit. His bright eyes shimmered pale gold in the dark and his tongue flicked in and out, tasting the air.

Kelmir's leonine instincts and fine night vision would help them find a path through the forest, while the little wyvern, with his heightened hearing, would let Kira know when danger was near. *Come, my brave hearts. Guide us to freedom.* Kelmir rumbled deep in his throat and padded into the darkness.

Kira climbed into the saddle, muscles taut as bowstrings. It seemed as if Trad's hooves found every brittle stem and leaf. But she knew from experience the noises they made were no louder than those of the usual forest animals.

She focused her mind on Kelmir, using her knees to guide Trad as they followed behind the stealthy hunting cat. Any other horse would have shied and run at the smell of the big feline. But Trad had hunted with Kelmir and Vaith many times, and he had no fear of his unusual companions. "Would that I could speak directly to you, too, Trad," Kira whispered. But her powers extended to only a few animals, and those few were all hunters and true carnivores. In the years that had passed since she'd discovered her strange gift, she had never been able to reach into the minds of grazing animals or scavengers.

No matter. Trad understood her well enough. He followed her lead now and began to pick his way without urging as they trailed behind the big cat that led the way, and they moved deeper into the woods.

Darkness hung about them like a heavy veil, and the quiet of the forest settled around them. The toneless churr of a nightjar sounded in the distance, but there was no answering call. There would be no moon tonight to cast a glow upon the world, and that would be to Kira's advantage. The men would be unable to track them until daybreak, and by then she and her companions would be several leagues away.

Kira knew the woods, knew the cycles of the trees and what plants and wildlife lived among them. Here, Toril's soldiers were out of their element. They were good in a battle, but when it came to stealth in the woods, a hunter could best a warrior any day.

Sensing her mood, Kelmir gave a growl of approval. *Yes, my dear ones*, Kira thought to both the big cat ahead and the dainty wyvern riding on her shoulder. *We are together again. You need not hide any longer.*

She was glad she had never told Toril about her gift. He saw her only as a healer's apprentice, one who had never finished her training. She shuddered to think what he might have done if he had known about her connection with Kelmir and Vaith. He would have trapped them, caged them, used them to control her, threatening them with harm to compel her obedience. He might even have killed them. He was capable of such cruelty. She wished she had known, wished she could have seen what he could be like. But he hadn't always been that way. At least, she hadn't seen that part of him when they'd met. Or had she? Had she really been that blind? That naive? Or had she just been headstrong, rebelling against Heresta's command to stay away from him?

She chastised herself for her stubbornness, her unwillingness to listen to reason. What was it in her that had made her run off with a man she barely knew?

She recalled the first time he'd kissed her, and her chest grew tight. More than rebellion had caused her to run to Toril. More than youthful stubbornness. It had been his charm, and the way his power had seemed to protect her. The way his promises had soothed. The way his presence had kept the world at bay.

Heresta had taken her in and cared for her, but despite the healer's kindness, she could not replace Kira's parents. What had driven Kira to Toril's side, and eventually his bed, had been the overwhelming desire to be loved and to feel safe again. The fear that followed her after the burning of her home was a haunting torment that woke her in the night and darkened her childhood memories. And what could be safer than to be protected by the man who had become the strength of the people? The commander who had led them to victory against the very marauders who had killed her parents and destroyed their home?

The first time she'd seen Toril, she'd been in awe. He was brought to Heresta for healing. When the men carried him into the healer's hut, he was badly wounded and unconscious. His blond hair glowed like a golden crown in the torchlight. Kira saw him as a sleeping hero, the man the bards sang about. They told stories of his bravery, his fierceness in battle, and his many victories. He and his men had turned the tide of war, sending the invaders scurrying back across the northern isthmus, dropping their plunder as they ran.

After Heresta had bound up his wounds, Kira had sat beside him, caring for him, changing his bandages. When he woke in the night, feverish, Kira had given him the soothing draughts and herbal brews Heresta had prescribed.

When at last he'd opened his eyes he'd smiled and called Kira his angel. He'd taken her hand in his, and a tingle of excitement had run through her.

Trad halted and Kira was jolted back to the present. Kelmir waited unmoving in the darkness ahead. Kira focused herself into the big cat's mind, allowing herself to sink fully into his senses. She felt herself merge with him, sniffing the air and staring ahead, ears twitching. There was a hint of wood smoke in the air and, in the distance, a flickering glow reflected off branches and leaves. People. Perhaps only a woodsman's hut, but she couldn't risk being seen by anyone so soon after her escape. She would have to turn aside and go around.

For the first time, she let herself think about where they were headed. Until now, she had only dreamed of being free from Toril. But now that the dream was reality, she wondered where she should go. Where could she truly be free? Toril held the entire northern region of Sedath in his control. She would have to travel a great distance to be safe.

She shifted in her saddle, easing her stiff muscles, feeling each bruise anew. The creak of leather sounded loud in the silence of the darkened woods. Vaith hissed softly in her ear, sensing her indecision. *What do you think?* she asked with her mind, turning her head toward him. His leathery wings were folded tightly at his sides, and he cocked his head to gaze at her. His round eyes glowed in the dark like disks of gold. Kira remembered the medallion that Heresta had given her. The golden medallion that had belonged to her mother. If the symbol was emblematic of her roots, why hadn't Heresta told her before? If it did explain where her powers had come from, why had the old healer kept it a secret? Kira's hand went to the pouch at her side. Could she really be descended from the strange folk who inhabited those distant lands?

She shivered in the cool night air, remembering how her mother had insisted that to tell anyone of her powers would be dangerous. Kira hadn't really understood, but the fear she heard in her mother's voice had made her vow never to reveal her gift to anyone. Now she was glad she had made that promise and, with the exception of telling Heresta, had kept it.

"West," she said, in a whisper. "We'll go west. If there is any haven for us, perhaps it lies in the land of my mother's people."

She knew she would have to travel many leagues to the south in order to cross the mountains. The peaks were high with few trails leading through them. She remembered studying Toril's many maps. A few showed all the explored lands of Lunari, including the outlying islands. She recalled that the nearest road over the Zendel Mountains led through the Kandurst Gap. But she would have to travel across a large expanse of open land to get there, unless she followed the Aikewall Forest south to the foothills of the Khepera Mountains. Then, if memory served her, she could follow the Sethern River to the west and turn north again to gain the pass. It was a long way around, but it would keep her from having to cross the open lands in the midst of the region controlled by Toril and his army. And the pass itself was not much used, which was an added boon.

But first, they would have to go around the inhabited area just ahead. Tomorrow she would take precautions to hide their tracks, for now it would be just as well to use those tracks to throw off the men who followed them. If Toril's soldiers somehow managed to pick up their trail, she didn't want them to know she was heading west.

In the stillness, a wood owl hooted. *Take us east, Kelmir, toward the rising sun.* Kelmir turned, his big paws padding silently between the trees. Kira gave a nudge with her left knee and Trad followed him, stepping carefully over roots and fallen branches.

Now and then she surveyed the forest to her right, watching as they traveled slowly past the flickering light, keeping a safe distance. The sight reminded her of her recent escape and the death of Heresta. True, Heresta had not been able to replace Kira's parents, but the old woman had cared for her. Kira hadn't understood it when the healer had first taken her in, but she had come to know that Heresta had loved her. A small sob escaped from her lips, and the tears that hadn't come as she'd sat beside her mentor's deathbed came now. She let them run freely down her cheeks, mourning the loss of the last person who had truly loved her. Vaith, sensing her distress, cooed softly in her ear, a warbling low-pitched sound. She reached up and stroked his neck. *Thank you for your concern, little one, but I will be well.* Leaning her head gently against him, she felt his cool skin on her cheek. *As long as I have my beloved companions with me, all will be well.*

She wiped her eyes with the back of her hand and wondered if it were true. Could she trust in her own words, or were they merely empty promises she tried to give herself? She hadn't been well for a long time. Ever since her parents had been killed, she'd felt fearful and unsure. And when she thought she'd found safety and protection with Toril, he had proven her wrong. Even if she managed to get through the mountains and across the Faersent Sea, would she find refuge?

Once they were well beyond the dwelling, they turned south and continued traveling through the dense forest. The glittering light that flickered from its windows grew dim and faded finally into the thick darkness behind them.

CHAPTER THREE

Shafts of morning sunlight pierced the thick canopy of branches and a golden haze dusted the shadowy spaces between the trees. Kelmir roved before Kira, scouting the way, as Vaith flitted from tree to tree, stopping only long enough for her to catch up to him before flying off again. Kira pushed aside the previous night's worries, forcing herself to focus on the present. "Easy enough to worry about tomorrow when it arrives," she quoted Heresta aloud. She smoothed a section of Trad's mane with her fingers. "Yesterday's tomorrow is here, and we're still free of Toril. That in itself is something to be glad of."

Her stomach growled and she grimaced. The pouch at her hip contained less than a handful of dried fruit. She glanced about, searching for a sign of late summer berries, mushrooms or anything else edible. It would have been easier to live off the forest in late spring or early summer, but there were still plants and tubers suitable for eating. She only had to find them.

Scanning the ground at the base of the tree trunks, she sighted a small patch of wild mother's grass. It wouldn't be filling, and uncooked it would be tough and sour, but the milky liquid that filled the stalks would provide some nourishment. She dismounted to gather the thick stalks,

26

pulling them up by their shallow roots. After brushing away the dirt, she cut the bottom from each fat stem, holding them upside down so the milk wouldn't drip out. Her mouth puckered as, one by one, she chewed the open ends of the stalks until the white pithy insides gave up their bitter liquid.

Beneath an old gnarled oak, she found a bush of trumpet berries. Most of the fruit was not yet fully ripened, and eating more than a handful would be unwise at any time, unless one were in need of a purgative. She picked only the ripest of the berries, eating a few and putting the rest into her pouch.

As she finished, Kelmir's mind brushed hers. Men ahead. The sights and smells of a settlement came through to her in wispy imagery. *Stay out of sight*, she told him. *You, too*, she sent a cautioning thought to Vaith. Shimmering scales caught the light and reflected it like rainbow colored fire as he flew up to perch on a high branch and wait in the shadows.

A settlement or hold might mean they were nearing the central road that led east and west through the middle of the woods. Kira pictured the maps of the region in her head. She couldn't recall seeing any villages or large holds marked on the map of the Aikewall Forest. The forest itself was close to sixty leagues wide and spanned more than eight hundred leagues from north to south. Several roads led along or through the forest, the main road east and west cutting through the center. The north-south road traversed the entire length of the wood along its western border, but only crossed deeper into the forest at the northern edge to pass around the edge of Lake Kaltes, which was so vast, it covered the land from the forest all the way to the foot of the Zendel Mountain range.

The holding was probably a small settlement of woodcutters or foresters who gathered brush and cut dead wood to sell as kindling and firewood. Kira weighed her options. Her stomach rumbled and she licked her lips. Wild fare wasn't scarce this time of year, but she hadn't asked Kelmir and Vaith to hunt for her, since she dared not take the time to stop and build a fire. But her hunger gripped her stomach like a fist, and she needed supplies for the journey, items she might be able to obtain from a settlement. She disliked the idea of hunting game for trade. Killing was distasteful, but a necessary fact of life, she reminded herself, and they needed supplies to survive. However, she would have to proceed with care. By now the soldiers would have sent a rider back to report her escape to Toril.

She grimaced in empathy for the soldier who had been chosen for the task. Then chided herself for her waste of compassion, reminding herself that he served Toril by choice.

As she once had.

The thought pulled her up short, bringing with it a mix of emotions. Shame commingled with pain and loss roiled through her. She felt cheated. Toril had lied to her. His words had promised love and kindness. His deeds had not fulfilled that promise. She shook with rage and gritted her teeth. A desperate whimper jangled inside her. Taking deep slow breaths to calm herself, she turned her attention to the present.

Kelmir, Vaith, we'll need to hunt fresh game for trading. A brace or two of rabbits or some plump wild fowl. She could feel their excitement at the prospect. They would work together as they used to. Kira sensed their anticipation and smiled. *Good. See what you can find in the woods away from the road and the settlement. I'll find some grazing for Trad and join you.*

She walked on, leading Trad in the direction of the holding, taking her time. It was only mid-day and it would be best to wait until evening to approach, when activities would be quieting down for the night. Fewer people would be out and about, most settling in for their evening meal. That would mean fewer eyes. And fewer questions. She also hoped that the evening gloom would help to hide her appearance.

She ran her fingers through her tangled hair. She considered her options. She would certainly need to do something about the color of her hair if she wanted to be less noticeable. The resin of an acacia would help to turn it brown, or at least darken the redness of it. But it would be easier to cover, if there were less of it.

The presence of Kelmir prowling in the distance and Vaith flitting quietly from branch to branch comforted her. The two hunters traveled silently, keeping out of sight, watching for the movement that would betray a small game animal. The years spent hiding from Toril had made the process of remaining concealed while hunting second nature to both of them. Out of bad comes good, Kira thought with a frown. She too had learned to make herself almost invisible, to hide her thoughts and emotions from Toril.

A league or so from the holding, she turned aside, taking a wide circular route around the settlement. Her feet were heavy, the long night of evading her pursuers having finally caught up to her. She rubbed at the back of her neck as a wide yawn escaped her. They would need to rest tonight, she thought, absently scratching under Trad's chin.

She came alert as she passed the point she knew would put her directly east of the settlement. Where she'd expected to find the main road, only a narrow cart track barred her path through the woods. A small swath of open sky followed its winding course through the trees.

Small drays and riders on horseback had made the track. The worn ruts were too close together for larger wagons. Perhaps she wasn't as close to the east-west road as she'd thought. She examined the trees for signs of cutting, but the forested area had only been picked clean of deadfall and bracken. Foresters or gatherers, not woodcutters. The settlement would be modest then and probably not on the main road.

After watching the track for a while to be certain it was empty, she crossed the path with her heart pounding. Once across, she moved with quiet steps, leading Trad in under the trees on the other side. She made her way to a point well beyond the hamlet, and found herself in a sheltered copse where the ground was soft and uneven.

She used a heavy stick to dig a shallow hole. Then she took out the knife and, with a grunt of displeasure, grabbed a handful of hair and pulled the blade across until the strands fell free. She repeated the process, dropping handfuls of coppery tresses into the hole, until a mere two fingers of length remained on her head. Then she covered the hole with dirt, tamped it down and scattered leaves over the disturbed soil.

When she finished, she felt dizzy with weariness and fatigue. *I need to rest a while,* she sent to Kelmir and Vaith. *Keep watch for me.* Yawning wide, she sat down with her back against a knobby oak. It had been a long day and night. She leaned back and let sleep draw her down.

* * *

She woke, swimming to the surface of sleep, her weariness dragging at her like an enormous weight. She sunk and rose several times before rousing. With the sudden realization of where she was, she came wholly awake, wondering how she could have slumbered so deeply.

The dusky shadows of early evening had merged into the forest as she slept. She would need to hurry. Entering the holding after dark would cause more commotion and curiosity than she wanted to stir up. She was about to stand when her fingers brushed against something warm and feathery. With a start she snatched her hand away and looked down. Four plump game hens lay beside her.

She smiled, reaching out for Kelmir and Vaith. *Thank you, my brave hearts. Well done.* Their pleasure at her praise swept over her as she passed her hands in a small circle over the fowl with a prayer of thanks to Troka for her generosity.

Standing, she stretched the stiffness out of her arms and legs, then checked on Trad. He nickered as she rubbed behind his ears. The forest was alive with the evening song of warblers and a woodpecker hammered in the distance. Kelmir and Vaith were alert and watchful, but they gave no sense of concern. She stooped to pick up the game hens. *Watch over Trad for me,* she told them before heading toward the foresters' cot.

She stayed in the shadows and surveyed the quiet settlement. The entire holding consisted of one large building, a work shed, a rough stable, a few flat-roofed cottages and several sturdy lean-tos. The group of buildings sat clustered in a clearing, a narrow track leading to the main cart road. A less than defensible position, and some of the buildings had been recently repaired. But then, with the outlanders having been expelled from Sedath, life had become more peaceful, if not necessarily more pleasant, thanks to Toril.

Lights glimmered from the windows of the main hall, glowing in the gray evening light. The work shed and most of the cottages appeared silent and empty. Kira squared her shoulders and stepped out into the clearing between two of the outbuildings, intent on heading for the nearest cottage. Perhaps there would be someone inside with whom she could barter.

A scuffling noise from the direction of the stable brought her to a halt. The buttery-yellow light of a small work lamp moved toward the open door, followed by a bulky shadow. Kira waited soundlessly, poised to dart back in amongst the trees.

The shadow emerged from the stable, followed by a short stout man in a leather tunic, a lamp raised high over his head. His deep-set eyes were dark in his round face, which held a large full nose and square chin. His shoulders were broad, and he appeared to be nearly as wide as he was tall, with arms so long they would have reached below his knees had they been down at his sides.

A bleating animal trailed after him, stumbling awkwardly and stretching its neck to reach something the man held behind his back. Kira smiled as she realized that the animal was a young goat and the man was not a man, but a gnome. An Uldast gnome most likely, she thought, as Uldast gnomes were known for their animal husbandry. The gnome was feeding the kid something from his hand as he walked, his rolling gait like that of a sailor fresh from the sea.

He stopped suddenly, sniffing the air, and the kid caught up with him, butting him from behind with its head and causing him to rock forward onto the balls of his feet. He stiffened and steadied himself, eyes narrowing as they came to rest on the shadows where Kira stood.

"What d'ye think yer doin' over there?" he asked, his voice a deep rumbling bass. "Com'on out where one can see yer with a clean eye."

Kira stepped from between the buildings, holding her arms out from her sides, the game hens held tightly in one fist.

"Who're ye? Eh? And why're ye skulkin' in the gloom?" The gnome's deep voice was gruff with suspicion.

"I'm sorry, I didn't intend to hide in the shadows as if I were spying," Kira replied. "I'm only a traveler passing through these lands. I saw your holding and thought I might barter some fresh game for supplies. If there is anyone here who might be open to a trade, that is," she spoke the words as politely as she could, keeping her arms outstretched and nodding at the dangling fowl.

"So, 'tis an accident ye were hanging in the shadows betwixt and between rather than comin' at us from the main road, eh?" He arched an eyebrow at her, his mouth held in a taut line.

"Well, not precisely," Kira said. "I was coming from the forest with these hens," she nodded again at the fowl. "Do you mind if I set them down? They're quite fat and heavy."

"Eh? Heavy is it?" he said, eyeing her with a smirk. "Well, they don't look all that large from here. Caught 'em in the woods nearby, did ye say?" He took a step forward and then rocked onto his toes. "Oof! Hold on there," he said over his shoulder. The young goat butted him again, attempting to wrest the food from his hand. "Ach. Take it, ye pushy youngling." He let go of the prize and wiped his hand on the leg of his brown woolen trousers. His eyes glinted with humor. "Well, now," he said, clearing his throat and turning down his mouth at Kira. "Let's see what yer've brought, and I'll tell ye if they're worth a naught fer trade."

Kira stepped closer, forcing herself not to smile as she held out the game hens to offer the gnome a better view. He grunted. "Not a bad catch for a day's work." He took the hens from her and held them up to test their weight. "All together, they might even make a small stew. What is it yer wantin' for them?"

Kira wasn't sure how much she should reveal about herself to this strange fellow, but there were several things she needed. She also knew that the gnomes held a high regard for negotiations and bartering. She tapped her chin with one finger as she thought, taking her time before replying. "Two blankets, a bag of grain, three measures of dried meat and a small cooking pot."

"What!?" exclaimed the gnome. "Have ye been eatin' Sanity's Bane? All that for some skinny birds?"

"A moment ago, they were not a bad catch," Kira said, amused by his reference to the intoxicating herb. "You'll feed a dozen folk with these skinny birds." She put a hand on her hip and clamped her jaw shut, waiting for his counter, a smile tugging at the corner of her mouth. Bargaining was a skill she'd learned well from Heresta.

"A dozen folk," he sputtered. "Perhaps where ye come from 'tis the way, but folk here are hardy and have need of a proper feed after workin' in the woods the day long." He held up the hens and eyed them disdainfully. "I'll tell ye what," he said. "I've always been a gen'rous soul. I'll give ye one blanket, and one measure o' dried meat."

"One and one?" Kira scoffed. "Then, I'll give you one hen."

"One for each, then," the gnome said.

"All right," Kira said, with a smile. "A deal. One for one. I have four hens, which I give for a blanket, a pot, a measure of dried meat and a bag of grain."

"I never said anything about grain or a pot," the gnome growled, shaking the hens at her.

"One for one," Kira said, standing her ground.

"Ach." The gnome tilted his head and smiled. "Agreed," he said. "It's what I get for bein' lax and underestimatin' ye. Ye bargain like a gnome, ye do."

Kira smiled. "I had a good teacher," she said, remembering Heresta bargaining in the markets as Kira carried their purchases from stall to stall.

"My name's Ryospar, and I'm pleased to make yer acquaintance. And truth be told, these are fine healthy hens ye've caught."

Kira hesitated for a moment, then said, "You may call me Ardea." She wasn't sure she should use her mother's name in such a way, but it was the first name that came into her head. She watched Ryospar's face, afraid he wouldn't believe her, but he only nodded.

"Would ye care to join us fer the evenin' meal before collectin' yer goods? Most are off deliverin' wood, but a few are here with me an' the youngsters."

Kira glanced up at the main building. Warm light spilled out from the windows, and the smell of wood smoke and cooking wafted on the evening air. A part of her longed to say yes, to sit by a bright fire and enjoy a fresh cooked meal, but she knew she shouldn't. No, she couldn't stay. Aside from the risk, there was the danger she might bring down on these quiet folk. "No, thank you. I truly must move on."

Ryospar peered at her, eyes squinted. For a moment, Kira thought he would probe further, but he only nodded.

"Come along, then," he said. "We'll gather yer goods and ye can be on yer way. Though I dare say, 'tisn't as welcoming in the woods as by a forester's fire." He turned toward one of the lean-tos, carrying the hens. The little goat trundled after him, and Kira followed.

Ryospar led the way into a small shed where he hung his lamp on a peg and set the hens on a nearby box. He picked up a small burlap bag from a stack in the corner, opened a barrel and began scooping out grain. When the sack was nearly full, he tied a cord around the opening and handed the bag to Kira.

She took the bag and hefted it in her hand, feeling the weight of it. Ryospar closed the barrel, but the little goat nudged him and he raised the lid just enough to grab a small handful of grain. He held out his hand to the kid. It lipped the kernels gently from his palm, licking it clean afterward. Ryospar scrutinized Kira, who was watching him with the young animal, and shrugged. "He's a nuisance, but I haven't got the heart to tie him up when I'm tending the stables." He wiped his hand on his trousers before gathering the rest of the items from the holding's stores. Placing a pouch of dried meat into a small but sturdy iron cooking pot, he turned to Kira and held the items out to her. "Ach, we'll have to be asking after the blanket up to the main hall," he said, as she took the proffered items. "We don't keep them stores out here." Intense curiosity crossed his face. "Are ye sure ye won't stay and share the eve's repast with us?"

Kira smiled wistfully at him. "No, but thank you again for the kind offer." She paused for a moment, casting a meaningful glance at the sack of grain in her hand. "And for the generous portions of grain and meat. I know you've over-measured both."

He raised both eyebrows and gave her a pointed look. "Ach, now don't go spreadin' that sort of rumor about the countryside. I'd ne'er be able to get another good bargain anywhere. Well now, yer goin' to have to come with me up to the hall, while I fetch yer blanket."

They walked to the main hall, the kid still following. "Ach, I almost fergot." He led the young goat over to the stable, ushered it inside and closed the lower half of the main door, so it couldn't get out. The kid bleated loudly from the other side of the door. "It'll only be a moment," he told it quietly. "Stop yer bawling. I'll be right back to finish the evenin' chores."

"I'm sorry," Kira said. "I didn't mean to interrupt your work."

"Ach, and how could ye not. 'Tisn't as if I could have planned fer yer visit, eh?"

Something about the way he said it, made Kira examine his face, but it was nearly full dark now and she couldn't make out his features clearly. It is a pity to be suspicious, even of such a kindly person, she thought, as she followed Ryospar up to the main hall. But she remained on guard.

The furnishings inside the main building were short and squat, built specifically for gnome comfort. The large central room was lit with lamps hanging from hooks along the walls that for Kira were at shoulder level, and the tables and chairs were low and wide. Three long tables were set up in a U-shape, with chairs set along the outside so those seated would all face the center of the room.

A broad fireplace sat at the back of the hall, with ovens set into both sides, where large meals could be cooked. There were trestle tables nearby, and fat rounds of dough set for rising near the fire. The smell of flour and yeast rose on the warm air, and the heady aroma of a hearty stew wafted across the room. Kira's mouth began to water.

At the fire, stirring the contents of a big pot stood a short stout woman about the same height as Ryospar. She glanced over her shoulder at them, nodding when she saw Kira. She lifted the ladle and rapped it on the edge of the stew pot before hanging it on a nearby hook. Wiping her hands on her apron, she turned and walked around the tables to meet them.

"Och, Ryospar," she said, her accent thicker than the old gnome's. "Who have ye got with ye?" Her round face held dark shining eyes over a pudgy nose, and her cheeks were red from the heat of the fire. A small bead of perspiration ran down the side of her face and she brushed it away with the back of her hand. Kira had at first thought she was a gnome like Ryospar, but she appeared to be human. There was nothing gnomish about her, except for her size.

The woman was obviously curious about Kira. She held her up chin, inspecting Kira, as if sizing up a potential scullery maid and not liking what she saw.

"Malla, we've a visitor. She's brought some fine game for trade," Ryospar held out the game hens to the woman. Malla scowled at the birds.

"Och, they be half-starved. Stringy, too, I expect." She took the hens, with a fierce look at Kira, as if she expected her to argue with her assessment of the fowl.

"I'd say they're plump enough to roast," Ryospar said cheerfully. "And I've already given my word on fair trade." He raised an eyebrow.

"Well, perhaps they'll serve," Malla replied more civilly. Then she dropped her voice and added, "Mayhap even Talya will find her hunger again."

Concern cut across Ryospar's face. "Still hasn't eaten?"

Malla pursed her lips and shook her head. Her eyes seemed to soften.

"Is someone ill?" Kira asked.

"Indeed," Ryospar replied. "'Tis my brother's youngest. For the past few days, she's been sleepin' more than a child should, not eatin'. And she's been coughin' deep in her chest. Now, she's taken on a fever. Malla's done all we know to do for such child's ailments as those we know of, but naught has worked." He shrugged helplessly.

There is no time for this, Kira thought. She needed to flee, to be gone from this place. She willed her heart to harden. But her healer's training prevailed. "I know something of herbs and healing," she offered. "If I could see her, I may be able to help."

Malla's eyes grew wide, her expression hopeful. "Are ye a healer, then?"

"I have some skill," Kira replied carefully, "but a true healer I am not. I was unable to complete my apprenticeship." She didn't say any more.

"It would be a kindness to us all, if ye could be of help," Ryospar said. "She's in the anteroom." He motioned to a doorway.

"I'll do what I can," Kira said.

The room was dim. A small candle guttering on a wooden table offered the only light. Kira knelt by a low pallet where a little girl lay, shivering beneath heavy blankets. Her skin was pale, and dark circles filled the hollows beneath her eyes. Her breathing was so shallow Kira had to hold her hand above the girl's mouth to feel the moist air that barely trickled from between her cracked lips.

Kira lifted the girl's hand and felt for the heartbeat at her wrist. It was weak and rapid, fluttering like a tiny bird's wings. The child's skin was hot to the touch, her forehead moist with sweat. A moan escaped from her small lips as Kira began lifting the blankets off. "This is no common fever," she told Ryospar who hovered nearby. She leaned over the girl, putting her face close to the child's, and sniffed. There was a sour scent to the girl's breath. "When did she fall ill?"

Ryospar rubbed at his chin. "It was a hand-span of days ago."

"Did she eat anything unusual, any wild plants or flowers, before she became sick?"

"Naught that I know tell of," Malla said from the doorway. "Och, but ye know children." She frowned. "They're all the time galavantin' about. Who knows what they're into from one moment to the next?"

"Have you given her anything for her symptoms?" Kira asked.

"Aye," Malla replied, wringing her hands in concern. "Honeyed tea fer the cough, an' white willow bark fer the fever. But she's barely drank a few sips o' neither."

Kira could feel the woman's eyes on her as she pulled back the blankets to examine the girl further. She placed her hand against the child's stomach. Her belly was distended, and hard to the touch as if it were filled with something solid. The girl moaned again.

Kira pulled one of the blankets back up to her chin, leaving the others piled at the end of the bed. "It isn't a normal childhood complaint," she said. "I think she's contracted something. A parasite of some sort."

Malla's hands went to her mouth and her eyes stitched with pained. "Och! I should have kept a better watch on the child!"

Ryospar turned to the distressed woman. "Nay, Malla. 'Tisn't yer fault. Ye can't be watchin' after all the younglings at every moment."

Kira eyed them for a long moment, uncertain as to what to say. She looked down at the child and decided on the truth. "I might be able to help her, but the remedy will make her even more ill for a time. She won't be able to have food for several more days, perhaps a week. And as small as she is . . ." Her words trailed off into silence as she watched Ryospar's jaw working. It was clear he was trying hard to keep his emotions in check, but Kira could see the fear in his eyes. "Have any of the other children had any symptoms?" she asked.

"Nay, naught that I've seen." Malla choked out the words and hugged herself, tears running down her face.

"Malla," Kira said. "I need you to boil a pot of water. After it boils for a few minutes, put two dippers of it into a clean wooden bowl. Add a small measure of white willow bark, and two of tansy. And mix a half-measure of powdered elf's garlic in it.' She reached into the pouch at

40

her waist and drew out a handful of garget roots and the berries she'd collected earlier. "Then chop these roots and mash the berries and toss them into the mixture."

Malla sniffled, wiping her eyes with the back of her hand. She crossed the room and took the roots from Kira, pausing to eye the berries suspiciously, "Nay," she said. "Yer not wantin' to give her those, are ye?"

"Yes," Kira said firmly, looking the woman in the eye. "I know they'll make her ill, but it will help to purge out the insects that are growing inside her."

Malla's eyes widened. She pursed her lips tight, but she took the berries and turned toward the door.

"Malla," Kira said.

"Yes?"

"If you have any peppermint and eucalyptus oil, please bring that as well."

Malla nodded and left the room.

Ryospar watched her go, then turned to Kira. "Is there naught fer me to do?" he asked.

"There is plenty, I'm afraid. First, we'll have to move her out of the main hall. Is there a small storage building we can clear out?"

Ryospar frowned, but nodded. "Aye, but ye want to move a sick child out into the night?"

"We need her away from the cooking area, in a place that's easily cleaned. We'll need everything else removed from the shed, and a thick bed of hay put down. Once the purging begins . . ." she spread out her hands to gesture at the room.

"Ach, I see yer meanin'," he said. He spun around and left the room.

Before long, Malla returned, a wooden bowl clutched tightly in one hand, a small vial in the other. Ryospar came in behind her. "'Tis ready," he said.

"Good. I'll carry her." Kira leaned over and lifted the little girl in her arms. Ryospar started to protest, but seemed to think better of it and turned to lead the way. The child's face shone ghostly pale in the flickering lamplight, and she made no sound as Kira carried her outside. She followed Ryospar to a work shed that stood near the edge of the woods. Several lamps already burned inside the shed, hanging from the low rafters, illuminating a narrow set of shelves along one wall. Ryospar had heaped a large pile of straw alongside the wall. A heavy blanket had been thrown over the straw. Several more blankets were stacked in the corner.

Kira gave the gnome a questioning look.

"'Twas an old bit of bedding, and not worth a stone." A catch in his voice belied his words and betrayed his emotions. "At least she'll not be chafed by the straw," he mumbled, facing away from Kira in discomfort.

Kira smiled at the gnome's obvious concern for the child. "It was very considerate of you." She laid the girl down on the makeshift bed, then gestured to Malla to bring the oils to her. Malla handed her the vial. "Ryospar, can you sit her up? I'm going to hold the oils under her nose to rouse her. Then we'll have to get her to drink as much of the tea as possible."

Ryospar did as she asked. Then Kira uncorked the vial and held the oils up to the child's nostrils. Talya's eyes fluttered, then she grimaced and pulled her head back, sneezing violently. Kira handed the vial to Malla and took the bowl from her.

"Talya." Kira held the girl's face with one hand to focus her attention on what she was saying. "Talya. You're very ill, and I know you don't want to eat or drink, but you must drink this in order to get well," she said firmly. "Do you understand?"

Talya blinked, face slack and eyes dull.

42

"Talya. You must drink as much of this as you can. Do you understand me?"

Talya nodded her head a tiny bit. Kira wasted no time and put the bowl to the girl's dry cracked lips, pouring the warm liquid into her mouth. Talya made a small face, coughed and pulled away. "Swallow it," Kira said. "It will make you better."

The little girl turned her bleary eyes up to Ryospar, who nodded back, reaching out to her. Her small fingers gripped his rough hand. She took a ragged breath, then leaned forward with her mouth open. "That's it," Kira said as Talya drank. "Good."

Kira tilted the bowl up and encouraged Talya to keep drinking until there was nothing left but fine sediment. "Well done," Kira said as Ryospar laid the weary child back onto the bedding.

"Now what?" asked the old gnome.

"Now we wait." She handed the empty bowl back to Malla. "She'll have some stomach pains at first, then she'll begin to purge. No food, only tea for the next three days. After that you can start her on weak broth. But only if the stomach swelling has gone down. If not, you'll have to make her another infusion to give her." She took out the rest of the berries she'd collected and the last of the garget root she'd taken from Heresta's stores and handed them to Malla.

The short woman cast her eyes to the floor and took the root without looking at Kira. "Och, 'tis a foul thing, them men a-chasin' after ye as they are," she said under her breath.

Kira jerked her head up. "What?"

Ryospar stepped between the two women, concern on his face. "Don't be alarmed," he said quietly. "They've been askin' after ye, in the outer holdings. I would've mentioned it to ye, but I didn't want to spook ye."

Kira felt the blood drain from her face. "I don't know what you mean," she said, giving Ryospar her best blank look.

He smiled. "They haven't made it this far south yet, but news travels on the wind in these parts, though I don't think they'll be comin' our way any too soon. We're not a bit more 'en a wide spot along the road, ye might say."

His voice was soothing, but Kira's stomach clenched. "You must be mistaking me for someone else," she said, as calmly as she could.

"Nay. The name may be wrong, but the descriptive fits ye close."

Kira combed her fingers through her fresh-cropped hair. The gnome's left eye twitched, as if he was winking at her. She should have used the acacia resin to color her hair before coming here! No matter what she did, it never seemed enough. Never seemed to be the right choice. She stood slowly, holding her hands down at her sides to keep from trembling. "Talya will need watching," she said with forced calm. "Someone will have to stay with her for the next few days."

Ryospar tilted his head to one side, watching her with a quizzical expression. He smiled again. "Yer still welcome to stay with us."

"I'm sorry, but I need to be on my way. My mother's family will be worried if I don't arrive soon," she lied.

Ryospar, shrugged. "Malla, d'ye see what ye've gone and done? Ye've affrighted our guest." Malla continued to stare at the floor. "Well, then. I suppose there isn't anything to be done about it now," he grumbled. "Malla, would yer be so kind as to fetch out the traveler's goods?"

Malla nodded slowly, then headed toward the main hall.

"Ye needn't be afeared of us," Ryospar told Kira after Malla had gone.

Kira struggled to remain calm. The gnome held completely still, in the unnerving way that gnomes do. It was one of the things that enabled them to get around without being seen. Right now, it reminded Kira of the stillness of a snake about to strike. "I'm not afraid," she said coolly. "I simply must be going. I've already stayed much longer than I had intended."

Ryospar backed a few steps away from the door. "I'm sorry ye feel that way," he said. "But I'll not hinder yer goin'. We'll owe our thanks to ye for Talya's sake."

Kira thought she heard kindness in his voice, but she no longer trusted herself. Her judgment had proven flawed with Toril. She dare not trust anyone. Not when her life and her freedom depended on it. And not when Vaith and Kelmir might be put at risk. "You don't owe me anything," she replied. "I only hope the child gets better."

Malla returned, carrying a small lamp. She held out a blanket and Kira's provisions.

Keeping Ryospar in sight, Kira sidled out the door.

Malla's red-rimmed eyes shone in the yellow lamplight. "Thank ye," the small woman whispered, her voice gruff with emotion.

"Just take care of her," Kira said, taking the provisions. "The wheel may turn without taking her for a while, yet."

Malla held out the lamp to her. "'Tis dark along the woods road. You'll be needin' a light to find yer way."

The lamp glowed in the night like a signal beacon. Kira shook her head. "No, thank you, Malla. There will be a waxing quarter moon tonight and enough light to see by."

She stepped out into the darkness, her heart pounding against the wall of her chest. When she reached the road, she walked along it for a short distance, then slipped quietly in among the trees and paused to listen.

There was no sound of pursuit, no noise but the call of a blackbird and its answering mate. She willed herself to be

45

still. It would do no good to have slipped unseen into the darkness beneath the trees only to go crashing and blundering through the underbrush. She reached out to Kelmir, asking him to come and lead her back to Trad. As she waited for him to join her, she grasped the woolen blanket and supplies, squeezing them tightly. She cursed herself for allowing compassion to overrule her caution. But Ryospar had seemed so friendly. And the child, Talya, had truly been sick.

But they knew her, knew who she was! Of course, the old gnome had been friendly, even letting her best him at bargaining.

She should have been more cautious. All her work to cover her tracks was lost. Even now, Toril's men might be hunting for her here in this part of the forest. How could she have been so foolish?

Something moved in the darkness. She tensed. A throaty growl rolled from the shadows and relief flooded over her. She'd been so distracted by her thoughts and fears, she hadn't sensed Kelmir padding through the trees to join her. One mistake after another, she thought. What was she doing? It was ridiculous to think she could escape from Toril. What he wanted was what he would have.

Kelmir stepped forward, rubbed up against her, purring. Tears moistened her eyes. *You're right, my friend. I'm sorry. We are not yet undone.*

A fluttering of wings brought her head up to see the dark form of Vaith alighting on a nearby branch. *Yes,* she told them. *I have you both. And Trad, too. And you all have me. We will find a place where we can be safe. Together.*

She reached down, kneading the back of Kelmir's neck. *Let's be off,* she told him. *We must be far from here before dawn.*

CHAPTER FOUR

Cold drops of water splashed onto Kira's face and she awoke with a sputter. It felt as if she'd been asleep for hours, but no glimmer of daylight pierced the heavy darkness. She couldn't see them, but she knew the dark clouds that had followed them throughout the day had caught up to them and hung overhead, a heavy sodden mass. An oppressive feeling of closeness pushed down on her and she shivered.

Kelmir raised his head and yawned as Kira sat up, wiping the moisture from her face and blinking into the darkness. Trad stood nearby, leaning in close to the large boulders along the river's bank. Just on the other side of the rocks, the Sethern River rushed past. She squinted in the direction of the sound. The rocks were dark shadows against the thick night.

The clouds suddenly erupted, dousing her with freezing rain. Kira jumped up, pulling her blanket from around her. "I knew we should have kept going. We might have found a cave or at least more of an overhang," she grumbled. Kelmir stood, stretched, and shook himself, sending another shower of water in Kira's direction. "Thank you so very kindly," she groused. Kelmir yawned.

Since leaving the woodcutters' holding, they'd followed the river's path, aiming for the Zendel Mountains. They were now on the southern bank of the Sethern. Kira hadn't intended to cross the river, but there was no cover on the northern side. The south bank offered a line of large rocks and boulders that formed a natural wall with few breaks. It wasn't much in the way of protection, but she'd been nervous and uncomfortable traveling in the open as they had since leaving the shelter of the Aikewall Forest. When they'd come to a narrow place where a fallen tree provided a natural bridge, Kira had decided to cross. Now the boulders along the southern bank created a shield between her and the lands to the north.

Kira shook the water off her blanket, folded it into a triangle and threw it over her shoulders as a short cape. She walked to where Trad stood and tightened his girth before scooping Vaith from the top of the tall gray rock where he'd been keeping watch.

"Come on, little one," she said, her voice tired and husky in her own ears. "Time to move on. We'll be just as cold sitting here getting wet as we will on the road, such as it is. And there won't be much sleeping to be had in this chill rain." She frowned. Sleep, at least good sound sleep, had eluded her since they'd left the woodcutters' holding. The wilds held many dangers, and not all of them wore the insignia of Toril's army.

Pulling the blanket tightly around her, she picked up Trad's reins and they set off along the bank of the Sethern. They settled into what, over the past several days, had become their usual routine of following Kelmir as he picked his way between the rocks, silently leading them westward.

They moved like ghosts through the thick shadows as the rain beat down on them from a starless sky. The sound of Trad's hooves became lost in the noise of raindrops splattering against rocks and into the churning river.

They hadn't gone far when Kelmir gave a low growl and stopped. Vaith cocked his head, glancing around with short quick movements, scanning the darkness beyond the rocks. Kira felt a cold prickling at the back of her neck. She let go of the blanket, slowly moving her hand to the hilt of her knife. As a weapon, it wasn't formidable, but any bit of rope will do in time of need, as Heresta had always said.

Kira reached out mentally to Vaith and Kelmir. Both were taut, nerves tense, but neither had any idea of what it was they were sensing. There was no sound or scent. Only the cold damp rain and the rushing river. She stood listening, groping for a sound, a movement, anything that might tell them what it was that watched them from the shadows. Trad shivered and a chill sliced through her.

Then it was gone. Whatever they had sensed seemed to have melted away. Kira loosened her grip on the knife. Her fingers tingled as the blood seeped back into them.

Kelmir's soggy coat dripped runnels of rainwater. He raised his head and looked into Kira's eyes. His questions tugged at her mind and she shrugged. *I don't know, but let's be watchful.*

She quested through her memories for some name to give to the strange sensations they had just experienced. Kelmir waited another moment, then gave himself a mighty shake, spraying water in every direction. Kira gave Trad's reins a gentle tug, and they set off once more.

Kira led Trad through the rest of the night and into a murky dawn. They stumbled across slippery rocks in the heavy wet darkness. She finally hauled herself shakily up into the saddle at dawn. The sun cast a weak light through the dull clouds overhead, but the chill of night clung stubbornly to the land. The feeble daylight that penetrated the thick expanse of clouds gave a pale cast to the landscape, dulling nature's colors as if the rain had washed them away.

The river widened as they traveled, and the great rocks on the bank were spaced further apart. The water churned angrily as it rushed alongside them. Trees and branches and other debris floated by, dragged along by the relentless force of water. Beside her, the land rose up in a steep cliff that ran with rivulets of thick slippery mud.

Kira sat astride Trad, shivering beneath her soggy blanket. The wet wool smelled of sheep and made her want to sneeze. She rubbed her nose. It's worth nothing, she thought glumly, clamping her mouth shut to keep her teeth from chattering. I should have traded for an oiled cape instead of a worthless blanket. She resisted the desire to fling it into the rushing river.

She considered dismounting. At least walking would help warm her. She pulled Trad to a stop, when something caught her eye. Squinting into the distance, she made out a pile of huge rocks that had tumbled down onto the sandy bank. Large blue-gray boulders had broken away from the cliff face and covered the bank all the way to the river's edge. They were strewn across the riverbank, as though some giant hand had deliberately placed them there to block the path.

Kira let out her breath with an explosive hiss. "Serpent's blood!" she spat. Leaping from the saddle, she threw off the cold sodden blanket and sank to her knees. "Great Troka! What have I done to deserve this?" she screamed at the sky.

Kelmir turned and walked back toward her, ears folded back against his head. He walked behind her and sat down, curling his body around hers. She leaned against him and pressed her face into his neck. It had been a long time since she'd needed comforting like this. After the death of her parents, when Heresta had first taken her in, Kira had spent days and nights out in the woods, burrowed into the soft warmth of Kelmir's fur, letting her grief flow out. Now, here she was once again, feeling like a lost child. What else could go wrong?

Rain splattered down and the numbing cold crept over her, bringing her back to herself. Kelmir stayed close, keeping his body in contact with hers. Trad stood still, head down; Vaith clung to the pommel of the saddle, eyeing her. She sat up. "Well, boys, this is getting us nowhere." Kira smiled weakly, giving Kelmir a brisk rub between the ears.

"We need to find some kind of shelter. Someplace where we can get out of the cold, at least." She dragged herself to her feet and stared up at the wall of rocks before them. "But first we need to find a way around that."

Kelmir stood up, following her gaze. He gave one glance back, then loped forward. Kira walked over to Trad and Vaith, stooping to pick up the blanket on her way. The sodden mass was caked in mud. She shook her head. "I just had to go and make things worse," she muttered, a sob pushing its way out with her words. She picked up Trad's reins and headed off to see if Kelmir had found a way past the barrier.

By the time she reached the rocks, Kelmir had climbed to the top of the pile and was cautiously making his way toward the far end. Kira shielded her eyes with her hands, cupping them close to her forehead as the rain continued to beat down. A low rumbling came from the south and grew louder as thunder rolled across the stormy sky. Kelmir continued to prowl along the top of the rocks, questing for a way past them. He stopped when he reached the top of the high embankment and gazed out.

Kira looked through his eyes, but land met sky in a blurring of dark grays and shadows. She stayed in his mind as he crept back along the rocks toward the river. Small stones loosened under his feet and rolled down the side of the rock pile. There was no way to get Trad over that

51

barrier, nor would they be able to climb it to the top of the cliff. The sides were too steep, the rocks too loose.

Kelmir reached the end of the rock pile and stood above the roiling river. Kira saw through his eyes that the rockslide continued down into the water. If the remains of the slide were less steep where the water rushed over it, it might be possible to wade out around the end of the pile that blocked their way.

Kira pulled away from Kelmir's mind and focused on the dark riverbank. She guided Trad to the river's edge, then stepped slowly out into the water, sliding her foot out in front of her to find a point of purchase. She gasped as the icy water rushed around her ankle, sucking at her calf as she put her weight down. She repeated the process with her other foot and found that she had to move further out into the rushing water to find a stable place to stand.

She inched her way out to the end of the rockslide, with Trad following behind her. By the time she reached the end of the slide and found a place to turn back toward the shore on the other side, the water was up to her hips. It pushed and buffeted her, as she stuck one foot in front of the other, seeking a solid foothold.

The going was agonizingly slow. Her legs stung from the cold and her feet were numb. She struggled to keep moving. Trad blustered behind her, blowing air out in an impatient whoosh. "Be patient," she scolded. "I'm cold, too. But I'm not falling into this river just because you want me to move faster."

Vaith clung to the saddle's pommel, nervously scanning the dark water and flexing his wings as if preparing to take to the air. Trad whinnied and once again the strange sensation prickled at the back of her neck. "All right, I'm moving," she told Trad over her shoulder, but it wasn't the horse's impatience that spurred her on.

Above, the comforting form of Kelmir appeared, a dark silhouette atop the rocks. She moved quickly now. If whatever was nearby decided to attack she didn't want to be caught in the water. Trad's hooves slipped on the precarious rocks and he lurched from side to side as the stones shifted beneath his weight. Each time she cringed, but each time he regained his footing.

The water rushed around the rockslide, creating a whirlpool of ghostly foam against the black water. The torrent tugged and grabbed at them as they struggled toward the shore. All the while Kira was unable to shake the sensation that something dark and sinister watched them.

As she neared the shore, it seemed as if everywhere she stepped the treacherous rocks shifted out from underfoot. She teetered, arms extended, trying to maintain her balance. If she slipped, the torrent would carry her away.

A sudden pull from Trad's reins brought her splashing down into the freezing river. Kira gasped as she hit the water. Trad foundered behind her, struggling to find a footing as the water dragged him alongside her. Suddenly, the bottom fell away and there was nothing to stand on. Vaith gave a loud squawk and leaped sideways in the air. Kira saw his silhouette pass her as he headed toward shore.

She hadn't thought she could be any colder, but as usual, things seemed determined to get worse. She kicked out with her legs, finally brushing the bottom of the river with the toes of her boots. She tilted her head back to keep her face above water, struggling against the swirling current. Trad came up beside her, swimming toward the riverbank. She let the reins slip from her hand and grabbed hold of the saddle.

As they neared the muddy embankment, Kira heard a roar and looked up to see Kelmir pounce from the rocks above. He landed with a resounding thud on what appeared to be a large dark boulder. A flash of lightning revealed the boulder as something more menacing. It swayed and toppled over, reaching out with bulky arms to grasp at the big cat.

The hulking shadow shoved Kelmir away and turned toward Trad and Kira as they labored to gain their footing on the shore. Kira watched it come, a dark heaving beast with burning eyes as bright as glowing coals. She let go of the saddle and reached for her knife as the dark mass lumbered toward her. Trad whinnied again, reared on his hind legs, and struck out with his front hooves. The shadow hesitated and Kelmir leaped at it from behind, knocking it off balance once more. It spun about and Kira slashed at its legs, but her knife glanced off the creature's tough hide.

Kelmir clung to the beast with teeth and claws as it twisted around. It let out a rough guttural sound as it reached behind to grab at the animal clinging to its back. Confusing shadows danced in the lightning-shattered darkness. Kira struck again, this time with a stabbing motion. Her knife pierced flesh and the beast let out a howl of rage. It bent over, trying to throw Kelmir off its back, but the fierce cat held tight, his teeth sinking deeper into the creature's neck.

Kira stabbed again and the beast flung out its thick massive arms, knocking her down. It threw its head back, striking Kelmir's skull with its own with a loud crack. Kelmir clawed at its face, but lost his grip and was flung across the muddy ground. Kira scrambled to get up, the knife slippery in her hand. She couldn't tell if it was covered in mud or blood, but she held on to the slick handle with stubborn determination as she backed away from the beast.

Leathery wings beat at the wet sky, and Vaith circled overhead. The monster flung its arm out and slapped the wyvern from the air. Vaith screeched as he thudded to the ground. Kira searched the darkness for him, but the monster lunged at her, forcing her back toward the river.

Trad had danced his way behind the hulking mass, his hooves sinking in the muddy riverbank as the storm raged on. The creature crouched to spring at Kira and Trad whinnied loudly, raising his forefeet to strike at the monster's back. It whirled on him, swiping at the horse's legs with vicious claws. Kira dove in again, thrusting the blade deep into its lower back and wrenching the knife upward. The blade sliced through with a sickening sound and the beast howled, reaching behind to claw at its back. It spun around, wrenching itself away from Kira's blade and struck at her.

She dodged sideways, but a heavy fist struck her face. The blow knocked her to the muddy bank. Her head reeled and the knife flew from her hand as she fell. She reached for the blade and the creature pounced. Kelmir dove past her. The beast tumbled back with the cat on top of him. They rolled over one another, screams mixing with the thunder, bodies silhouetted against flashes of lightning that tore from the sky. Kelmir clung to the monster's torso, his teeth sunk deep into its right arm. Trad leaped to the side as the two plowed past him. Whirling quickly around, he struck out, hooves flashing. Kelmir hung on. His claws raked across his adversary's chest while the beast struggled to ward off the blows of Trad's hooves.

Kira's face burned with pain. A part of her wanted to give up, to let the struggle end here. But somewhere deep inside her a sense of purpose welled up and she knew she must overcome this beast, or die trying. Her fingers found the knife. She grasped it by the hilt and gritted her teeth in resolve. Heaving to her feet, she stumbled toward the fighting, the knife raised overhead. She searched for an opening, but neither Trad nor Kelmir slackened their attack. Kira stood ready. The monster rolled away from

Trad and its head appeared on the ground before her. She stabbed desperately at its eyes and the sharp blade slid deep into soft tissue.

The beast lashed at its face and wailed. Kelmir gave it one last shake, then let go. The monster lay dead. With a sideways step, Kelmir moved cautiously away, circling the beast's carcass, watching for movement.

Dizziness danced inside Kira's head. Her skull was afire. She swayed for a moment. Her legs weakened and gave out. She fell on her knees in the mud and sobbed. Cold rain ran down her face as she raised the knife and stabbed it into the mud, over and over, until her arm shook and the pain and fury burst out of her in a ragged scream.

The rain poured down. Her breathing slowed and became more regular. She took a few deep breaths, blowing them out through her mouth. Trad stood over the creature, his body quivering with exhaustion. Kelmir crouched nearby, watching her, the tip of his tail flicking back and forth. Kira glanced around, searching for Vaith. A whistling chirp came faintly from above and she turned toward the rocks that had blocked their path.

Vaith stood on the edge of the slide nearest the cliff, his eyes glowing dimly in the distance. He tugged at her with his mind. Kira tried to reach out to him, but a heavy darkness clotted her brain. She crawled over to the rocks and used them to pull herself up. She leaned back against the rocks and turned her hot face to the icy rain, letting it cool the fire in her head.

Another chirrup brought her attention back to Vaith. She turned toward him, reaching out with one arm to lean against the rocks as she walked toward the cliff. A bolt of lightning lit the sky, outlining the mouth of a cave. Blackness rose up before her and she thought she was going to faint, but she kept moving toward the dark spot in the side of the cliff. She knew there could be danger, knew she should move carefully, but she was exhausted. If more danger lurked inside, she was too weak to fight it. They all were.

She kept moving, dragging her feet like someone drunk or under the influence of madweed. When she reached the mouth of the cave, she turned back to call the others, but her throat was raw, and all she could do was croak out the words so low she couldn't hear her own voice. Kelmir stood up and walked over to Trad, nudging the big horse's flank. Trad moved obediently, as if he had no will of his own. Vaith perched on the brink of the rocks. Kira nodded once, then stumbled into the cave.

CHAPTER FIVE

Kira crept forward, brushing her fingertips against the rough cave wall to guide her. A few steps in from the opening, she stopped, repelled by the stench of animal musk and rot. There was no way to tell how far back the cavern extended, but she had no intention of exploring. She wanted only to rest. She sank down, but caught herself at the scrape of Trad's hooves on the stony floor. He needed to be unsaddled and she needed to check him and the others for wounds.

She led Trad beside the wall and loosened his girth. After sliding off his saddle and halter, she rubbed feebly at his back with the wet saddle blanket. She stroked his flanks in the darkness, then ran her hands lightly over his chest and down each leg. He had a number of scratches, but none that seemed too deep. But she would have to wait until daylight to perform a more thorough examination.

Kelmir sat near the mouth of the cave. As she leaned over him a dark shadow swooped in through the cave entrance. Startled, she lost her balance and landed hard on the dirt floor. She heard a small thud and the scrabbling of claws beside her. Vaith. She tried to see into his mind, but the mental effort was too much for her. She reached out her hand and he waddled toward her. His left wing hung awkwardly out to the side. He allowed her to gently search for injuries, but squawked in pain as the tips of her fingers brushed against a rip in the fragile membrane of his wing. The wound was minor and, luckily, a straight tear that would mend well, but it would be a while before Vaith regained his normal grace and speed in the air.

She turned her attention to Kelmir. The big cat stood still as she sat beside him, running her fingers along his back and legs. He flinched from her touch, but she didn't feel any broken bones. The shallow cuts and scratches he had could be best cared for by his own ministrations. Kira leaned her back against the wall. The stone was rough and hard and she was cold and wet, but it was a relief to be out of the incessant rain.

She let herself slide down, curled up on the stony floor, and peered into the depths of the cave. Flashes of lightning illuminated only the first few feet in from the opening, but despite the weight of the looming darkness, she could feel the space open up around her. She wondered if her voice would bounce back at her if she spoke, or if the gloomy corners would gobble up the sound of her words. She remained silent, unwilling to find out.

A shiver ran through her and she drew up her knees and hugged herself. Outside, the storm still raged. Against the intermittent flashes of light in the sky beyond the mouth of the cave, Kelmir was a shadowy wraith, circling in front of the opening as he prepared to lie down. Kira turned away and closed her eyes. Her head ached and she was cold and sore and tired. Her hunger seemed a distant echo. A buzzing started inside her head and she drifted off, the clicking sound of Kelmir's sharp claws on the stony floor growing distant and hazy.

* * *

Kira opened her eyes, wincing in pain at the light before quickly shutting them again. Light? She raised a hand to shield her eyes. Pale rays of daylight spilled into the cave. Water still dripped from the rocky overhang, but the dark clouds had lightened to a silvery gray and a pale blue streak of morning sky was visible on the horizon beyond the river.

Her damp clothes clung to her. She shivered in the cold of the shadowy cave and rolled her neck to ease the stiffness, gasping when a burst of pain shot across the side of her head. Gently, she put her hands to her face. The left side was tender and swollen. She worked her jaw gently back and forth. Nothing broken, but the pain was fresh and raw. She moaned and sat up, testing her joints and muscles in what had become a daily ritual, an intimate survey to see how much damage had been done the day before.

Kelmir lay just inside the cave mouth. His ears twitched in her direction as she stirred, and he opened one eye to a narrow slit. Trad stood against the opposite wall, sleeping, his breathing slow and steady.

Kira swallowed hard. Her throat was ragged and her lips burned. How can I be so thirsty after spending hours in the rain? she thought, squinting against the brightness. The rushing river called to her and she pushed herself to her feet. Head throbbing, she staggered out of the cave.

She caught her breath as she emerged into the light and saw the dead creature lying in her path. It was huge and foul. The rain had washed much of the body clean, but dried mud and blood still matted its fur in places. She stared at the gray skin and thick bony ridging along its spine in startled recognition. A rock troll. She'd heard stories, gory descriptions of ten-foot tall beasts that could shred a human with one swipe of its vicious claws, but she'd never seen one. The dark and the rain had been as

60

much good luck as bad. If she had known what they were fighting— Kira closed her eyes. No. She and her companions would have fought just as hard, no matter the danger, or the size of their foe.

She gaped at the beast. The troll's stature, much less than ten feet by Kira's reckoning, was far from the height such creatures were supposed to reach as adults. Perhaps the stories she'd heard had been exaggerated.

But, what if they weren't? She shuddered. Trolls were supposed to be territorial, but what if there were more of them about. If this one wasn't full grown—

She skirted the body slowly, careful not to touch it. Her reasoning mind knew it had been dead for hours, but part of her was still afraid. A small hoot made her jump. She flinched, bringing her hand up quickly to her pounding head. *I'm fine*, she thought at Vaith, then grimaced. *At least I was until you startled me.* Vaith trilled low in his throat and, sensing his hurt, Kira regretted her scolding words. She gritted her teeth as she made her way to the river's edge. "I'm sorry, little one, I'm just in a foul mood. It isn't your fault I'm in pain," she whispered to keep the echoing in her head at bay.

Kneeling on the riverbank, she cupped her hands and scooped up freezing water, sipping as it dribbled through her fingers. The icy water tasted sweet, but numbed her fingers. The morning sun glowed high in the sky, and the stones along the river cast shadows that seemed to ripple and dance between bright patches of sunlight.

Kira stretched her legs out behind her, lying on her stomach on the sandy shore to lower her face to the water. The cold made her flinch, but she pushed her face into the icy river. When she could hold her breath no longer, she pulled her head up, gasping for air, then plunged her face back into the water over and over until the throbbing finally subsided to a dull pain. She took a long cold drink and rolled onto her back, allowing herself to doze in the warmth of the sun as it peeked out between scattering clouds.

When she woke once more, her clothes were nearly dry. She opened one eye, then the other. Her face was still sore, but the throbbing ache was gone and the sunlight was tolerable.

A shadow passed over. Vaith fluttered above her for a moment, and then made an awkward landing beside her. "Show off," she told him with a smile. He folded his wings carefully, shrugging his shoulders, and Kira noted stiffness in his movements. He could have been hurt far worse by the troll than he'd been.

She sat up as Kelmir limped out of the cave. He had cleaned some of the mud off himself, baring fresh claw marks on his right shoulder. Kira berated herself for not seeing the extent of the wound earlier. She was making too many mistakes. Mistakes they couldn't afford. She tended to his wound, using what was left of her store of herbs. Afterward, Kelmir sprawled out to sleep in the sun.

Muttering to herself about her stupidity, she led Trad out into the light and reexamined him. A long scratch on his left forefoot had become red and puffy. He wasn't limping, but Kira didn't like the look of it. She wrapped it in damp moss to reduce the swelling and covered it with sticky mud dredged from the river.

Vaith sidled up to her, tilting his head and flicking his tail. His hunger spilled out and her stomach growled in response. "Yes, you're right. It's high time we caught something to eat." She sat up. Her head was clearer, but her face was tender and her body ached. She tried to remember a time when she didn't hurt. It seemed as if, since leaving the home she had shared with Heresta, her life had been an unending series of beatings.

She stood and wiped her hands on her shirt. "This journey's been rough on all of us, little one. But things

62

could be worse. At least we've managed to elude Toril's men this far."

The swollen river rushed by, still carrying branches and other debris, but the fish would be settling back into feeding now that the storm had passed. She saw herself as a child, sitting beside her father on the bank of the stream near their farm, watching as he baited his line and dropped it into the water. He would speak softly to her, telling her about fish and their ways, when they fed and when they didn't, which ones tasted best in stew, or roasted over an open fire. His quiet murmurings entranced her and she would feel the hush of the trees and flowers as she watched and waited for her father's line to become taut with the next big catch. The two of them would both jump when the pole jerked, and then they would laugh together as he pulled in the line with a wriggling fish on the end of it.

Her mouth watered at the thought of hot fish stew and she scanned the area for something to use for a line and a pole. She had a short length of waxed thread taken from Heresta's stores. The thread was normally used for stitching wounds, but would be strong and fine enough for line. Only, she had no hooks. She recalled sitting by the fire, watching her father make his own hooks, heating and hammering small metal nails into the correct shape, but she had nothing like that. She knew there were people who could spear a fish with a long pole, but she wasn't sure her battered body was up to such a physical feat.

There wasn't enough line for a fish net. She glanced back at the cave, wondering if there might be something inside she could use to catch a fish, then discarded the thought. From all the stories she'd heard, trolls weren't generally that industrious. Especially rock trolls. They much preferred to take something warm-blooded and feed on it before it was cold. She shivered at the thought.

Still, a quick search might provide something useful. She stood up and started toward the cave, but stopped near the fallen troll. It lay on its stomach, one arm under its body, the other extended out to the side. Its curved claws were wide at the tips of the fingers, but narrow and sharp on the ends, and perhaps she could scrape one down. She crept closer, reaching for her knife, but her hand came away from her belt empty. Another stupid mistake. She'd dropped her only weapon in the cave. She rushed to retrieve the blade. How long before such a mistake would cost her her freedom, or worse, one of their lives?

With the knife in her hand, she pushed aside her revulsion, and crept up to the beast's outstretched arm. She tried slicing at the claw on the first finger, but the nail was thick and strong, and she resorted to hacking at it. Her blows glanced off the smooth surface. In frustration, Kira placed one foot on the monster's hand to hold the finger steady and brought the sharp blade down in a chopping motion. The knife missed its mark, sinking into flesh and through the joint. The fingertip came off, bouncing a few inches away and lay in the dirt, an oozing lump ending in a shiny curve that glinted in the sun.

Kira stepped away from the troll. Dark gray fluid oozed from the finger where the tip had been severed and a sickening sweet odor drifted up. She clamped her mouth shut to keep the bile from rising past her throat, squared her shoulders, and picked up the clawed fingertip. It was far less menacing detached from the troll's hand. Using the knife, she pried the nail from its fleshy bed. She held her breath, trying not to inhale the foul smell, and worked the nail against a rock until the base was almost as narrow as the sharp tip. As she worked, she thought about her father. Those quiet days by the river had been a pleasant diversion, unlike what she was doing now. She set her jaw and finished her work, carving a neck into the base of the claw where she could attach her line.

A tree branch that had washed ashore provided a flexible pole, and she gathered bait from under the stones by the river, scooping up the insects that scrambled from the light when she lifted the rocks. A short distance upriver, she found a deep eddy near the bank where she dropped the makeshift hook into the water and sat down to wait.

Fat heavy flies drifted about, making low buzzing noises as she sat staring at the spot where her line intersected the water. As her eyes adjusted, she could make out a huge boulder, just beneath the surface. Around it, the water slowed and eddied. She heard her father's deep voice telling her that this quiet swirl of dark water was a perfect hiding place for fish. She pulled her line over, inching it closer to the side of the rock. The line pulled tight and she clamped her hands around the pole.

Kira muttered a prayer that the line would hold, as she moved closer to the water. If only I can work it around the rock, she thought, stretching her arms out over the deep water and trying to lead the fish around the other side of the boulder. It struggled against her, and she let it have its way. Then as it swam toward safety under the shielding presence of the rock, she led it around the other side. After repeating the process a few times, the fish grew tired. Sensing it had about given up, Kira gave one last yank, and a speckled fish flew out of the water and landed flapping at her feet.

She bowed her head and gave thanks for the life she was taking, then eyed the fish hungrily. It was too small to feed all three of them. Her stomach grumbled as she pried the fish from the hook and tossed it up on the bank where it couldn't flop back into the river. Her arms shook with fatigue by the time evening shadows stretched across the river, but five fat fish gleamed on the shore.

At the water's edge, she cleaned her catch as Vaith watched. She wasted nothing, placing the guts onto a flat rock and nodding to the little wyvern, who leaped forward and ate greedily. All living things were sacred, every life a spoke on the wheel. From Heresta, she had learned to show the proper gratitude for every plant and animal that gave its life to sustain hers. She cleaned three of the fish, saving the last two for Kelmir. The big cat would eat them whole.

She skewered her three cleaned fish between thin green branches, opening them up to expose their fleshy insides, and stuck the ends of the branches in the sandy soil. "Keep an eye on these for me, little one, and I'll share some with you once they're cooked," she told Vaith, who hopped from one foot to the other as she worked. "I think we can chance another fire. It will be dusk shortly, and the smoke won't be seen. If we build it just inside the cave, the flames will be hidden from view, as well." Picking the driest pieces she could find, she gathered enough firewood to make a small blaze and keep it going long enough to cook their meager meal.

As the sun cast the last of the day's long shadows across the river, Kira knelt beside a dancing blaze, holding the skewered fish close enough to roast without burning. When they finished eating, she sat back and watched the flames turn to coals, and the coals to ash as the fire died. Life is that way, she thought. Burning bright one moment, then fading into nothing the next. A black mood stole over her as she fell into a feverish sleep beside the cooling ash, and her dreams were filled with a deadly fire that fell from the sky, raining down on fields and villages. Burning people ran in every direction, trying to escape the destruction and death all around them. In the midst of all the heat and chaos stood Toril, and fire filled his eyes.

CHAPTER SIX

Early next morning they continued their journey, following the river toward its source. The skies cleared, but the nights grew colder as they trekked across the upward-sloping terrain. From what she remembered of the maps she had seen, she knew they would need to turn north again to make the main pass through the Zendel Mountains. Kira stared ahead. The ground continued to rise ever more steeply, and the rocky cliff towered above them. Worry gnawed at her. They wouldn't be able to head north if the cliff didn't recede.

There were other passes through the mountains besides the Kandurst Gap. But each potential option held its own dangers. The Gap traversed the mountains at a low elevation that allowed passage most of the year, which made it physically less dangerous than other paths. However, it was also heavily used. The trail that followed the river might take them to a pass less traveled because it led high up into the mountains, which could be treacherous. The pass, if it existed, might not even be open. A rock fall might have closed it, or it might already be covered in snow and ice. This wasn't the way she would have chosen to travel to the Faersent Sea, but the rising cliff was leaving them no choice.

The river narrowed, splashing past in white torrents, while the ground grew rough and rocky. The trail followed the river's zigzag path as the cliff rose up, leaning at a precarious angle overhead. They climbed steep inclines and threaded narrow rocky places where the trail became difficult and unsafe. Kira often dismounted, leading Trad instead of riding. His leg was still inflamed and she worried that the strenuous journey kept it from healing.

Every morning, Kira had to renew her resolve to go on, wavering between the worry that they would reach an impassable point and the fear that Toril's men might have picked up their trail. At each turn they came to, she hoped they would find the water's source and the narrow gap beyond, and that they would be over the mountains and on their way down to the western sea. But around each bend, there was still no sign of the pass.

On the morning of the tenth day after leaving the cave, the snow began. It started as a slow flurry of flakes, drifting out of the sky like a swarm of dying butterflies. Kira pulled the blanket closer. Above them were the cold gray clouds, ahead the endless narrow trail. *Vaith, can you fly further ahead and scout for us? If the snow gets worse, we'll need a place to wait out the storm.*

He shot her a sleepy-eyed glance from his perch on the saddle horn, blinking his eyes open and shut, rousing himself from his chill-induced stupor. With a slow spread of his wings, he launched himself into the air and flapped off.

As Vaith took flight, Kelmir bounded forward and batted at a large flake of snow that drifted past his nose. The snowflake stuck to his foot and melted. Kira found herself laughing as he licked the wetness from his paw. She'd forgotten the joy that snow could bring. Snow had been rare in the vales where she'd grown up, but when it did fall the children would leave their chores to play in the white softness. Even some of the adults had joined in, building snow mounds and carving out cold sculptures that they would pour water over, turning them into icy statues. But there had always been a crackling fire to run to and something hot to drink when her hands and face turned rosy from the cold.

Vaith's thoughts nudged her memories aside and she gazed through his eyes at the path ahead. The river continued, but there was no sign of a pass, and no place to shelter. *Come back,* Kira told him, trying to keep the worry from her thoughts. Darkness was falling and she knew they wouldn't survive long if the snow flurry became a blizzard. The pass had to be near. Trad seemed reluctant as she urged him forward. "We'll rest, soon. I promise." She patted his warm neck. She had carefully tended his wounded leg each morning and night, but the swelling remained and the scratch had begun to fester. She no longer rode, but walked beside him, keeping a watch on his gait.

Trad blew out, his breath rising in steamy wisps, and she stroked his ears. Things could be worse, she kept reminding herself, repeating Heresta's words over in her mind. But the words were only words and they did nothing to soothe her. Certainly things could be worse, she thought. I could be lying bruised and tortured in Toril's tent. Or dead.

Snowflakes reeled in the air and she leaned against Trad's warm flank, pulling the blanket over her head so it covered her face. Her fingers shook from the cold and she blew into them for warmth. "Come on, Trad." She tugged gently at his reins.

Vaith returned and landed on her shoulder. His claws dug into the padding of her vest. Gladness flowed through her, even as they hurried into the unknown. It was good to have him on her shoulder again. She relaxed and watched the road ahead.

The snow continued to fall and the wind picked up as midday turned toward late afternoon. Kira began searching for a place to camp, but there seemed to be no place that would shelter Trad from the wind and cold.

They turned a corner and Kira pulled Trad up short. A distant rumbling filled the air. Ahead, a tall white streak sliced down the mountainside. A waterfall. They were near the summit at last.

Large flakes continued to fall and the snow drifted, filling in their footprints as they passed beneath the waterfall and on through the thick forest. The trail narrowed to a foot track, becoming overgrown with roots and bracken, but continued to wind through the trees. The path turned westward and before evening began to descend. Kira's mind buzzed. After all they'd been through, it couldn't be that easy, could it?

They emerged from the dense covering of woods to find themselves at the top of a steep cliff, with the only way down a narrow ledge that cut back and forth along the rock face. Kira peered into the shadows that filled the valley below. Through the heavy haze, she could make out a dense forest and, farther off, open land.

She leaned down to check Trad's leg. His swollen ankle was hot to the touch and he stood still, keeping his weight off his foot. The poultice she had applied the day before had dried, and dark yellow pus oozed out from the edges. She rubbed his withers. His coat was wet with sweat and he shivered at her touch. "I'm sorry, Trad. What you need is a hot soak in a strong drawing fluid to pull out the toxin and then a long rest, but I can't give you that here. Hopefully, we'll find a cot or 'stead in the valley."

She turned to Kelmir. The big cat sat on his haunches a few feet down the path, waiting. "It's up to you, Kel," she told him. "Scout the way down. We'll follow behind."

The trek down was woefully slow, but Kira took her time, making sure the ground was solid enough to hold Trad's weight as he limped along behind her. The sky brightened as the morning sun rose toward its zenith, but the air refused to warm. Kira stared out toward the flat expanse that lay beyond the trees. It was hard to tell from this distance, but the ground seemed to have been cleared for planting. She hoped it meant they would find a farm or holding nearby. Preferably one with a warm fire, Kira thought, blowing on her fingers to warm them.

Trad's limp had deteriorated to a hobble. The only possibility of finding help now lay in the valley below them.

They passed below the haze and finally the numbing chill abated and the air grew warmer as they made their way down toward the valley. Stretched out below them, deciduous trees dressed in brilliant colors grew among the tall evergreens. Fall had already come to this valley. She stopped to let Trad rest and admired the colorful display of red and gold. For a moment she let herself forget she was fleeing a gang of mercenaries bent on returning her to imprisonment and abuse. When she was young fall had been her favorite time of year. The warmth of summer had always lingered on the farm as she helped her father and mother tend the fall crops they would dry and preserve for the winter. But in fall the sun set early, and there were stories by a warm fire and hot mugs of mulled cider to hold between cold fingers after coming in from evening chores.

Her reverie was broken as Trad tried to put his weight down on his foreleg and stumbled toward the trail's edge. "Whoa, Trad. Whoa." The edge of the trail shifted and collapsed in a rattle of dirt and rocks that slid toward the valley below. With shaking hands, Kira eased Trad back toward the cliff wall. It was a good thing she hadn't been able to ride. The treacherous path was barely able to hold Trad's weight without her on his back.

"Okay, boy," she said as he grew steady. His breathing was heavy as she rubbed his muzzle. "Let's move on. The sooner we reach the valley, the sooner I can tend to that leg." He snorted and stepped forward at her urging, but he was unable to put his weight on the foot. Kira walked backward down the trail, keeping her eyes on his progress as he hobbled toward her.

"Come on Trad," she said, when he slowed. His coat was covered in foamy sweat that spattered her in small flecks as he shivered. A few hundred strides more would bring them to the valley floor. "We're nearly there," she whispered, but Trad stopped and leaned against the face of the cliff, refusing to move. His foreleg was swollen and dripping with pus. Kira knew how much it must hurt. "You can do it, boy. Just a little farther," she urged.

She pulled at Trad's bridle. "Come on," she begged, her voice breaking. But Trad refused to budge. Kira clenched her jaw and pulled again, but a spattering of dirt and rocks rained down on them. She stopped and peered up through the gray mist. On the cliff far above them were the silhouettes of three men on horseback. And they were starting down the trail toward her. She heard a shout and more dirt showered down the cliff side. For one terrible moment, she thought she heard Toril's angry voice, felt him battering her. The men had to be Toril's soldiers. Who else would be following the trail through this pass? Trad started and whinnied as gravel and rocks pelted him. Vaith flapped up from the saddle with a terrified squawk. Kira tried to calm them, but her own fear and the dust from the cascading dirt choked her.

Trad broke free, yanking the reins out of her hands, and bolted down the trail. He careened along the path, dangerously close to the edge. The trail seemed to shift beneath Kira's feet as she ran after Trad, calling for him to slow down. She watched in terror as he bore directly down on Kelmir. The big cat sprang out of the way, leaping down to the next level and running ahead as Trad turned the corner and continued headlong toward the bottom. As he neared the valley floor, an entire section of the cliff above them gave way in an angry roar. Horses screamed and men yelled as the shower of debris turned into a rushing fall of dirt and rocks that crashed down toward the valley floor.

More dirt fell on Kira and she yanked the blanket up over her head and pressed herself flat against the cliff as the rush of stones and debris poured past. The dirt slid down in a torrent that pelted her head and shoulders. Dust rose up and filled her nose and mouth. She squeezed her eyes shut and tried not to breathe. Sliding debris tumbled over her, pushing her toward the edge of the trail. She dug her fingers into the rock wall. The trail gave out beneath her feet and she leaned back, bracing herself against the cliff, waiting as the dirt slid past her, slowed to a trickle, and stopped. She opened her eyes and peeled back the blanket. A thick brown haze obscured everything. She coughed and spit, clearing the dirt from her mouth. "Troka, please let Trad be all right," she prayed.

She slid one foot back, testing for solid ground. Found nothing. Behind her, the trail had been shaved down to a narrow strip just wide enough for her to clutch with her toes. With tiny steps, she inched sideways along the cliff, gripping the wall as best she could. After a few feet, the trail widened out again. She stepped cautiously away from the cliff, testing first to see if the path would hold her, shook the dirt from her face and looked up. Through the haze she could make out a single man, peering down from the top of the cliff. Of the other two men, there was no sign. All the way down the side of the cliff, a gaping section of the trail had been obliterated. A wide swathe of the cliff wall had been shaved smooth. There was no way back up. But no way down from the top either. Fear gave way to relief. Toril's men would have to go back empty handed. The man at the top of the cliff yelled something, but his voice was only an echo. Then the mist closed in and obscured him from view.

Kira shook dirt from her blanket. She needed to get off the ledge. The slide might not have been intentional, but that didn't mean the men above her wouldn't try to cause another one. They might be tired of chasing her and ready to return to Toril with news of her accidental death.

But the lower part of the trail was completely gone. Where before it had crossed the side of the cliff, there was now a long slide of dirt and rocks. It wouldn't be a pleasant way to travel, but there was no other way to reach the valley floor. She wiped at her face, but her filthy hands and sleeves only ground more of the gritty dirt into her skin.

Putting one foot in front of the other to be sure the trail would hold her weight, she inched toward the pile of rubble. She stared across the debris to where a section of the trail was still intact. It might be possible to cross the slide and reach the trail again on the other side, but then she would still have to recross the mound of dirt farther down when the trail cut back again. Below her, Trad stood trembling on three legs. The quicker she reached him, the better. Besides, the mass of dirt and rocks didn't appear stable. And she couldn't possibly get past the debris at its widest points. She might just as well ride it down from here.

She made certain her pouch was tied securely at her waist and drew the blanket around her. She leaped forward and leaned back. The dirt slid out from under her feet as she skidded down the rushing debris. She bent her knees as she picked up speed, tilting from side to side to keep herself from toppling over. Small rocks and sand filled her boots. Dust flew, creating a cloud as the valley floor rose to meet her.

She sat back hard to slow her descent as she neared the bottom. When she stopped, dirt and rocks continued to slide down and pile up. A brown dusting of powder settled around her. She coughed and sneezed as she dusted herself off. Trad stood off to her right with Kelmir pacing nearby. Vaith called to her from a low tree branch. Relief washed over her and the aches and scratches from the rockslide faded. They were all here. All safe. She grabbed Trad's reins and pulled him toward the copse of trees where no arrows could find them.

Once under the cover of birch and hazel, she sat down and pulled off her boots, shaking out the rocks and dirt before putting them back on. Worry began to crowd at her. They'd all made it down the cliff and Toril's men would be unable to follow for the time being, but now what? Her scrapes and bruises were minor, but Trad could barely walk. If she didn't properly care for his leg soon, he could be permanently lame.

She limped over to where he stood shivering. His leg was a swollen mass, hot to the touch, and he jerked away from her, eyes wide and nostrils flaring. "Shhhh," she whispered, limping after him. "Come on, Trad." Slow and easy, she gathered the reins in her hand. "There, now." She kept her voice steady, but her hands shook as she guided him deeper into the thicket where Vaith perched.

CHAPTER SEVEN

The settlement spread out before her, large and prosperous. It was certainly bigger than any of the farms or holds she'd seen near her home. Late afternoon sunlight shone across the clearing that surrounded the hold, a typical defense line where the forest had been cleared for hundreds of strides around the high walls that circled the main buildings. Kira paused just inside the tree line to give her tunic one more swipe. She knew it was a wasted attempt, there was no way she could get clean, and there wasn't any time to spare. But she couldn't afford to be turned away as a beggar, either. She squared her shoulders, hefted the small pig onto her back, and strode forward across the clearing, feeling vulnerable in the open space. Casting an air of confidence over herself that she didn't really feel, she headed for the main gate.

Vaith had flitted from branch to branch, scouting the edge of the forest. He'd discovered the hold shortly after they set out from the cliff side. Kira had sent Kelmir out for game. He'd returned with a wild peccary large enough to impress the holder, she hoped, but small enough that she would be able to carry it. She pushed away the thought that she was trading one life for another. Trad was a faithful companion. She would do what was necessary to save him.

Kelmir stood guard over Trad. She wouldn't have brought the big cat with her at any rate. Most people were frightened of Kelmir, particularly the first time they saw him.

The main gate was open, which wasn't unusual for a settlement at peace—the gates would probably be shut at sunset—but she hesitated before entering. Where was the gatekeeper or a watch? Her skin prickled. What if it was a trap? Stop it! she commanded herself. Her worries were foolish and gained her nothing. The men on the cliff had no way down and the mountain range extended at least a moon's ride in either direction without another pass. It would take time for them to get a message back to Toril. He was certain to have other men out hunting for her, but those others still had no way of knowing where she was headed. She hadn't really known herself. No, this was just a sleepy little hold.

She shifted the weight of the animal on her shoulders and walked into the main yard. A low growl stopped her. A powerful mastiff with a muscular chest stared at her from just inside the gate. She sensed protective anger and fear from him, mixed with curiosity and excitement at the scent of fresh game. Watchdog or hunter? Both? Of course, his reaction could be pure instinct. She tried to touch his mind with hers, but it was a jumble of emotions, and she was unable to calm him. Dogs were often difficult for her to reach. Not true carnivores, they could sometimes be impossible to connect with. She could sense more from them than she could from an herbivore, but usually not enough to communicate. This was the sort of thing that made her ponder the strangeness and the limitations of her gift. Why carnivores, and then only those that hunted? Was there something about her that gave her an affinity with creatures that killed? Was that what had attracted Toril to her? She shuddered. The dog growled again.

Kira slowed her breathing, then mentally reached out once more. The big dog crouched as it prepared to leap. She gripped the legs of the pig, ready to swing the carcass at the dog.

"Whoa, Cadge, back!" Kira heard a deep male voice. The dog stopped growling, but stood its ground as a tall man came around the corner of the nearest building scattering a flock of speckled yard fowl. His black hair was pulled back from his face and his shirt was open, the sleeves rolled up, revealing the dark curling hair of his chest and arms. His skin was tanned, and his shoulders broad. As he drew near, Kira saw his blue eyes narrow.

"What business do you have at Tem Hold?" he asked as he came to stand beside the mastiff.

"I wish to barter for shelter and supplies," Kira replied. "I have fresh game." Slowly, she lowered the peccary to the ground, then took a step back.

The man glanced at the dead animal. "And if I said that the wild game in the forest surround is already mine as Land Holder and that I would not bargain for what belongs to me, what would you say to that?"

"Then I would give my apologies to you and ask for your pardon," Kira replied. She hoped her desperation wasn't obvious. "I'm a stranger here. I did not know that Holders in this region laid claim to the forests as well as the tilled lands."

"I claim what is my birthright," he said in a harsh voice.

"I meant no offense, Lord Holder." Kira nodded in a gesture of respect.

"In this holding we do not use that title," he snapped. "You will call me Holder Tem. But do not call me Lord." His voice changed almost to a whisper.

Kira nodded again. "Holder Tem, I have nothing to bargain with, yet I would still ask for shelter and aid, as a traveler in need. At least, for the chance to mend my mount's wounds."

"I see no mount," he said, suspicion in his voice.

"My horse is in the forest. Lame. I didn't want to walk him farther without knowing I would be able to tend to his injury."

Holder Tem set his jaw. His eyes darkened to a deep indigo. "I would not let it be said that Tem Hold refused a traveler in need, especially on the eve of Fall Turn," he said in a cool voice.

Kira was startled. Was it truly the eve of Fall Turn? She hadn't realized how many days had passed since her escape.

"You may bring the animal here," he continued, "though you will have to tend him yourself. My stable master has gone to market, and we have no healer in this hold for man nor beast." There was sadness in his voice.

"Thank you, Holder Tem," Kira said. "I believe I can manage. Know that I am in your debt and will seek to repay you in some way."

"I'll send for the stable master's apprentice to help bring in your horse," the Holder offered.

"It may take some time for me to return with him and I would not want to keep the apprentice from his work. There are, however, a few items that might make the trek here easier, if you would allow it."

"Harl," the holder called. "Harl!" he yelled again, and a young boy came running across the courtyard.

"Sir?" he said. He was out of breath and wisps of straw clung in his tawny hair.

"Sleeping again?" the holder asked sternly.

"No, sir. I was cleaning the stalls just as Master Jarret instructed me."

"Yes, of course," The holder seemed unconvinced. "See to the needs of our guest. She will need a stall for her horse tonight." He gave Kira a final sharp look. "And bring her what she needs to tend to the animal." He turned on his heel and headed back toward the main building. The mastiff growled and the holder called over his shoulder, "Come, Cadge!" The dog sniffed the air in Kira's direction before padding after the man.

The stable boy led Kira across the yard and into a supply room adjacent to the main stable. She gathered some strips of cloth to bind Trad's leg and a small bag of oats to use as a lure. The boy, Harl, watched with obvious curiosity. Then she gave Harl instructions to boil a pot of water, add basil, alum, meadow mint and chamomile, and let it steep.

"But where shall I get these things?" he asked her.

"Do you have a cook in this hold?"

"We have a fine cook," he boasted, puffing out his chest. "Her name is Brilissa."

"Then go and ask Brilissa," Kira said, giving the boy an encouraging smile. "Those are common herbs, often used in cooking and preserving. A cook as fine as yours will have them on hand. I'll return as soon as I can." She went out through the main gates and hurried back the way she'd come.

The hold was large enough that they would most likely have all she needed to tend to Trad's leg. Holder Tem claimed to own all the game in the woods, but perhaps she could still barter her skills in exchange for a few days rest. If not to hunt, perhaps to tend the ill. If the hold had no healer, then there would surely be a few folk who could use a poultice or a healing draught.

The stable boy had watched her inquisitively, but without fear. This must be a peaceful land, she thought. And it appeared that the folk of Tem Hold had not heard of her flight from Toril. Perhaps she could rest here, for a few days at least.

CHAPTER EIGHT

Kira sat on a wooden crate. An oil lamp burned low, its small glow struggling to push back the darkness. She leaned forward in the dim light, head heavy with fatigue. Trad's wound was still inflamed, but the oozing pus had lessened. Harl had done well, preparing the herbal tincture just as she'd requested. Trad had balked at first, skittering sideways when she touched his leg. After a great deal of coaxing he'd finally allowed her to settle his foot into the bucket of drawing fluid. The herbal concoction had done its work, pulling out the pus and purifying the wound.

She wrapped the wound, using clean strips of linen cloth soaked in a fresh mixture of drawing fluid and winding them around Trad's ankle. As each cloth cooled, she removed it and replaced it with a fresh one. The sour smell of sickness mixed with the aroma of herbs.

Kira sat up, stretching the stiff muscles of her back. She was about to toss another used bandage onto the pile of discarded rags when something in the folds of fabric caught her eye. A long black sliver gleamed darkly against the pinkish yellow stains of bloody drainage.

A shard from one of the troll's claws! She hurled the rag down in disgust. No wonder Trad had been in so much pain. The filthy beast had left a part of itself embedded in

Trad's leg. She grimaced, then realization and relief spread through her. Now that the source of pain and inflammation was gone, the wound would heal.

Harl lay curled in the straw, snoring quietly. The trek back to the hold had taken until well after full dark, but when Kira had arrived at the gate, cajoling the big gray one step at a time, Harl had been waiting. He'd helped her settle Trad into a stall and stayed with her, lending a hand, far into the night. He'd asked Kira intelligent questions about what she was doing. It was obvious he wanted to learn what she knew about animals. Even after she'd seen him yawning wide, his eyelids drooping, and had urged him to go to his bed, the boy had remained. When he could no longer keep his eyes open, he had refused to leave the stall, telling her it was his responsibility to watch over the animals in the stable when the stable master was away.

Kira gave Trad a gentle pat on the chest. He was still feverish, but his shivering had lessened. With the crisis passed, what he needed most was rest. She leaned her head against the wooden slats of the stall. Closing her eyes, she reached out to Kelmir and Vaith to let them know she and Trad were fine. She soon found herself drifting in and out of their thoughts, the sights of the forest mixing with hazy dream images as she fell into a half-waking sleep.

A rustle of straw pulled her back to wakefulness. Harl was awake and sitting up, brushing wisps of straw from his hair. "I didn't mean to disturb you," he said. "But if I don't get to the kitchen soon, there'll be no hot morning meal for me."

"It's all right," Kira said. "I was only resting my eyes."

"The horse. Is he all right?" the boy asked, studying Trad.

"It seems he will be," she said, sitting up. "The fever has nearly broken and I think we've removed the cause of the swelling." She pointed to the cloth on the stable floor. Harl crept forward to peer at it.

"What is it?" he asked, wrinkling his forehead.

"A piece of claw," Kira said with loathing. "From a rock troll."

Harl jerked his head up and his eyes grew round. "A rock troll? When? How?"

"We were attacked in the night as we made our way along the river on the other side of the mountain pass. There was a storm and we didn't see the beast until it was too late."

"How did you escape?" he asked in awe.

"My companions and I fought the beast and won our lives," Kira cringed at her slip of the tongue. She hoped the boy hadn't noticed her use of the plural.

"But—"

"You'd better hurry, or you'll miss your morning meal," she leaned back and shut her eyes. He was just a young boy, thirsty for adventure, but Kira was tired and she didn't want to relive her battle with the troll.

There was silence for a moment, then the rustle of straw followed by the click of a latch as Harl left the stable.

Kira waited until he was gone before getting up. She gave Trad another pat, then stretched the knots from her muscles. Cool morning air had seeped into the stable and she stamped her feet to bring life back into them. She rubbed at her arms to shake off the chill and began cleaning up from the long night's vigil. She'd just finished dumping the last of the herbal infusion and was returning from the midden heap when Harl returned carrying a steaming mug and a plate of food. Her stomach rumbled at the sight.

"Brilissa sent this for you."

"That's very kind of her," Kira said, her mouth watering. She paused for a moment, wondering if the boy was telling her the truth. She wouldn't want to deprive him of his breakfast. "Harl, are you sure the cook sent this for me?"

"Oh, yes," he said, quickly. "She said to ask you to come to the kitchen after you've eaten and rested. That is, if you would. She was curious about the herbs you used to mend your horse. When I first asked for them, she thought you were trying to make some kind of soup." He grinned at her.

Kira took the food from him. The plate was filled with thick slices of dark bread and wide strips of roasted pork. The food's heady aroma filled her nostrils and Kira wondered if the meat was from the animal she'd brought to the hold the day before. "Thank you, Harl," she said. "Please, thank Brilissa for me, and tell her I'll be happy to speak with her." She sat down on the crate, balancing the plate on her knees. The mug was filled with tea and cream and the rising steam carried the scent of aromatic spices. She wrapped her fingers around the warm mug and blew across the top before taking a sip. Hot creamy liquid filled her mouth, and rolled down her throat. Its warmth spread through her.

As she ate, Harl worked in the stable, turning out the old bedding and replacing it with fresh dry straw, and filling feed bins. The rustle of hay and the rattle of grain brought back her days on her parents' farm. She hadn't been much younger than Harl when the raiders had come burning their way across the land. She remembered the smoke and the fear in her mother's eyes when she took Kira by the hand, running with her into the woods. She'd hidden Kira in the cleft of a hollow tree. The opening had been wide enough for Kira, but her mother had been unable to squeeze through the crevice. Kira clenched her eyes shut and forced away the rest of that painful memory.

She finished eating and stood up, swaying with exhaustion. She set the mug and plate down on the crate and, after swathing Trad's leg once more, lay down in the straw and sank into a deep sleep.

*   *   *

Late morning sunlight streamed in through the door, casting a golden haze into the building. Kira sat up, disoriented. The memory of the past day and night came back to her and she jumped to her feet. Trad chewed contentedly on a mouthful of fresh hay. The feed bin inside his stall held a few kernels of grain. Harl had apparently fed Trad with the rest of the animals. Kira checked Trad over once more. Thankfully, the swelling and fever hadn't returned.

The stable was quiet. She took one of the clean linen cloths, dipped it in a nearby water bucket and washed herself. The empty dishes still sat on the crate where she'd left them. She picked them up and set off in search of the kitchen.

The yard was empty except for a few ducks and geese, pecking at insects and seeds. Most everyone must be out harvesting, Kira thought. She headed around the back of the main hall, where smoke rose from the stone chimneys of a large out-building and the rich smell of simmering stew wafted on the air. She heard the clatter of pans and a woman's commanding voice.

Kira stuck her head in at the door. Several men and women bustled about, preparing the midday meal. In the midst of all the activity stood a sturdy blond woman, her hair pulled up and pinned on top of her head, several strands breaking free to hang loose about her face. A long apron was tied around her waist and her shoes were dusted with flour. People were kneading dough, stirring pots, and carrying trays piled high with fruit, bread, and cheese.

Kira considered slipping away until the kitchen was less busy, but she spied a large washtub just across from the doorway where she stood. She might as well return the dishes while she was here. She stepped in through the doorway and edged along the wall, staying out of the way. As she placed the mug and the plate on the sideboard next to the tub, the blond woman called out to her. "Hie! What are you doing in my kitchen?"

Kira wheeled and found herself face-to-face with the head cook. "Your pardon, I was just returning your dishes. Brilissa, is it?" She kept her voice polite. The cooking staff had all stopped to watch, and the kitchen was filled with a tense silence, broken only by the hissing of steam that came from several large pots.

"Yes, I'm Brilissa." The woman raised an eyebrow. "You can't be the stranger we've been hearing all the tales about." The cook regarded her with a crooked smile. "You're tall enough, but not the warrior I was expecting."

"I don't know what Harl has told you about me," Kira said. "He did say that you wished to speak with me, but I can certainly return at a more convenient time."

"In Tem Hold's kitchen? There's no such thing." The cook's laughter was like the clinking of dishes in a washtub, a surprisingly musical sound that made Kira smile.

"Come along. I'll fetch us a cup of tea, and we can talk." Brilissa gestured at her kitchen staff. "All right, now. What are you all doing standing around when there's a meal to prepare? Alyn, you take charge until I return." She took Kira by the arm and led her into a small anteroom away from the noisy kitchen. "And mind nothing burns," she called over her shoulder.

"But I'm taking you away from your duties," Kira said.

"Of course you are," Brilissa replied. "Probably the only chance I'll have today to get away from them, and I mean to take complete advantage." She busied herself with a mixture of herbs, which she set inside a heavy clay teapot. "Just a moment," she said and bustled out the door. She returned a moment later with a steaming kettle. She poured a slow stream of hot water into the teapot, then set the kettle aside and fell into a heavy wooden chair.

"Sit, sit," she said, gesturing to a matching chair on the other side of the table.

Brilissa's interest in herbal remedies seemed endless. While she plied Kira with a stream of questions, a young girl came into the room, her head tilted forward so that her long brown hair covered her face. She peeked up at Brilissa, brown eyes spying through the shiny wave of hair. The cook smiled at the girl and nodded at a low stool that stood in the corner of the room. The girl crept over to the stool and sat down. She was thin and gangly, her long fingers worrying constantly at the hem of her wrinkled skirt. Kira caught the girl peering at them through her long tresses. But each time Kira looked directly at her, she ducked her head and turned away. Brilissa took no further notice of the girl, so Kira let her be, as well.

Before long, one of the kitchen workers came in and nodded to the cook. Brilissa stood. "I would like to speak more with you, but it's time to serve the midday meal, and I must make sure that all is in order. I'll send another plate to the stable with Harl," she said as she left the room.

"Thank you," Kira said to the woman's back. She sat for a moment longer, drinking the last of her tea. When she reached over to clear the cups from the table, the young girl jumped up, grabbed the dishes and, with an unintelligible murmur, swept out of the room.

Kira stared after her, a little startled. What an odd child, she thought.

She returned to the stable and removed the bandage from Trad's leg. The wound was still raw, but the inflammation was completely gone. Relieved, Kira wrapped a fresh cloth around his leg. She went to the far side of the stall and called to him. He stared at her with his large dark eyes. "Come on, Trad. I need to see how well you can walk," she said. He took a tentative step in her direction and stopped. His ankle was still sore, and he refused to put any weight on it. He flicked his tail nervously.

"All right, boy. I'll speak with the holder. Perhaps he will find it in his generosity to extend us another night or two in his hold. But I'll have to wait until after he's eaten. In the meantime, maybe I can find some place to get cleaned up a bit before I talk with him."

Trad snorted at her. "Well, it doesn't hurt to make a good impression," she said. "Especially when asking someone for a favor." She patted him on the withers, then went in search of a place to wash up.

She crossed to the pump in the corner of the yard. The dozen or so spotted hens that had been scratching in the dirt near the pump flapped their wings and clucked their displeasure as she strode past them. The pump still held a prime, and a few short pulls filled a wooden bucket to overflowing. Kira bent forward and poured the cool water over her head, then scrubbed at her hair with her hands. If Brilissa hadn't run off so fast, Kira might have asked for some mint or lavender to use as a scrub, but just getting off the layers of dust and dirt was a relief. She shook her head and smoothed the water from her hair. It had grown and was no longer cropped short against her head. She wondered if she should re-cut it. It probably needed to be darkened again, too. She gave the pump handle another swift pull, then stuck her arms under the flow and scrubbed them. With her sleeves rolled up she could see all the scrapes and bruises she'd acquired on her journey. At least none of these are from Toril's hand, she thought, drying herself off.

Harl caught up with her on her way back to the stable. He held a plate of bread and a bowl of rich-looking soup. "Brilissa sent you more food," he said, a little out of breath.

Kira's mouth watered at the soup's woodsy fragrance. Thick slices of carrots and dark mushrooms floated in a seasoned broth. "Thank you, Harl." She took the plate and bowl from him and he produced a wooden spoon from his pocket.

"I'm afraid my hands are full," she told him. "Could you carry it to the stable for me?"

The boy grinned. "Will you tell me more about the troll?" he asked as soon as she'd settled herself onto the stool to eat.

"There's nothing more to tell," she said between mouthfuls.

"You only told me that you fought with it and won," Harl said. "What I want to know is how. Rock trolls are as tall as trees, stronger than full-grown bulls. Won't you please tell me how you defeated it?"

She tore off a piece of thick bread and dipped it into the soup. "You were right about Brilissa's cooking," she said. "Her soup is wonderful."

"Why won't you tell me about it?" Harl asked.

"I told you, Harl, there's nothing more to tell. Why are you so interested?"

"Because no one here has ever seen such a creature, much less killed one!" Kira heard excitement rising in his voice. "No one here has ever gone anywhere or done anything," he said with a frown. He watched her, eyes bright. "Someday, I'm going to be a great warrior and slay a hundred men just like Warlord Toril."

The bowl slipped in Kira's hand and soup splashed onto the straw. "Killing is not something to aspire to," she said quietly.

"But all great warriors do great deeds, killing men in battle and—"

"A truly great warrior kills only in need, not to count the heads of those he has slaughtered," she snapped.

He bowed his head and his hair fell over his eyes.

"I'm sorry," he said. "I didn't mean to anger you."

Kira let the anger flow out of her. He was only a boy. "No, Harl," she said. "I'm sorry. I have no right to tell you what you should or shouldn't want. But this land has seen too much of war and death."

"But Warlord Toril drove out the invaders," the boy said, raising his eyes to meet hers. "He and his men have done great deeds, haven't they?"

"Yes, I suppose they have." Kira set down the bowl of soup. "Yet they have not disbanded. They continue to march across the land, taking what they want. How are they better than the invaders they drove away?"

"But they protect us," he said. "They keep the invaders from returning and others from coming."

"Do they?" Kira shook her head and stared into her bowl. How could she take away a boy's dreams of glory? How could she explain what she had seen? The way that Toril had reveled in the admiration of the people until he could no longer live without it. The way he embraced his power, as if it were a treasure beyond reckoning. She spooned the last of the soup into her mouth, but now it tasted bitter.

CHAPTER NINE

Kira stayed with Trad throughout the afternoon. When she offered to help Harl with his work, his face flushed, so she let him be. Later, when she went to the kitchen to ask for fresh herbs, there was such a flurry of activity, she decided it would be best not to bother Brilissa. As she returned to the stable she glimpsed someone following her. She slowed her pace and turned her head in time to see the young girl from the kitchen slip around the back corner of the building.

As she sat down beside Trad, a door creaked and a rustling of straw moved toward her, then stopped near an adjacent stall. Someone watched her from the shadows. She waited for the girl to approach, but the child remained quiet and out of sight. "You needn't hide," Kira finally said. "I won't harm you."

There was a small catch of breath, then silence. Kira shrugged and rewrapped Trad's leg. The wound was healing, but Kira hoped the holder would allow them to stay another night or two in the hold. If not, they would have to rest in the forest before heading for the coast. She searched with her mind and found Vaith and Kelmir. Fully fed, they rested deep in the woods. When she came back to herself, two eyes shone from between the slats of the adjoining stall. Kira smiled at the lurking girl and the eyes disappeared.

No matter what Kira did, the girl in the shadows would neither speak nor come closer. It was a relief when Harl finally came for her late in the afternoon. The tension of being watched had begun to try her nerves. She followed Harl into the main hall.

Bright lanterns cast a warm flickering glow against wooden walls and a high vaulted ceiling sloped upward into shadow. The hall smelled of fresh bread and roasted meat. The remains of the evening meal were still visible on the long tables set in rows. Small clusters of people sat about the hall, talking quietly or laughing together, and a group of young children chased one another around a tall chair on a dais at the far end of the room. In a distant corner a well-dressed woman sat alone, working at some sort of sewing. People stopped talking, turning to watch as Kira entered the room. Even the children stopped for a moment, before resuming their game. The woman in the corner seemed to take no notice. She continued to sew, pulling her needle and thread smoothly through the fabric, but Kira detected a tense watchfulness in the woman's posture.

Holder Tem sat alone at the end of a long table. He looked up at Harl's approach. Kira waited a respectful distance from the holder as he spoke under his breath to the stable boy. Harl nodded then turned to Kira. "Holder Tem offers you a seat at his table," the boy said in a formal tone, gesturing to a seat near the holder.

She moved to a chair and sat facing the man across the corner of the heavy wooden table. She waited for the holder to speak first as respect required, but he merely watched her over his wine cup. His face was stern, but his blue eyes were bright with curiosity.

"How is your horse?" he asked.

Kira was taken off guard. She hadn't expected the holder to ask after Trad, but then he would want to know how soon his unwelcome guest would be ready to leave.

"He is mending, Holder Tem, thanks to your hospitality and the aid of your people. He could use a little more rest, but if you wish us to leave, we will."

The man's jaw tightened. "Nothing has been said of your leaving," he said.

"My apologies, Holder Tem. Once again, I have erred. I didn't mean to assume."

"Yes," he said. "I'm sure you didn't." He grew calmer. "You carry no weapons, aside from the dagger in your belt. I'm curious how you took down the animal you brought to us." His voice was flat, holding no emotion, but there was a glint in his eyes that made Kira uncomfortable. She wondered how much she should tell him, how much he knew, and whether or not the story of her encounter with the troll had already reached him.

"I am a simple hunter, Holder Tem, but I am skilled at my trade," Kira said, hoping he would let the question go.

"Skilled is one thing. But to bring down one of the wild peccary in this region, even a young one, is no small feat. I don't believe it could be done by anyone with naught but a single knife." He leaned forward and folded his hands on the table.

Kira hesitated. He was trying to read her reaction. She kept her face blank, the way she'd learned to do when Toril was in one of his foul moods.

"What are you hiding?" the holder asked suddenly. "Do you hesitate because you are fearful, or is there some darker purpose that I need be wary of? As holder of these lands it is my duty to care for the land and the people. And to protect them from harm." His eyes narrowed.

How much of what went on in his land would escape his attention? How much should she tell him? How much might he know? Neither Vaith nor Kelmir had alerted her to the presence of anyone in the forest, but the woods belonged to this man. If word of her flight from Toril had already reached this far, why would he be asking these questions? She would answer enough to put the man's worries to rest.

"I have trained two animals to hunt with me," Kira said. "They wait in the forest until I return."

"So, you're not as alone as you would have us believe, and you have trained beasts to work game with you," he said. "Are these animals the same companions that helped you to defeat the rock troll?" He sat back in his chair, watching her.

Kira felt as if she were being stalked by a cunning hunter. Telling Harl about the troll had been another mistake. It seemed the holder kept a close watch on the happenings in his hold. She wanted to flee, but instead she answered calmly. "They are."

He stiffened. "Tell me, how tame are these animals? I won't have wild hunting beasts among my people, or on my land."

"They are well-trained, though not as tame as a domesticated beast might be. They are still hunters," Kira said. "I've hunted with them for many years. They were born in the wild, but you and your people need not fear them. Though, most people fear the moon cat when they first see him. The other is a wyvern."

"A moon cat! Trained?" His face hardened. "I've never heard of anyone taming such a beast."

"It's true, they're dangerous when wild, but Kel is no danger to anyone, unless they threaten him. Or me," she said.

The man was silent, as if considering all that Kira had said. She waited.

"Have you eaten?" he asked finally, surprising her.

"Not since the midday meal, Holder Tem."

"I would not have it said that Tem Hold does not feed its guests, particularly when the kitchen has prepared a special feast to celebrate Fall Turn. Harl, please ask Brilissa to send out food for our guest."

"Yes, sir." Harl grinned and scurried off toward the kitchen, quickly returning with a fresh platter of meat, a loaf of bread, and a bowl of boiled vegetables. A plate was set before Kira along with a cup filled with deep ruby liquid. Kira took a sip of the wine, rolling it around on her tongue. It was mild and fruity.

"I see you like the wine," the holder said, his mouth twitching almost into a smile. "Tem Hold boasts a good store. This wine is from the southern coast."

"It is very good, Holder Tem. Thank you."

"Please, eat." He waved a hand at the food before her.

Kira filled her plate and began to eat, taking small mouthfuls and chewing slowly as the holder sipped at his wine. He watched her, leaning back in his chair. "I see you are a cautious person," he said. "A virtue not all can claim," he added, and Kira wondered at the note of sorrow in his voice. He was silent a few moments, waiting while she ate.

When she finished her meal, Harl picked up the empty plate, but before she could turn and thank him, he was gone.

"My stable boy must think much of you," Holder Tem said when Harl returned from the kitchen to stand beside her. "He is rarely so attentive to our guests." Harl studied the floor.

Kira smiled up at the boy. "He has been a great help to me in tending to my horse. I'm sure you're proud to have such a bright and willing young man in your hold." Harl blushed, and the smile on his face told Kira that he was warmed by the praise.

"Yes, well, it seems he has shown you qualities he rarely exercises with his daily responsibilities. But boys are ever at odds with themselves at Harl's age." He threw the boy a stern look, before returning his attention to Kira. "Now that you have eaten, I would like to know where you are traveling at this time of the year."

Kira thought about her mother's medallion and the land that beckoned from across the western sea. "I am headed for the coast. I intend to sail for other parts." Once more she tried to be evasive.

"Then you will have to wait out the season. The fall and winter storms are violent on the western seas. The last ship of the year will have left harbor some weeks ago."

Kira was crestfallen. Now what? Her hand drifted to the pouch that held her treasures. Simple trinkets all, except for the medallion. "When does the storm season pass?" she asked, trying not to betray her frustration and worry. Any delay could cost her and her companions their freedom, and keep her from ever discovering who she truly was.

"Three moons from now, at least. In a bad year, as many as four or more." He took another drink. "I see you're disappointed, but perhaps we can help one another."

"I am already in your debt, Holder Tem. How might I be of service to you?" Kira replied cautiously.

"We have no hunter at our hold. It would be good to have fresh game, and a larger supply of wild meat would allow us to take more of our stock to market next season. With your skills you could provide a useful service to the hold and, in exchange, you would be welcome to stay on until the storm season has passed and the harbor reopens."

Kira was thoughtful. It could be the perfect opportunity. With the pass down the cliff destroyed, it would take at least two moons, perhaps longer, for Toril's men to backtrack from there and make their way north to the main gap. Another moon would likely go by before they managed to come this far south. Trad could heal in comfort and she and her companions could wait out the winter. She would have to make arrangements for Kelmir and Vaith, but there was time to deal with that before harsh weather set in. However, there would still be the problem of paying for passage on a ship. "It is a generous offer, Holder Tem, but I could also offer the hold my services in the healing arts."

He set his cup down roughly. The ruby-colored contents splashed over the rim and onto his sleeve. "Healing arts? More like conjuring and luck, and all of it bad. No, Hunter. We have no need of a healer here."

Kira took a calculated risk. "I cannot work the season for food and lodging alone. There must be other holds in this region that would welcome the skills of a healer as well as a hunter." She took another sip of wine.

The holder seemed to struggle with himself for a moment, then his expression grew wary. "And what else would you ask?"

"Food and shelter for myself and my horse and the cost of ship's passage," Kira said quickly.

He set his jaw. "For that, you would need to do more than hunt for the hold." He relaxed into his chair, a slight smile pulling up one corner of his mouth. "Tell me, are you learned in the matters of reading and writing?"

"I am, but—"

"Then I will agree to your terms, if you will also tutor my niece and nephew in those subjects."

Kira chewed her lower lip. She had never taught anyone before. And tutoring two children? She remembered the children she had known growing up and embers of old anger stirred inside her. Some of them had been mean and others merely spoiled. They had all bullied her, but then she'd been young and shy.

The holder waited for her answer, poised like a hungry wyvern ready to swoop down on a defenseless rodent. Kira wasn't sure she wanted anything to do with children, but what other option did she have? "It's a bargain, and done." She slapped the table in front of her.

"Done and done," he said, striking the table with the flat of his palm, his eyes locked on hers. "But if you bring the other animals into my hold, the moon cat must be restrained."

Kira wanted to argue, to tell this arrogant holder what she thought of his fearful ignorance, but she held her tongue.

The holder stood and nodded to her. "A bargain, then," he said. A few faces turned curiously in her direction as the holder left the room. After a moment the people went back to their conversations, but the well-dressed woman in the corner had stopped sewing and stared at her with cold eyes.

CHAPTER TEN

Mayet stared at the embroidery in her lap, toying with the stitching. Milos could make her eat with these people, but he couldn't force her to be social with them. Aside from the special foods, it hadn't been much of a Fall Turn feast anyway. When she'd been a girl in her father's hold there had been dancing at even the least special occasions, dancing and courting. She glanced over at Milos.

He was still speaking with the strange dark-haired woman in tattered garments. What was he up to now? Was he smiling? Since his brother's death the man never smiled. A momentary sorrow pulled at her heart, then anger swept over her. How could Kamar have left her in such a state? No money, no property of her own. Left to be cared for by his inept brother who had no lordly skills. A man who would let the people rule themselves. While she and her children were expected to treat commoners as equals. Worst of all, with his new policies, he'd slowly been eating away at Mayet's domain, charging others with the duties of managing the household's daily business. He'd even given over the run of the entire kitchen to that brash hag, Brilissa. Not that Mayet had ever cared about counting sacks of flour, but she no longer had the control over the servants she'd once enjoyed. Not that she couldn't still put them in their places, but their deference to her was no longer the appropriate show of respect for their better, but obvious patronizing placation. She clutched at her sewing, twisting the small embroidery frame till it snapped. She froze.

Loosening her grip on the broken frame, she thrust her anger down. It would be unseemly to display her emotions where others could see. She smoothed her skirts and straightened her shoulders, glancing around to see who might be watching her. Farmers and servants sat talking and drinking while their brats chased one another on the dais. She should be sitting at table upon that dais with Milos, her children beside her, not down here on the main floor among the peasantry. If Kamar were alive, she'd have her rightful place, and her son would be heir to Tem Hold and all its lands. But all that had been stolen from her. Now, Tem Hold's place of honor sat vacant except on the rarest of occasions.

She pasted a tolerant smile on her lips. She must bide her time. Milos would see things her way once they were wed. She would see to it. He'd soon take her as his bride and restore her to her lawful place as Lady of the Hold. There were no other women who were worthy of the station his title would provide. She toyed with the gold signet ring on her left hand. The Tem family crest shone against her skin. The symbol of her true place. It was only a matter of time before Milos would see that she was the only woman fit to be his wife. She need only find a way to stir the flame in him.

He hadn't sought out the company of any woman since his brother's death, despite that he'd earned a reputation for romantic dalliances before taking over the responsibilities of Tem Hold. She pulled her needle and thread deftly through the heavy fabric. It was only a matter of time before a man's hunger for a woman's touch would drive him to seek companionship. No proper man could remain unwed forever, especially one as young and virile as Milos. She needed to win him before he began thinking of one of those women he'd courted in the past. Courted? A fine and civil word for the gallivanting of a young man. Holding her needlework up to the light, she stared beyond it to where Milos sat.

Why was he still speaking to that barbarous female? What could he possibly find interesting about her? Disgusting. Where were her tresses? She barely had any hair on her head and her skin was so pale. And what kind of woman wore breeches? No man could be attracted to that.

Look at her sitting there, eating like a meticulous cat. How obvious could she be? Mayet clasped her hands together in angry frustration. Could that strumpet really think that Tem's Holder would want anything from someone like her? She was clearly lowborn and base. Mayet heard a tittering laugh and realized she'd been staring. She glanced around to see who was laughing at her, but no one appeared to be taking any notice.

How dare they! They should be paying her compliments and seeing to her needs, waiting on her requests. Instead they sat about her hall and ignored her. She would put an end to their lack of respect one day. All she needed was to show Milos what she could offer him. It wasn't as if it were unheard of for a man to wed his brother's widow.

Perhaps I should begin taking more notice of his views and policies, she thought, become more involved with running the hold. If she showed him she was open to discussing his plans, shared some of his interests, he would see that they were meant to rule together. And she could temper his more drastic ideas, like his program for land sharing and the ridiculous notion that these peasants should have some say in the way they're ruled. She stroked the sleeves of her gown, brushing up the fine velvet nap. I've waited long enough, she thought. If he was too thick to see they belonged together, then she would have to find some way to show him. Wild horses must be caught to be broken.

She turned toward the holder, a smile on her lips, and stiffened. He seemed to be coming to some sort of agreement with that terrible woman. What could he possibly want of her? Mayet watched in horror as he slapped the table with his open hand. A bargain? Her face grew hot. There was no way she would allow that horrid creature to profit from a bargain made with Milos. Mayet clutched at her sewing. She would have to get rid of the slattern.

She shot an angry look in the direction of the main table. That mangy stable hand is waiting on the wretch. He probably knows what kind of bargain Milos has made. What was it they called him? Karl? Larl? No matter. Tratine would know. She could always count on her son. Such a sweet boy. He'd do anything she asked.

* * *

Mayet rose early the next morning, a plan taking shape in her mind. It seemed unnatural to awaken with the household servants rather than lie abed being waited on, but she had work to do. She donned a pale gold chemise and a red velvet overdress, lacing the bodice tight. She still had her figure, she thought contentedly, running her hands down to where the skirts flared out at her hips. And the crimson of the dress would set off her dark hair and eyes.

She found Milos working on some documents in his library. She knew he used the room to maintain a bit of privacy, but soon the hold would belong to both of them and he would have no need of privacy from her.

She paused before the door, pinching her cheeks to bring them a blush of color, and swept gracefully into the room. He was surprised to see her, but she was sure she saw admiration in his eyes when she gave him her most charming smile.

"Mayet. What are you doing here?"

"I simply wanted to see you, Milos. We spend so little time together."

"I'm busy at the moment." He gestured at the stack of parchment before him.

"Perhaps I might help you," she offered.

"As I recall your Lady's training did not include much in the way of letters and sums," he said.

She opened her mouth to reply, but he cut her off.

"In addition to supplying the hold with fresh game, the new hunter will tutor Tratine and Milvari."

"Milvari has more than enough skill at reading for a proper Lady and I don't want Tratine to spend a single moment with that creature." Mayet patted at her freshly coifed hair. At least that kitchen girl was good for something, she thought, turning coyly away from Milos to admire herself in the mirror.

"Tratine needs scholarly learning and the discipline of daily lessons," Milos said, his jaw tightening. "And there is nothing improper about learning. I believe Milvari has a talent for it. A lady, as well as a lord, should learn to read and write properly."

"But Milos, that woman! She isn't fit to tutor my children."

"You know nothing about her," Milos replied flatly.

Mayet watched his reflection in the corner of the mirror. Sitting behind her, he had his elbow propped on the table, chin resting on his fist, a large pile of papers set before him.

He was a muscular man, more fine boned than his brother had been, but his face was careworn. She turned toward him. "Nor do you. I can see what she is."

"Do not presume to tell me what I know," Milos warned.

Mayet could see the tension rising in him and heard the veiled anger behind his words. "But Milos," she said in her sweetest voice. "You can continue to teach the children, can't you? There isn't anything they need to learn that you don't know well enough to teach."

"I am too busy to tutor anyone, Mayet. I haven't had the time to spend with Tratine and Milvari for several moons, as you well know."

"If you would just make those farmers do their own work, you'd have plenty of time." She realized her mistake before her words faded.

"I am still holder here, and I, not you, will decide how best to fulfill my responsibilities."

Mayet tilted her head to the side and gave him a winning smile. "But, Milos—"

"I am done speaking on it. The hunter will teach the children, and you will see to your own . . . duties."

The way he nearly spat the last word at her was insulting. As if correcting the servants all day, trying to teach them to behave properly was nothing, but Mayet held her tongue. They'd argued in the past, but he'd never before lost patience with her so quickly. She nodded once curtly, then grabbed up her skirts and left the room. See to my own duties, indeed! As if I were allowed to run this hold as I should, she thought. He might think this was settled, but she was not finished with it yet. What this hold needed was a good cleansing.

* * *

The fire blazed brightly, pushing the night's gloom into the far corners of the sitting room. "Come and sit by the fire with me, Tratine," Mayet crooned. "Tell me everything you've done today." She smiled up at him as he crossed the room.

Tratine sat on the cushions at her feet, and leaned against her legs. Mayet stroked his fine hair. It was comforting to have him near. "You've grown so these past few seasons," she said. "Soon you'll be as tall as your father was."

"Taller," he said. "You always say I'll be taller. Like the men in your family, Mother. Right?"

"Yes, my dear. Much taller." She stared into the fire as she ran her fingers through his hair. The warmth of the flames filled the room and she shrugged her shawl off her shoulders. "Tratine."

"Yes, Mother?"

"Your Uncle is suggesting that you take lessons from that strange woman who arrived at the hold two days ago."

"What kind of lessons?"

"Reading and writing, I believe he said. Though I should think he could teach you himself, he claims he's too busy to do so,"

"Reading and writing?" he whined. "Why should I take schooling from a hunter?"

"Hunter?"

"Yes, Mother, that's what they call her. The Hunter."

"What else do you know of this hunter?"

"I heard she killed a rock troll!" Tratine said excitedly.

Mayet snorted. "A troll? Do you really believe that?"

"Well, Harl says—" Tratine tilted his head up toward her.

"Harl? The stable boy?"

"Yes."

"And what have I told you about listening to the tales of your lessers?"

"Always listen, but never believe without proof," he said in a low voice.

"Do you have any proof?"

"Harl showed me a piece of the troll's claw. It was sharp as a knife and black as night." There was admiration in his tone.

"How do you know it was a troll's claw?" Mayet asked sharply. "Have you ever seen one before?"

"You know I haven't." His voice cracked and his shoulders slumped.

Mayet rubbed the back of his neck, gently kneading the pudgy flesh. "Tratine, I'm not bullying you. I'm only trying to teach you what you need to know to be a proper holder."

"But Mother," he whined, then stopped. "Yes, of course," he corrected himself. "But I'm not a holder, Mother." His tone had become sulky.

"You will be one day," she assured him. "You are the heir to Tem Hold."

"But what about when Uncle Milos marries? If he has a son, I will be only a cousin to the true heir."

Mayet sat up sharply. Her fingers dug into his neck. "What do you mean, when your uncle marries? Do you know something, Tratine?"

"Ow! You're hurting me!"

She let go. "Mother didn't mean to hurt you, my dear," she crooned. "But if you know something about your uncle, if he has plans, you need to tell me."

"I don't know anything," he said. "I was just asking."

"Then what made you ask such a question?"

"I was just thinking, wondering, what I would do if I wasn't to become a holder."

"I don't think you'll have to worry about that much longer, Tray." Using her pet name for him made her smile.

As a baby, he'd swung from one title to the other, between using Mama and Mayet, and had finally called her May. In return she'd called him Tray and the name had stuck. Only recently he'd asked her not to use that name in front of anyone. "I'm not a little boy anymore, Mother," he'd said. "The other men will have no respect for me if they hear you call me that!"

At first she'd been offended. Then she'd smiled, intending to tease him, but he'd been so serious. It was the first time she'd realized how much he'd grown since his father had died. That was the moment she knew she would need to do something soon to insure his inheritance. But it wasn't the day she'd begun to plan. No, after Kamar, she'd always intended to find a way into Milos' wedding bed. But winning him had proved more difficult than she'd anticipated.

Before Kamar's death, Milos had rushed here and there, laughing, drinking, hunting, wooing. Just as with his other interests, he roamed from one woman to the next. He seemed to be searching for something or someone. But each time Kamar confided to Mayet that he thought his brother might finally have found a potential bride, Milos would be off again, gadding about, drinking or hunting.

He'd even convinced Kamar to go with him on some of his hunting escapades, deep into the forest. Then one day, they'd brought Kamar back to the hold, mangled by a vicious boar. The local healer worked night and day with his poultices and remedies, but Kamar had died.

Mayet hadn't noticed it at first, lost in her own grief, but it had become clear that Milos had changed. When he'd assumed his place as holder, he had grown serious. He stopped hunting and took little notice of any woman. And now he rarely smiled.

The sitting room door creaked open. Mayet watched out of the corner of her eye as Milvari crept across the room.

"What are you doing?" she snapped, rousing Tratine. "Now you've awakened your poor brother. How often must I tell you not to go sneaking around like that?"

Tratine glared at his sister. Milvari stood still, head down, hair hanging over her eyes.

"Come over here. Stand up straight! Why can't you keep your hair tied back like a proper lady?" Milvari inched her way across the room and stood beside her mother's chair.

Mayet pulled roughly at the girl's skirt, trying to straighten out the wrinkles. It was useless, the edge of the garment was frayed and dirty and smelled of horses. She grabbed Milvari by the arm. "You're a mess. Who will ever want to marry you, if you go about behaving like some dull-witted peasant? Do you want your uncle to throw us out because you cannot act a proper lady?" Milvari whimpered and continued staring her feet. "Oh, go to bed," Mayet growled in frustration. She pushed Milvari toward her bedchamber.

Milvari stumbled, then dashed from the room. Mayet sighed and turned back toward the fire. The child was an embarrassment. Ever since Kamar's death, she'd been impossible. "I wish your father could see how you've grown," she said, gently patting Tratine's shoulder. He leaned back, resting against her.

Mayet stared into the fire, thinking of the ways she might bring Milos to her bed and guarantee Tratine's inheritance.

CHAPTER ELEVEN

Kira gnawed the inside of her cheek in frustration. She'd made a bargain, which she intended to fulfill, needed to fulfill, to earn enough to pay for ship's passage when the storm season broke. But how was she to teach these two resisting, unruly children? After a full week, neither of her students had yet responded to her. Milvari hung her head, hiding behind her hair as usual, while Tratine stared out the window, a scowl on his face. Kira sat across the table from them, worry knotting her insides. She'd been surprised to discover that the awkward young girl from the kitchen was Holder Tem's niece and dismayed to find his nephew to be so spoiled and arrogant.

At first she'd felt sorry for the two. She'd learned from Harl that their father had been injured in a hunting accident three years before and had died from his wounds. Now she was angry and frustrated at her inability to reach the youngsters. While Milvari seemed at least to listen to her, Kira hadn't been able to get the girl to speak a word or look directly at her. There was no way of knowing what the girl understood of the lessons.

Only the Holder's direct order had compelled Tratine to join Kira and Milvari in the main hall each day after the midday meal. Even so, the holder's nephew refused to respond to any of her directions. He was big for his thirteen years, large-boned and awkward. No longer a child and not yet a man, he clearly took the cue for his arrogant behavior from his mother.

Mayet was a lithe woman with angry eyes and a cold pride that she wore like a shawl. She made no attempt to hide her resentment of Kira, refusing to acknowledge her when Kira bid her good day. After the first few attempts to discuss her two students with their mother, Kira had given up.

She picked up one of the books the holder had provided for the lessons and leafed through it. Tratine continued to stare out the window, but Milvari peeked out from under her hair, sneaking quick glances when she thought Kira couldn't see her. Kira walked past her to gaze out the window over Tratine's shoulder. From this vantage point, she could see out through the open gate into the fields beyond. The last of the harvest had been piled in ricks and the short-cropped stalks that remained reflected the golden sun. It reminded her of home.

It was a pity these children had lost their father at such a young age. Kira knew the pain of that loss. She understood the reticence they might feel in permitting themselves to become attached to another person, but that was no reason for them to be allowed to be rude or to shirk their lessons. Yet, she thought, how long had it taken for her? How long had Heresta given of herself without return before Kira had responded to her? She let out a heavy breath and frowned as Tratine's shoulders stiffened.

"Don't worry, Tratine. I'm not going to berate you. In fact, it's such a beautiful afternoon I think we should continue our studies outside."

Milvari cast a glance at her, and Kira almost thought she saw the girl smile. Perhaps a nature lesson would help Milvari to open up. She certainly seemed to spend as much time as possible outside away from other people, at least when she wasn't skulking in the shadows.

"Come along," Kira said, grabbing a small book from a nearby shelf.

Tratine sat frozen in his seat and Milvari twitched nervously. "And leave your paper and quills, you won't need them," Kira added, heading out the door.

In the yard, a group of women winnowed the new grain. Holding the corners of heavy cloths, they tossed the grain into the air where the breeze could blow away the chaff as the heavy kernels fell back onto the fabric. Their good humor filled the yard as they worked, chatting and laughing at a bit of cleverness or some small joke. Beside them, children sat in a circle, singing a riddle song, the timbre of their voices rising and falling as they sang out the questions and answers.

Kira stopped at the main gate, letting the sun's rays warm her as she waited for the two youngsters to catch up. She could almost hear Tratine's grumbling, and pictured Milvari's nervous movements as the young girl put away her papers and ink. As soon as she heard their footsteps approach, she started off, her two students following slowly behind.

She led them out across the open field toward the wide river that passed along the edge of the hold-lands to the north. In the distance, men and boys loaded the sheaves of grain onto wagons to bring into the hold for winnowing. The folk of the hold worked together in a balance of rhythm and harmony that made Kira long to be a part of their quiet world.

She dragged her thoughts back as she reached the riverbank, settled herself onto a large rock, and stared out across the water. The river ran slow and shallow. Sunlight glinted off the cool, green surface. Were she to stay here, her presence would destroy the calm of Tem Hold the way a rock would shatter the smooth surface of the river.

Tratine clomped up beside her. "What are we doing out here?" he asked in a petulant voice, as Milvari crept up to join them.

"We are observing," Kira said, concealing the emotion her thoughts had stirred within her.

"There is nothing to see out here," he said, kicking at a clump of dry grass.

Kira looked over at him, shading her eyes with her hand. "Do you really believe that?"

His eyes narrowed and he kicked at the turf again, shoving it loose with the toe of his boot. "What do you see then?" he asked finally.

"There's a brush hen with her brood in the tall weeds on the far side of the river."

"Where?" He squinted. "I don't see anything," he said and kicked the clump of grass up into the air. It arched out over the water, landing with a splash. A rustle erupted in the brush on the far bank.

"Oh!" Milvari pointed toward the sound. A large brush hen ran across the meadow followed by six speckled chicks.

"How did you know that?" Tratine asked.

"I saw them, Tratine. Just as I told you." Kira opened the little book she'd brought from the hall. She held it out for Tratine to see. There was a small neat drawing of a brush hen on one of the pages, along with a description of the bird and its habits.

"Late summer and early autumn are good seasons for bird sightings. What other wild fowl might we expect to see out here by the river?"

"Why should I bother to know that?" Tratine snapped. "I have no use for such knowledge. Brush hens serve no purpose except to be plucked and roasted. Only a hunter needs to know how to find them and catch them, not a

Holder." He stuck out his chin and scowled at his sister. Milvari was crouched near the water, peering at the ground. Before Kira could call a warning, the girl stroked the leaves of a light-green plant with her finger. She quickly drew back her hand with a sharp intake of breath.

"Take care, Milvari." Kira stooped beside the girl. "Let me see." She took Milvari's pale hand, turning it over in her own. A tiny bead of blood had formed on the tip of her finger. Kira indicated the plant with its soft-looking leaves. "That is a pino plant. A trickster dressed in velvety green. It appears soft, but the hairs on its leaves hide sharp thorns." She took Milvari's hand and guided her downriver, scanning the ground before them.

When she found what she was hunting for, she stopped. "What do you think this one is?" she asked, pointing to a mass of thin branches tangled together in a twist of knots.

Milvari bowed her head, letting her hair drift down over her face.

Kira knelt, pulling Milvari down with her. "It doesn't look like much, does it?" she said, coaxing some of the branches apart and breaking them off. White liquid oozed from the broken ends. Kira dabbed some of the liquid on Milvari's bleeding finger. It dried almost at once.

"It's called harz," Kira told her. "It helps to stop bleeding and dulls pain. A very handy little plant."

Milvari stared at her finger for a moment, her eyes wide. For the first time since Kira had met the Holder's niece, Milvari looked directly at her. There was a glimmer of excitement in the girl's face.

Is this what Heresta finally saw in me? Kira wondered. Milvari's look of profound curiosity and exhilaration at knowing something new reminded Kira of her days with the old healer.

They spent the rest of the afternoon hunting new plants. Milvari would point and Kira would explain the properties of the leaves, stems, roots or flowers. Tratine watched from a distance, glowering. It seemed to somehow anger him that his sister had found something to be interested in and someone willing to teach her about it.

At the usual time for ending their lessons, Tratine left Kira and Milvari by the river. He stalked off across the field, fists clenched at his sides. Kira glanced at his receding figure as she continued to instruct Milvari. At least the girl showed some spark. Perhaps the boy would come to take part, as well. Kira simply needed to discover what interested him.

The afternoon sun was well on its path toward the horizon when Milvari finally seemed to notice that her brother was gone. She stood for a moment in silence, watching Kira pluck small bundles of helmet flowers.

"What do those purple flowers do?" Milvari's voice was barely audible.

Kira kept her head down, trying not to show surprise that the girl had spoken. She continued to break off the stalks of flowers, leaving the base of the plant to spread and grow again. "This is helmet flower. It will help a nervous person relax and sleep. It must be properly dried and stored. Then it can be made into tea." She braided the plant stalks together. "Here." She held out the bundle of green and purple. Milvari dropped her gaze. "Go ahead, take it," Kira said, smiling. "Hang it with the flower ends pointing down so the oils will seep into the leaves."

Milvari reached out and gingerly took the flowers. She lifted them up to her face and sniffed, then wrinkled her brow. "It doesn't smell," she murmured.

"Ah, you have discovered a truth. Just as not all plants that appear inviting are friendly, not all flowers smell the way they look," Kira told her.

Milvari cocked her head to one side, and then nodded, a small smile twitching at the corners of her mouth. "Like you?" she asked.

"Like me?"

The smile slipped from Milvari's face. She shrugged, and cast her eyes down at her feet again. Her dark hair fell over her face like a thick curtain.

Kira watched the girl retreating back into herself, remembering her first few months with Heresta. It made her heart ache. "If you mean that I am different than I appear," Kira said thoughtfully, "I would say that you are correct."

Milvari raised her head and smiled. Then she turned and ran back toward the hold.

Kira watched her go. What had just happened? Had she gained the girl's trust or merely amused her? Getting Milvari to speak to her was a breakthrough, but Kira knew she would still need to go gently with the girl.

If only she could find a way to make a similar connection with Tratine. It would certainly make their time together easier. Soon the winter storms would come inland and she and her students would be spending a lot more time together. The Holder had already discussed a new teaching schedule with her, one that would occupy much of his niece's and nephew's time during the long winter months.

She would think on it later. Now, she was late for her visit with Vaith and Kelmir. She set off across the field, skirting the hold and heading into the forest beyond. She could have brought Vaith into the hold, but her two companions had seldom been parted in the past few years. Since in his ignorance Holder Tem refused to allow Kelmir into the hold unrestrained, the two animals stayed in the woods together. She smiled suddenly. Perhaps Vaith could help with Tratine. Boys were always fascinated by snakes and other wild animals. As for a wyvern, what boy could resist? It would be worth the attempt at least. But for the time being, she set aside all thoughts of Tratine and let Kel and Vaith know she was on her way.

CHAPTER TWELVE

Milvari ran back to the hold, the bundle of flowers gripped in her hand. She glanced down at the white sticky layer covering her fingertip in amazement. This was a whole new world to her. Plants that healed, plants that calmed, even plants that could make a person or animal rush around in a mad fit. She knew Brilissa used plants to flavor the hold's meals. The kitchen was always filled with the rich scent of spices and seasonings. But she'd had no idea that the things growing in fields and forest could be used for so much else.

She stopped and stood panting outside the main gate, fearful someone might notice her. Head down, she hurried to the stable and slipped inside. Harl was in the back, raking out the stalls and humming to himself as he worked. She had often watched him, following unnoticed as he fed and curried the horses. She'd even seen him slip under a layer of fresh straw to nap now and then. Sometimes when Harl was asleep and no one else was about, Milvari would take down the brushes and combs and stroke one of the horses, brushing its hair and combing out the long mane and tail. She loved the feel of the horse's muscles as they rippled under her hands and the way the animals listened as she talked to them, sharing her secrets.

But for most of the past half moon, instead of Harl she had watched the hunter, fascinated. There were no women like her in all of her uncle's land. At least, none that ever came to Tem Hold. Her mother insisted that proper ladies wore fine dresses and never dirtied their hands. *Fine ladies sew. They direct the work of others. They do not deign to kneel in the dirt,* she'd told her.

She looked down at her dusty skirt and dirt streaked hands and frowned. If not for Uncle Milos's firm insistence, Milvari's mother would not have even allowed her to learn to read and write. But this hunter was different. She rode a fine horse. She knew how to read, how to write. And she did not expect others to do work she herself would not.

Milvari took the flowers into the storage room and hung them in the corner behind a stack of wooden crates. People rarely went into the back corners of the room. The little bundle of stalks would dry safely out of sight. Milvari knew she would never be what her mother called a proper lady. She wanted to run like the boys in the hold, to wear breeches, to ride out over the fields and meadows, to have her own horse to curry and brush. The hunter did all these things and more.

Milvari longed to be like this tall pale woman who had come down the eastern pass before it had collapsed. She'd heard Harl telling the other boys about the troll the hunter had fought and killed. She couldn't imagine anyone committing such a heroic deed. She remembered how she'd watched from the shadows as Harl told the other boys the story.

The thin piece of claw had glinted in the lamplight as Harl held it out in the palm of his hand.

"It's all lies," Tratine said.

"It's true," Harl insisted. "How else did she get this?"

"How do you know that's even from a troll?" Tratine asked. "You've never seen one."

One of the other boys laughed.

"It's the wrong shape for a bear," Harl said. "It's too big for anything else. And it's sharp as a knife blade." He drew the claw across a piece of hardened leather, demonstrating to his audience the keen edge of the black shard.

Milvari had stifled a gasp at the sight, not wanting to make her presence known. She would have liked to see the claw close up, but Harl kept it with him, and Milvari couldn't ask him to show it to her. She wouldn't know how to talk to him. And if her mother found out, she'd surely be punished. Besides, she had always learned more by sitting quietly out of the way and listening to others talk than most people did by asking questions. She reached up and stroked the soft petals of the helmet flowers dangling from the beam. It had always been better to watch from the shadows.

In the main hall, during their daily lessons, Milvari had watched the strange woman expectantly. She hadn't known what she was waiting for, only that there should be something more to this tall female who was so unlike the proper ladies Milvari's mother chatted about at length. It was only a feeling, but it had settled in the pit of her stomach, curled tight with anticipation. But each afternoon's lessons with the hunter had been merely ordinary, reading, writing and a smattering of sums practice.

Until today.

Today's lesson had begun the same as the others, but then everything changed. Out in the sunshine, as Milvari trekked across the cleared fields to the river, the anticipation inside her had uncurled, becoming a stirring of excitement and curiosity. She had followed behind Tratine as usual, but this time she struggled to keep her feet from running away with her. Her brother stood by in his usual haughty manner, unaware that the hunter revealed to them magical secrets and wonders beyond anything they'd been shown before.

She touched the flower petals once more, then wrapped her arms about herself, as if to hold in her new knowledge. She closed her eyes and, leaf and flower, went over each detail of the day's lesson in her mind. As she pictured each plant, she began to see a pattern, the way they were connected to their medicinal properties and where they grew in relation to the river and to one another. This was learning she understood better than sums or reading. She hugged herself tighter. Would the hunter be willing to share more of her wondrous knowledge?

Milvari thought about the small book with the brush hen's picture. She opened her eyes and jumped up. Just inside the storeroom doorway, she paused and peeked out. Harl continued raking out the back stalls, still humming off-key. Milvari slipped out of the stable. The late afternoon sunlight was still bright enough to make her blink after the darkness of the storeroom as she made her way toward the main building.

The hall was a flurry of hustling and bustling. She skirted around tables being readied for the evening meal, dodging kitchen staff carrying plates and cups, baskets of fruit and pitchers of ale that glistened with beaded moisture. No one paid her any heed. Milvari was used to being invisible. Since her father's death, she kept to herself and tried not to be seen by anyone, especially her mother. She walked quietly over to the side of the room used for their afternoon lessons. The small stack of books that the hunter taught from sat on the shelf. Milvari picked them up one at a time and sifted through the pages. There was nothing about plants.

She thought again about the little book and wondered if the hunter had brought it with her, or if it was one of the books Uncle Milos had provided for their lessons. Perhaps there were others like it tucked between the scrolls and books in her uncle's study. She had to find out, but she'd never been allowed in her uncle's personal rooms. The study was in the west wing off the main hall and part of her uncle's private rooms, the one place in the hold reserved for the holder alone. She refused to think about what might happen if her uncle found her there. Milvari bit her lip to keep herself from shaking. She would have to be truly invisible to get into the library without being seen.

CHAPTER THIRTEEN

Mayet held the crimson cape up in the late morning sunlight that reached through the unshuttered window. The red silk brocade shimmered exquisitely, but the fine fabric was clearly not heavy enough to provide the warmth she would need. Fall was no season to be married. Lisana should have told that overblown fool, Kaer Sasson, that he would have to wait until spring. But her cousin claimed to be enamored with the brute. More like enamored with his property! Mayet dropped her arms. She well understood Lisana's hurry. Holder Sasson was past his prime seasons. His first wife had passed on without leaving an heir. Lisana needed to bear a boy child of Sasson's line as soon as possible.

The room was strewn with clothes and not one garment fit for a wedding. Mayet tossed the cape aside and picked up a long wool cloak. Pale fur trimmed the royal blue fabric. A golden clasp would make it more formal if worn with the right dress. Mayet tossed the cape over her shoulders. Lisana could have at least given her more time to prepare. It was too late to have a proper dress made. And who would keep an eye on Milos and that short-haired harlot while she was gone? She couldn't possibly go without taking Tratine, and Milvari was less than useless. If only the invitation had come later, there would not have been time to make the trip at all. Family obligations indeed!

She flung the cloak onto the floor. It would take a half moon to reach Sasson Hold and the same for the return trip. The wedding celebration would take more than a fortnight. There was no telling what that so-called hunter would be up to while Mayet was gone for more than a moon. The witch was hunting all right. But not for wild game.

Mayet surveyed the mound of clothing on the bed. She reached beneath the pile and pulled out a silver gown encrusted with tiny pearls. She held the glittering garment before her and eyed herself in the mirror. It wasn't meant for travel, but if she must leave, she would make certain Milos knew what he would be missing.

She called for her maid. When the young girl entered the room, Mayet pointed at the pile of dresses slung over her traveling trunk. "See that these are packed and loaded on the wagon. And have Brilissa send up that kitchen girl to dress my hair." She pushed her long locks back over her shoulders.

"Alyn will be busy with the midday meal, m'Lady," the girl said quietly.

"She'll be busy dressing my hair," Mayet growled. "There are enough people in that kitchen to feed two holds. Go and tell Brilissa she's to send the girl up now."

The young woman curtsied and left the room.

The very idea of a servant telling her that another servant would be too busy to wait upon her was infuriating! "This is what comes of making the lower classes believe they are better than their station," she said through clenched teeth.

She stared at her reflection and relaxed, trying to smooth the lines of her face, and her eyes brightened. Lisana's wedding might be worth the trip, after all. This might be the opportunity she needed to reach even higher. Some of the richest lands lay just north of Sasson Hold. With the last of the harvesting done, who knew what other unattached holders might attend? She pulled off her dressing gown, tossing it aside. "There are better holders than you, Milos Tem. And I deserve better!" She stepped into the pearl-decorated dress. As she yanked it up over her hips she heard a loud ripping sound.

Her foot had caught the hem of the underskirt and torn it away from the bodice. She stomped her feet, shaking the dress down to the floor. Pulling her legs out of the glittering fabric, she stepped back and heaved a kick at the ridiculous gown. Pearls scattered across the floor and Mayet threw herself into a chair. As she did, the pile of satins and silks beneath her shifted and sent her sliding to the floor with a thud. She sat unmoving, momentarily stunned, surrounded by shimmering fabrics. Reaching behind her, she gave the offending chair an angry shove. It leaned back, teetering for a moment before crashing to the floor. Mayet scowled at it. There was no satisfaction to be had in bullying the furniture.

The constraints of Mayet's world wrapped around her like a mailed fist. Without Kamar, she had nothing. As the past holder's widow, she had no real standing. She and her children were allowed to remain in Tem Hold only by the good will of its current holder. And now, by allowing the peasants to have a say in the governance of the hold, Milos was making changes that would remove even that small bit of security.

She aimed another kick at the dresses by her feet and a constricting knot rose from her chest and into her throat. There was a knock at the door and she choked back the sob that ached for release.

Pushing herself up from the floor, she snatched up her dressing gown, wrapping herself in its silken folds. She might be only a woman, but she was still a noble woman. By the time Alyn entered the room Mayet had regained her composure.

CHAPTER FOURTEEN

As Kira stepped through the door, the heat of the kitchen wrapped itself about her and pushed aside the clinging predawn chill.

Brilissa sat alone at the wide board, sipping a steaming cup of spiced tea. "What are you doing here so early?" the jovial cook asked, as she dribbled honey into her cup.

"I could ask the same," Kira responded warmly, inhaling the scent of boiling porridge and fresh clipped herbs. She liked this woman who ran her kitchen so efficiently. And she liked the cordial feel of the kitchen with its pungent aromas so strong she could taste the savory scents floating in the air. "I'd have thought that one of your apprentices could build up the fires and start the morning's work."

"Oh, by the wheel, they certainly could," Brilissa said. "But then when would I find a moment's quiet?" She pushed the pot toward Kira. "Tea?"

"No, thank you," Kira said. "I can't stay. I only came to see what scraps I might have."

"Scraps indeed!" Brilissa placed her hands on her chest, feigning horror. "Not from my kitchen. But provisions you may have." She smiled and pushed herself out of her chair, stretching.

126

"I would hate to bother the head cook with such a request." Kira nodded in respect.

Brilissa laughed. "Who better?" She put a finger beside her nose and winked. "The head cook always knows where the best stores are kept."

Kira left the kitchen with a much larger bundle of food than she had intended.

* * *

Trad snorted, his breath steaming in the crisp morning air. The big stallion's leg had healed rapidly and he was no longer content to remain in the stable when Kira went out to hunt. He was filled with nervous energy and needed more exercise than the short walks around the hold had provided. Kira had barely been able to keep him from running off at a gallop when they'd ridden out in the early haze of dawn.

Kira shivered in the worn cloak Harl had found for her. Luckily, the morning's hunt had gone well. Along with the brace of fat hares they had caught, Vaith and Kelmir had brought down a fine buck, which was now slung across Trad's back. Once more, Kira bowed her head to offer thanks to the animals that gave their lives so others on the wheel might live. She considered heading back to the hold, but it was still early and the more game she could bring in before the snows came, the better provisioned the hold would be through winter. Along with tutoring his niece and nephew, Holder Tem had hired her to help keep the hold supplied with meat. Kira intended to fulfill both bargains.

Mist rose from the fields, covering the forest path in a gauzy fog. Kira walked ahead. It wouldn't do for Trad to trip and re-injure himself. The path narrowed as it meandered though the woods. A small crackle of twigs off to the left told Kira where Kelmir prowled. Vaith flitted from tree to tree, suddenly swooping low over the path ahead of her, his eyes glowing and his thoughts filled with hunger.

"I suppose it's about time," Kira said, opening her pouch. The smell of meat and bread reminded her that they had set off that morning without eating.

Kira settled herself on the gnarled roots of an ancient oak and unrolled the heavy cloth Brilissa had given her. It was filled with sliced meat, dark bread and fragrant cheese. The cook had also given her several large apples. Kira pulled off a large chunk of bread and ate it with a thick slice of meat. The cheese was tangy and she nibbled at it between bites of apple, feeding the cores to Trad.

When she finished her meal, Kira leaned back for a moment. Kelmir snoozed nearby, lying in the dappled sunshine that filtered through the trees. Vaith sat a short distance away, eyeing the remaining meat. She tossed a scrap of meat high into the air and he streaked from his perch, catching it before it began to fall. He landed on another branch and ripped the meat apart, stuffing pieces into his mouth.

"Slow down, you little glutton." Vaith eyed her, a piece of meat dangling from his pointy teeth, and Kira laughed. "All right, finish it so we can get back to work," she said, rolling the rest of the food in the cloth.

Kelmir raised his head and stood, slowly stretching out his front legs and arching his back. He padded off along the path in the direction they had been heading. Vaith watched the big cat, turning his head while he stuffed the last morsel into his mouth before taking to the air. He swooped down low, soaring close by Kelmir's head before winging up the path. Kelmir gave a small growl and leaped after him.

By late morning, the hunters were tired. Trad had begun to sag under the weight of the game he carried. Kira turned back toward the hold satisfied that they had gathered enough meat for one day. If their hunting remained productive, she would easily be able to request a warmer cloak and additional bedding before the winter season.

She offered the fattest of the hares to Kelmir and he took it in his great maw. "Here you are, Kel," she said. "We've had a good day." She turned to Vaith. "I want you to come with me, little one. There's someone I want you to meet. You can eat along the way." She held up the rolled bundle containing their remaining provisions and patted the pommel of Trad's saddle.

Vaith landed gracefully on the leather perch and watched expectantly as Kira unrolled the cloth and tore off a piece of meat. He took the morsel from her and ate it as they headed back to Tem Hold. She talked along the way, telling Vaith about Tratine and Milvari. She sent him mind-pictures of them, showing him how Milvari had finally awakened to Kira's teaching, while Tratine remained distant. She tried to show Vaith her hope that Tratine would be as interested in wyverns as Milvari had been about plants.

Vaith finished eating, then licked his claws till they glistened, his long black tongue snaking between his toes. He sat tall on his perch, gleaming in the midday sun, when they reached the main gate. Kira called out for Harl as she passed the stable. She stopped Trad beside the kitchen door and began unloading the morning's catch.

Harl jogged over and reached up to help, then stopped, mouth agape. "Is that a . . . wyvern?" he asked, staring at Vaith.

Kira smiled at Harl's wide-eyed excitement. She liked this young man. He made her feel welcome and at ease, and his reaction to Vaith was exactly the one she hoped to get from Tratine. "Vaith," she said, "this is Harl. Harl would like to know if you're a wyvern."

Vaith turned his head toward the boy and stared at him. Kira chuckled. "Harl, this is Vaith. He is a longtime companion of mine and an excellent hunter."

Harl stood still. "I've seen them from a distance, but never so close."

"You could come closer."

"Won't he fly off?"

Trad blew impatiently, staring back over his shoulder at them. "Not unless he has a reason to," Kira replied, untying the rope that held the remaining game on Trad's back. "Here, help me with this. Trad needs to rest." She patted the horse's rump and he shook his head, whipping his mane with eagerness. "You can help get this game into the kitchen while I see to Trad. Vaith will still be here when we're done with our work."

Harl helped Kira lift the deer and hang it on the dressing hook beside the kitchen door. As they unloaded the smaller game, he kept watch on the bright winged creature before him, as if he thought Vaith would disappear if he looked away too long. "When you're done here," she told Harl, "see what scraps of meat Brilissa will part with for our guest."

"Really? Do you think he'll let me feed him?"

"I don't think he'd let me stop you," Kira said, smiling. Trad headed toward the stable and Kira followed. "Now hurry up. Sooner done is sooner on," she called over her shoulder. Her smile wavered. She was quoting Heresta again. A breath of cool air ruffled her hair. "You'll always be with me, old raven," she whispered to the wind.

Vaith perched on a railing while Trad was rubbed, brushed, blanketed and fed. Harl hadn't come into the stable by the time Kira finished, so she took Vaith and went in search of him. She peeked in the door of the kitchen and saw him talking with one of the cooks. Harl grinned and waved when he saw her and Kira returned his wave. She started to step inside to see about getting a plate of food,

130

but remembered Vaith and ducked back out. It wouldn't do to have Brilissa see her bringing an animal into the kitchen.

She was about to send Vaith off to perch nearby when Harl came tumbling out of the kitchen door. "Hunter!" he called. "The midday meal will be delayed." He eyed her and an impish grin spread across his face.

"I don't suppose you'd care to tell me why," she responded.

"Well, if you must know," he said with a playful air. "The household is busy with travel preparations. The present Lady of the Hold and her retinue will be leaving on the morn," he went on. "She will be accompanied by her son, the heir apparent, and they shall not return for more than a full moon's time."

"Oh," Kira said.

"What's wrong, Hunter? I thought you'd be pleased at having one less student."

"Nothing is wrong," Kira said, but she couldn't keep the disappointment from her voice. She'd been so sure she could win over Tratine by introducing him to Vaith.

Harl glanced around. "There are some who are quite happy at the prospect of a moon's turn without the company of certain persons," he confided.

His humor was contagious, but Kira gave him an innocent look. "Are there?" she asked.

Harl laughed. Kira knew she should admonish him for his behavior, but couldn't keep herself from laughing with him. She coaxed Vaith onto her wrist and held out her arm. "Harl, how would you like to take Vaith out for a flight?"

CHAPTER FIFTEEN

Milvari tarried, waiting for everyone to finish the evening meal. She nibbled nervously at her food, glancing now and then in the direction of her uncle's library. Each night for the past week she'd sat here, trying to feel brave and waiting for a chance to slip into the hallway unseen. The hall that led from the main room to the library was filled with shadows, a few flickering candles providing the only illumination. Unlike the great room, which was hung with bright oil lamps, the hallway sconces held heavy wax candles. Tonight, as on most nights, only every third candle was lit and thick shadows danced in doorways and beneath the furnishings that lined the walls. Milvari had often lurked in those shadows and knew intimately where the gloom lay heaviest and could obscure even the largest of mice.

As the hall began to empty, she helped clear away the plates and cups from the table. Her mother wouldn't like it if she knew Milvari was doing kitchen work, but as usual no one in the room took notice. With Tratine gone, Milvari didn't have to fear her brother's tattling, and none of the cooking staff had ever told her mother about the times that Brilissa allowed her to help in the kitchen.

Everyone else in the household took little notice of her. Only Brilissa seemed to see her. Most of the time, Milvari sat alone in the corner of the kitchen, out of the way. But sometimes Brilissa would hand her a bowl of something to stir, or a container of flour and a sifter. Neither she nor Brilissa would speak. Milvari would simply set to work. When she finished the task, she would drift back into her quiet corner.

Milvari loved the kitchen. It brought back hazy memories of her father. Winter mornings when he rose early, she'd followed him down the cold hall to the cozy room filled with the scent of baking bread and simmering porridge. He would fix them both tea and hot bread with butter and jam, and then carry her back to bed where he would tuck her in before leaving on his errands. Milvari shuddered. It had been later on just such a morning that the men had brought her father back to the hold, wounded and bloody. Her mother hadn't let her go to him. The healer tried for days, but none could stay the turning of the wheel. Their morning meal together had been his last.

A log crackled in the grate and she glanced toward the hearth. A few people tarried by the fire, talking in quiet voices. Nearby, several children played a game of Spokes. They laughed and chatted as they took turns dropping slender colored sticks into a circle outlined with string on the floor. She set her stack of plates on the end of one long table and watched in fascination as the children vied to see who could complete the best pattern in one throw. Milvari had played the game as a young child, but always alone, or with her brother, never with any other children. Her mother had always kept her and Tratine apart from the other children, telling them, *Lords and Ladies shouldn't mix with the lower classes.* Delighted laughter erupted as one young girl completed an almost perfect star in one toss. Emptiness raked its claws through her. She longed to sit beside them and play.

She turned away abruptly, remembering her purpose. She hoped that tonight she'd be able to steal into her uncle's library and search the shelves for more books on plants and animals. She thought of asking the hunter, but each time she'd tried, she'd choked on the words. Since that first time, their lessons had gone back to the way they'd been, reading, writing and sums. They hadn't gone out to the fields again. Milvari knew her mother had had something to do with it. She had berated Milvari at length after Tratine had recounted their lesson out by the stream. Uncle Milos was always so distant and unapproachable. She couldn't possibly ask him. Besides, he might say no. Or worse, tell her mother she had asked

Milvari composed her face into the blank mask that kept others from seeing her emotions. Nothing hurts, nothing hurts, she told herself. But her chest was tight and pain bubbled up inside. Raw memories scurried around inside her head and vicious voices shouted at her. The voices were all jumbled together and she could never catch the words, but they were filled with anger and loathing. All their disapproval was directed at her, descending on her like thunder rolling down a mountain. Her head was ringing and she wiped her hands on her wrinkled skirt in an effort to push the voices down and away.

Nothing hurts, nothing hurts, nothing hurts. She sank down into a chair and squeezed her eyes shut. The angry sounds slowly subsided. She sat unmoving for a long time, afraid the ugly voices would return.

After a while, she sensed movement, and someone picked up the stack of plates she'd left on the table and carried them toward the kitchen. The room grew quiet. Cautiously, she opened her eyes. The tables were empty and she was alone.

With a single glance toward the kitchen door, she slipped into the dark hallway, not giving herself time to change her mind. Sliding in and out of the deep wavering shadows, she stole up to the library and stopped. She stood outside the door, listening. There was no sound and no light shone from under the door, not even a glow from the fireplace. Her hand was stiff and cold as she gripped the doorknob and slowly turned it.

CHAPTER SIXTEEN

Red and gold streaked the western sky as the coach creaked toward Sasson Hold. Mayet strained to sit up straight, head held high. She had forgotten how uncomfortable it could be spending day after day traveling. There were few settlements of adequate size between Tem and Sasson Holds, and the roadside inns and cots left much to be desired in the way of accommodations. The last inn they had stopped at had barely had enough room to house them for the night. And the food! Atrocious. Brilissa wouldn't have slopped hogs with the fare that innkeeper had provided.

That at least was one thing Tem Hold offered, well-cooked meals. And more than common fare, too. Brilissa's cooking was almost enough to make it worthwhile to put up with the woman's uppity nature. Almost.

At least the inn had been able to provide her a place to bathe, although the innkeeper's wife had no idea of how to properly press and steam a garment. Mayet ran her hands down the fabric of her skirt, to flatten out the wrinkles.

As they neared Sasson Hold, she stared out over fields filled with golden stacks of wheat and barley. Lisana was indeed a lucky young woman. Sasson Hold was one of the richest settlements in the Western Reach.

Tratine rode beside the carriage astride his father's charger, looking older than his fourteen years. Several times already she had asked him how she looked. Each time he assured her of her beauty, but she remained nervous. She needed to make the best possible first impression to catch the eye of a worthy holder. Men had no idea what women must endure! The hours of endless worry over what to wear and how to behave. A man throws on a doublet and hose and everyone scrapes and bows, but if a woman isn't perfectly dressed and coifed she's considered plain and drab.

She shifted her weight on the cushions to ease the stiffness in her back. Days of rough roads and uncomfortable sleeping quarters had taken their toll. Her hand went to her face as she realized that age was catching up to her. Gently stroking the corners of her eyes with her fingertips, she searched for the telltale feel of wrinkles in her once-smooth skin. It was fortuitous that they had left the inn so late in the morning. Arriving after dark would give her a night to rest and recuperate, and time to make herself beautiful before anyone saw her. She sagged against the seat, letting her hands fall back into her lap.

Her mind began to wander. She had been born and raised on the western side of the great Zendel Mountains. There had never been any question of her not marrying a holder, someone with at least as much property as her brother would inherit, and remaining on this side of the mountains. But there was a time in her youth when she had wondered what lay on the other side of those great mountains. She would listen greedily to the stories and songs of traveling bards, trying to appear as bored as her mother. Those dreams were certainly past. She could barely endure two weeks in a carriage now. Crossing the Zendel range would be a torment. She sat up straighter.

Fortunately, she had been raised a proper lady and had grown out of such silly childhood notions.

The coach gave a final heave and stopped bouncing. The road into Sasson Hold grew smoother and bright torches lit the roadway. Mayet leaned back. Some of the tension eased out of her aching muscles, and she moaned in relief.

They began to pass other travelers, mostly commoners, traversing the road, some herding fattened animals. A few men on horseback rode by and Mayet tilted her head demurely away from their gazes until they had passed, peeking out at them from under her dark lashes. More than one of the men were richly dressed and several were certainly wealthy landholders. She smiled. She would have to make inquiries to discover who the eligible holders were. A fresh sense of purpose skittered through her with a tingle of anticipation. It had been some time since she'd last sparkled on the floor of a bright hall lit for celebration. She began to anticipate the wedding festivities.

CHAPTER SEVENTEEN

Milvari inched the door open and peeked into the room. Ruddy light flickered from the low fire and shadows rippled across the floor and walls. A heavy desk sat draped in darkness in the center of the room. She licked her lips and glanced back down the hallway. Fear beat upon her like a drum as she stepped inside. Holding onto the knob, she slowly closed the door, cringing at the audible click as it shut.

She brought out the taper she'd hidden in her skirt pocket, tiptoed to the hearth and touched the end of the taper to a bright red ember. The wick flared. She stepped away from the fireplace and held the slender candle before her. Pale light pushed toward the edges of the room. On one wall stood a tall wooden shelf filled with scrolls and books. Milvari took a step toward the shelf.

A dark figure loomed out of the shadows in the corner and a low voice growled, "Who's there?"

Milvari gasped, nearly dropping the candle. Her uncle sat in a high backed chair. He leaned forward into the circle of light that seeped outward from the candle's sputtering flame. His eyes were red rimmed and he blinked as if he were rousing from a deep sleep.

His hair was unkempt, his eyes bleary, and he looked like a demon in the dim light. Milvari's breathing grew rapid. The flame flickered as the candle shook in her outstretched hand.

"Milvari?" His voice was gruff.

Milvari struggled to catch her breath.

Uncle Milos stood up, towering over her in the darkness. He moved toward her.

Milvari stared up at him. A small whimper escaped from her lips.

He knelt before her, lowering himself down onto one knee to peer at her. "What's wrong, child?" His voice had softened.

Milvari shook her head and sobbed. "I-I-," she stammered.

He put his hands on her shoulders. "Milvari," he said. His dark eyes shone in the firelight. "Don't be frightened." His brow drew down, but he seemed more concerned than angry.

Milvari stared into his dark eyes. There was something there she didn't recognize. Her mouth moved, but no sound came out.

He stiffened. "Why won't you speak to me?" His voice cracked.

She swallowed her fear. "I wanted books," she whispered. "About plants. For healing."

His hands fell away from her shoulders. "I have none. Not since . . ." His voice trailed off.

"I-I'm s-sorry," she stammered.

He bowed his head. "No, Milvari. It is I who am sorry. Your father should be here for you, not I. Not I." His voice fell so low she could barely hear him.

Was that sadness in his voice? Milvari gaped at him and some of the fear washed out of her. Was it sorrow she'd seen in his eyes?

He stood suddenly, rising once more to tower above her, then turned away. "You should be abed," he said, his voice hard. The voice of her uncle once more.

Milvari glanced up. His shoulders were set, his back an insurmountable wall. She barely noticed the hot wax dripping from the thin candle onto her hand as she fled from the room.

CHAPTER EIGHTEEN

Kira entered the hold's kitchen to prepare for the day ahead, shaking off the frosty morning air that crept inside with her. More than once in the past few weeks, Brilissa had pointed out that Kira was providing more game than the hold had seen in years. The kitchen was alive from early morning until late into the night. In between preparing meals, the kitchen staff kept busy with salting and preserving the extra meat for the winter months. Kira thought she saw new faces among the bakers, cooks and fire tenders.

"They're not new," Brilissa said, wrapping Kira's morning provisions. "They're from the outlying crofts." She smiled. "You didn't think Tem Hold sat alone in the region without crofts to support it, did you?" She put two ripe golden apples on the table with the rest of Kira's food.

"I hadn't thought about it," Kira confessed, taking a sip of her tea. The tang of lemongrass was a surprising contrast to the sweet ginger flavor of the brew. As the mornings had grown colder, Brilissa had finally convinced her to have a hot drink before heading out into the woods. "I know the holder's sister-kin, Lady Mayet, has relatives to the north and that she's gone there to attend a wedding. I assumed there were other holds like this one."

"Not quite like this one," Brilissa laughed, setting a dish of dark red jam onto the table. "I don't suppose there are any other holds like Tem Hold."

"How do you mean?" Kira took another sip, wrapping her hands around the thick mug to let the heat flow into her fingers.

Brilissa poured fresh water into a bowl of fragrant spice bark, wiped her hands on her apron and sat down at the table across from Kira. "First, let me tell you how Tem Hold is the same as other holds," she said.

Kira glanced out the small window at the dark sky and nodded. Dawn came later each day as winter approached and the woods would keep for a while yet.

Brilissa poured herself a mug of tea from the steaming pot. "All holdings have a main hold, the place from where the holder manages his land and his people. All the lands about the hold belong to the holder, though they are farmed by crofters. The crofters are allowed to live on the land and farm it. In exchange, they help provide for the hold. And in times of trouble, they aid in the defense of the hold. In turn, the hold offers safety and support in hard times."

"It sounds much like the country where I grew up," Kira said. "Before the marauders came." She set down her cup, unwrapping her fingers from around it.

"That may be," Brilissa picked up a loaf of brown bread and sawed a thick slice off the end as she spoke. "But that leads us to where Tem Hold is different, or is becoming different, I should say." She offered the bread to Kira.

Kira shook her head.

Brilissa shrugged and slathered a spoonful of rich jam on the bread. "The Lord of Tem Hold has determined to make some changes in the way the hold is managed."

"Changes?"

"Our holder has ideas about the governance of his holdings that are rather . . . uncommon."

"What do you mean by uncommon?" Kira asked.

Brilissa took a bite of bread and closed her eyes, smiling as she chewed. "Are you certain you won't have some?" she asked when she finished swallowing. "This year's brambleberry jam is some of the finest we've ever made."

Kira reached over and sliced a piece of bread from the thick loaf. "It's been a long time since I have eaten so well."

"It's my job to make sure the folk in this Hold are well-fed." Brilissa pushed the jam toward her.

Kira smiled. "It's clear that you are dedicated to your work." She smeared a dab of jam on the bread and then bit into it. A rich burst of sweetness filled her mouth as she chewed.

"In most holds, the holder is considered the Lord and Master, and treated as such. His decisions are law and are rarely questioned." Brilissa continued with a frown. "In some holds no one dares."

The head cook paused, a distant look on her face. Kira stopped eating and waited for the woman to gather herself. After a moment, Brilissa, smiled. "Oh, I must have been dreaming," she said, wiping at invisible crumbs on the table before her. "Where was I?"

"You were telling me how Tem Hold is different."

"Yes, well, Tem Hold was ever the same as others. Even when Lord Kamar was Holder, may Troka hold him gently." She bowed her head and invoked the Goddess, waving her hand in a circle before her to make the Sign of the Wheel.

Kira bowed her head and said a silent prayer to the Goddess.

Brilissa waited until Kira was finished. "Milos was the younger brother and had no desire to rule. He was always satisfied to let his brother, Kamar, lead even when they were lads," she continued. "When he took up the rule of Tem Hold after Lord Kamar's death, it changed him."

"You mean he wasn't always so—"

"Dour," Brilissa finished for her.

"I was going to say serious."

"Yes, of course." Brilissa winked at her.

"Even so, I still don't see how that makes Tem Hold so different."

"Oh, it isn't his demeanor. No, no, no. It's this new form of governance he's introduced. People's Rule he calls it. He holds meetings and lets every crofter and worker have a say in the running of the hold's business, land and livestock alike. It's got the other holders worried. They're afraid it'll spread like a grassfire on a breezy day." A satisfied smile lit up her face. "Even the Lady Mayet's been at him about it. For all the good it will do her."

Kira wondered if all the people in the hold disliked its Lady as much as Brilissa and Harl seemed to. A pale streak had begun to spread across the eastern sky, signaling the dawn. Kira reached for the roll of provisions Brilissa had packed for her. "Thank you for the food, Brilissa," she said.

"You are welcome, as always," Brilissa replied. "Though, with all the extra work your hunting has caused me, I'm not sure I should keep furnishing you with provisions."

Kira started to apologize, but stopped when she saw the cheerful glint in the other woman's eyes. "Well, I wouldn't want you to waste away with nothing to do," she retorted.

Brilissa slapped the table with her hand and chuckled merrily. "And speaking of nothing to do," she said, rising from her chair, "it's time I sent you on your way and got to work."

Kira threw on her cloak and headed for the door.

"Oh, one more thing," Brilissa said. "I would appreciate if you didn't clutter up my kitchen with your garments." She took a dark brown cloak from a chair by the table and held it out to Kira.

Kira inspected the heavy wool garment. "You know quite well that isn't mine."

"Ah, but it is," the cook said, holding it out to her once more. "I won't have it said that I sent Tem Hold's hunter into the freezing cold with no more than a thin rag for a cloak."

Kira started to protest, but recognized the stern set of Brilissa's jaw. As a child she had seen that same stubbornness on Heresta's face many times. It always signaled the end of an argument, with Kira on the losing side. She handed over the thin garment for the heavier one. The new cloak was thick and warm and would keep out the harsh winter cold much better than the old one had.

"Thank you, Brilissa," she said. "I would like very much to repay you for your generosity."

"You might bring me another fine boar in time for Season's Turn," Brilissa told her. "And a measure of fresh juniper berries. I have a new recipe I should like to try for the Turning feast."

"I will do my best," Kira said, throwing on the wool cloak with a flourish before heading out the door.

Trad stamped in the cold, eager to get moving as Kira tied the bundle of provender to the saddle. As she rode out of the main gate, she thought she saw a dark shape in the shadows, but when she looked back, the hold lay still and silent.

CHAPTER NINETEEN

Mayet sat rigid, trying not to scowl as couples swept by, spinning and weaving across the floor to the music of pipes and strings. Lisana's laughter still rang in her ears. Her stinging remarks echoed in Mayet's mind. "But he's so young! Surely a woman of your years should aim at a man more her equal in seasons."

Mayet had merely asked who the handsome gentleman was, not whether or not he might wish to wed her! Not that the thought hadn't crossed her mind. And why shouldn't it? While she wasn't as young and ripe as her plump cousin, Mayet was by no means a worn-out old crone.

Lisana waved at her from across the room. Mayet managed to smile and nod courteously, but her cheeks were hot and her nails dug into the palms of her clenched hands. Lisana, flushed with happiness, was speaking to a dark man, a mischievous smile on her pink face. What was that little cow up to? The man turned his narrow face toward Mayet and eyed her like a hungry wolf. His dark eyes stared at her from above a long nose and thin pale lips. Mayet shuddered. She rose quickly, leaving the room in a rustle of silk, anxious to distance herself from the vulgar-looking man.

The spacious entry hall was cool after the warmth of the crowded main room, and she pulled her wrap around her. Lisana was right about one thing. All the marriageable men at the wedding were pups, most of them far from any inheritance. Mayet frowned. It had been a foolish thought, the idea that she could sweep into one large social gathering and immediately find a worthy husband. She sighed. Milos was still her best chance to remarry, reclaim her rightful place and guarantee Tratine's inheritance.

Music and laughter swirled out of the main room as the door opened behind her. Mayet turned. The wolfish-looking man strode toward her, a hungry smile on his face. Mayet glanced around. The previous solace of the vacant hall had suddenly changed to a menacing emptiness and a cold chill fell over her.

She took a step back as the man approached. Dark eyes glinted from the shadows of his face. She tried to step aside, but he swerved, cutting off her escape. He made a sweeping bow before her, but his eyes never left her face. "Lady K'Tem." His voice was deep and raspy.

Mayet was startled at hearing her widow's name. She hated the sound of it, but of course, Lisana was certain to use it. Mayet knew it was the proper way to address her, but she'd been away from a proper hold for a long time. Perhaps this was some sort of cruel joke her cousin was playing. If this was the sort of man Lisana would send her way, Mayet might as well have stayed at Tem Hold. She draped herself in her lady's air of composure. "I see my cousin has given you my name," she said haughtily. "She has not, however, given me yours."

"My pardon, Lady." His thin lips curved into a cold smile. "My name is Lago Surrat."

The name wasn't familiar. Clearly, this man was not a holder, nor was he seeking a bride. "What is it you wish of me, sir?"

"Lady K'Tem." He took a step forward, closing the space between them, dropping his voice to a conspiratorial whisper. "I am a seeker of lost things, a finder of the wayward."

A cold prickle skittered along the back of Mayet's neck. "I have no need of your services. If you will pardon me, I believe I shall return to the celebration." She moved to go, but he blocked her way.

"You may have no need of my services," he rasped, "but I may still be able to be of assistance to you. Your lovely cousin tells me that you have an unwelcome guest at Tem Hold."

Mayet glared. It was just like Lisana to prattle every word uttered in confidence. "What do you mean?"

"Your cousin, the Lady Sasson, mentioned that you have had a recent visitor. A woman."

"What is your interest in that?"

"I am seeking an indentured servant who was parted from her master. A tall pale woman with flame-red hair. Her master will pay handsomely for her return. I would be willing to provide recompense for your help, if your guest is indeed the person I seek." The man's nose twitched as he spoke, which made him look more like a rodent than a wolf.

Tall. Pale. Yes. The hunter's hair, though dark, had shone with a red sheen when the sun struck it. What little she had of it. Mayet's mind began to spin, calculating the possibilities. Had Milos made a bargain with a fugitive? The woman had been ragged when she'd arrived at Tem Hold. Mayet stroked her chin with a forefinger, contemplating the man before her. What might it be worth to this Lago to find the woman he was seeking? Having the wretched hunter removed from Tem Hold would certainly be an improvement, but it would in no way guarantee Mayet's place as Lady Tem. There might be more to gain by working with this man.

She rested one hand on the man's arm. "Might we talk over a cup of wine?" she asked. Perhaps it was time for her to strike a bargain of her own.

CHAPTER TWENTY

Kira glanced over her shoulder. The gnawing sense of being watched made her muscles twitch. When she'd first decided to stay at Tem Hold, she had thought she'd be able to forget about Toril and his men for a moon or two. Now she couldn't shake the tightness in her chest. Trad's ears flicked as she squeezed in with her knees, urging him to a faster pace. The deeper into the forest they went, the nearer they drew to Vaith and Kelmir, the more at ease Kira became.

The spaces between the trees grew narrower and Trad had to slow to a walk to navigate between them. Ahead, through the shadows, Kira could see where the glade opened up and late afternoon sunlight warmed the entryway of the abandoned cave that Vaith and Kelmir had found while searching for game. It was deep in the forest a fair distance south of the hold, but Kira was grateful they had found shelter from the weather before the coming winter.

Kelmir yawned and stretched, raising his back haunches high into the air with calm ease, as Kira rode into the sunlit space. Tall trees surrounded the rocky hillside and grew above the cave mouth, which led through a narrow tunnel and opened up into a space large enough for several people and animals. Kira had crawled inside when they'd first discovered it, and had swept out the debris left by the previous inhabitants. A low ledge jutted out on one side, providing a perch for Vaith, and she'd brought straw to cover the floor and provide a layer of bedding for Kelmir. Kira would have preferred to have her companions near her, but the cave would provide a warm shelter for them through the cold winter.

She dismounted and left Trad to graze at the edge of the glade. Kelmir rubbed against her thigh and Vaith flew above her, circling and trilling. Neither of her companions seemed nervous or concerned. Kira dropped down onto the grass and the tension in her body dissipated, like a puff of cloud before a summer's breeze.

Scratching between Kelmir's ears with one hand, she held out the other to Vaith, who flew down to land on her wrist. He snaked his head down and eyed the gauntlet Harl had given her, squeezing the new leather experimentally with his talons. Kira smiled. "Yes, little one, a lovely gift. It seems our young friend was quite impressed with you."

Vaith puffed out his chest. "Don't let it go to your head," Kira teased. "Young boys are easily impressed."

Vaith let out an insulted squawk and launched himself from her arm to land on an overhanging branch. He furled his wings and turned his back on her.

"My apologies, oh prince of dragonets. I meant no disrespect," she said with mock sincerity. "I don't know what came over me. You are and have always been the most noble and impressive of wyverns."

Vaith stood still.

Kira rolled her eyes. "Your scales glow in sunlight like priceless jewels."

He cocked his head.

"Your talons are as sharp as fine-honed blades."

He peeped at her out of the corner of one eye.

"You fly like the wind and your eyes are glowing moons."

Vaith leaped off the branch, soared down and paraded before her. Kelmir yawned and flopped over on his side, then stretched out his legs, nearly tripping Vaith with his paws. Kira laughed out loud.

* * *

It was nearly dark when Kira started back. Kelmir ranged ahead, leading the way through the gloaming forest, and Vaith rode on Kira's shoulder, trilling quietly in her ear. They'd gone only a short distance when Kelmir stopped short, his tail twitching furiously. Vaith quit singing and Kira pulled Trad to a halt. The nervous prickling returned. *What is it, Kel?*

Kelmir growled low in his throat and bounded off, rushing past Kira and heading back the way they had come. A flurry of crashing brush and breaking twigs exploded off to the right. Kira tried to connect with Kelmir, but the cat was too focused on his quarry for her to reach him.

A scream erupted from the darkness, followed by a rush of sliding rocks and splashing water. Vaith launched himself overhead and fluttered out of sight. Kira closed her eyes and tried again to reach Kelmir.

Kel?

Her thoughts moved through a thick haze and finally found him, moving into his mind. He sat hunched over the edge of a ravine. Something whimpered in the darkness below.

Kelmir crouched low, staring down into the thick shadows. His nostrils filled with the sharp tang of sweat and fear. Slowly, his eyes separated the shades of gray, and focused on the silhouette of someone hunkered down at the bottom of the ravine. *Friend or foe?* Kelmir sensed only fear.

Kira was fully alert to the possibility of danger, but a nagging thought plagued her. It had been little more than a half moon since she'd come to Tem Hold. Surely Toril's men couldn't have found her so soon, and it seemed unlikely a mercenary soldier would cower, mewling, in a dark ravine. Whoever Kelmir had chased into the ravine might need help. Heresta's voice floated inside her head repeating the healer's oath: Healer to the wounded and sick, harbor to those lost in the storm, helper to those in need, hearth to those alone.

Reluctantly, she turned Trad in the direction of the sounds. They picked their way through the heavy brush and fallen branches until they came to the edge of the ravine. They rode along the rim until they reached the spot where Kelmir lay, muscles tensed, head hanging over the edge. He stared into the darkness, tail twitching back and forth. Vaith fluttered down and settled on the ground beside him.

Kira slid out of the saddle and took a few cautious steps, testing the ground with her foot. When she reached Kelmir's side, she peered into the gulf, but in the twilight the deepening shadows seemed to dance and shift. Even through Kelmir's keen eyes, she was unable to identify the motionless figure below.

Aside from the trickling of the stream, there was only silence. "Hello?" Kira called out. No answer.

Kira grew concerned. "Are you hurt?" she asked. There was a small movement, followed by the rattle and plash of gravel and dirt sliding into the water. The silence returned as Kira waited, frowning into the darkness. She thought of sending Vaith down to take a look, but it could be dangerous for him, or frightening for the person hiding in the dark. A forlorn sob rose from the shadows.

Kneeling on the embankment, hands gripping the edge, Kira spoke in even tones. "Please, let us help you," she said.

A familiar voice whispered up from the shadows. "I'm afraid." There was another sob, followed by low weeping. Kelmir stopped flicking his tail and bent his ears forward as he stared at the sound.

Kira was thunderstruck. She had only heard the girl speak a few words and half sentences, but she recognized the voice at once. "Milvari?"

"Y-yes."

"Are you hurt?"

"I-I don't think so."

"What are you doing out here?"

"I-I followed you. To see if you would gather more herbs." Her voice cracked with fear and sadness.

Kira was sorry she had allowed Harl's warnings of Mayet's disapproval stop her from teaching Milvari about herb lore. She knew how it felt to have a door open and then close just as one began to step through it. "Oh, Milvari. You could have asked me."

"I didn't—I didn't know h-how. I'm s-sorry."

Kira ached for the poor girl. "Never mind. It's all right. Let's just get you out of there. Can you climb up?"

"I-I'm not sure. Is it still there?"

Kira was puzzled. "Is what still here?"

"The-the giant cat. The one that chased me."

"Kelmir won't hurt you. He's one of my companions. And my friend." She touched Kelmir on the shoulder and the big cat's ears twitched.

"But—"

Kira stroked Kelmir's head. "I promise you, Milvari. Kel won't hurt you. He only chased you because you ran. He was merely trying to protect me."

Milvari was quiet.

"Would you feel better if I sent him away?"

155

There was no response.

CHAPTER TWENTY-ONE

Milvari huddled at the bottom of the ravine, shivering, her wet skirt weighing her down. Her face and arms burned from the branches that had lashed her as she ran, and her knees were scratched from the fall. She'd dropped her cloak as she scrambled between the trees and now she shivered in the cold night air. Should she ask the hunter to send the frightening animal away? Could she?

She shrank back. She was such a fool. Her mother was right, she wasn't good for anything. She had so wanted to be like the hunter! Strong. Brave.

"All right, Kel. I guess you'll have to go." The hunter's voice seemed filled with disappointment.

"N-no. It's all right."

"Are you certain?"

"Yes." Milvari tried to sound confident, but her voice came out a high-pitched squeak.

"All right, Milvari. Try to climb up. Just go slowly."

She reached up, trying to find a handhold, but the rocks and gravel loosened, a shower of dirt tumbled down on her. She coughed.

"Are you all right?" the hunter asked.

Milvari spit dirt out of her mouth and then almost laughed. Her mother would be mortified. She grew braver at the thought of her unladylike plight. "I'm fine," she called out. "Except I keep slipping back down. The rocks are all loose."

"Try moving farther along the ravine. The embankment might be more solid."

"But I can't see." Milvari's budding courage wavered.

"Try to feel your way. Stretch your arms out to the sides and use your fingers to guide you. It might help if you close your eyes."

Milvari squeezed her eyes shut. Reaching out with her left hand, she inched her way along the bank until her fingers touched firm ground. "I think I found a solid place," she called.

"Good," the hunter said. "Keep talking so I can find the spot above you."

Keep talking? What should she say? Milvari had been told over and over by her mother not to speak unless spoken to. She'd already said more in the past few minutes than she had in months.

"Milvari?" Her name floated down to her, rousing her from her thoughts.

"I'm here. But I-I don't know what to say."

"Try telling me what you recall about the plants we found in the field. Do you remember?"

"Oh yes!" She went over every plant and the properties associated with each. The shape of the leaves, the color of the flowers, the places where they grew. The words seemed to jump out of her.

"Milvari," the hunter interrupted from above, "you need to try climbing up now."

"I'm sorry," Milvari's cheeks burned with embarrassment. Had that been her rattling on like a child?

"Don't be. I'm very impressed. You seem to remember everything I taught you. Come along, now. Give it another try. I'll be here to give you a hand at the top."

CHAPTER TWENTY-TWO

They left Vaith and Kelmir at the edge of the forest. Milvari sat behind Kira, wrapped in Kira's cloak and clinging to her as if she feared she would fall off Trad's back. Kira reached down and patted the girl's cold wet hands. "We're nearly home," she said to sooth Milvari's fears.

They drew near the hold. The heavy gate stood open to the night. Lanterns were lit and hung along the tops of the walls, causing strange shadows to bounce and weave. People rushed about in disorder. The hold looked like a roiling kettle about to boil over. Kira urged Trad on. Whatever was going on, Holder Tem would be relieved to have his niece safely back inside the walls of Tem Hold.

They rode through the gate and Kira halted Trad in the main yard. Someone called Milvari's name. A shadow loomed across the ground as the stable door slammed opened and light spilled out. Kira recognized the silhouette. Holder Tem strode forward to meet them. He folded his arms across his chest, an angry aura billowing around him.

Kira tensed. Milvari's grip tightened and she leaned out to look past Kira at the irate man standing before them.

In the light from the lanterns, Kira saw the muscles in the holder's jaw working before he spoke. His words

159

scraped through clenched teeth. "It's late to be out, Hunter."

She gripped the reins in her fist and steadied her nerves. She let every trace of emotion fall away from her face. Keeping her eyes on the muscular man, she reached back to help Milvari dismount. Still shivering, the girl clung to Kira's arm as she slid off the horse's back to stand before her uncle. She seemed small, huddled in Kira's heavy cloak.

Kira slipped out of the saddle to stand beside the young girl. Fear tingled its way along her skin. She put a hand on Trad's shoulder to steady herself. The holder stared at her and she wanted to run, to escape. Memories of the way Toril had glared at her before the beatings returned, mixing with the pounding of her blood. Her breathing grew shallow. A part of her knew Milos Tem had never given her any reason to fear him, but neither had Toril. At first.

"I am sorry if we worried you, Holder Tem." Her mouth was dry and she hoped he wouldn't hear the fear in her voice. Her fear had always enraged Toril, driving him to greater brutality. "I had intended to have your niece back before dark, but we had a small mishap."

Milvari glanced up at her, then looked down again. Kira hoped Milvari wouldn't spoil the lie. It was only a small tale, after all, and might save the girl some trouble.

"I can see that," the holder snapped. "Milvari, go inside."

"But Uncle—" she began, looking directly at him.

His eyes grew dark and his jaw tightened, and Milvari dropped her head.

"Go, now." His voice was low, but seemed to hold less anger. "I will speak to the hunter alone."

Milvari drew off the cloak and handed it to Kira. "Thank you," she said. "I look forward to our lessons tomorrow." She glanced at her uncle, lifted her chin, and set off toward the main building.

As Milvari walked away, Kira steeled herself, waiting for the storm of the holder's anger to unleash itself. But Milos stood mesmerized, staring toward the hall long after the girl had gone inside. When he turned back to Kira, his eyes shone in the lamplight. "I don't know what has happened," he said, his voice as quiet as a mountain lake at dawn. "I cannot condone that you have put my niece at risk, but I—" He glanced back toward the hall.

The holder's face seemed to change before her eyes. The worry and anger appeared to melt away, leaving a mingled expression of sorrow and joy. For a moment, her fear fell away. Then his face resolved into its usual stern countenance and the moment passed. Kira wondered if the change she had seen had only been her imagination.

"In the future," the holder said, "you will notify me if you plan to take my niece out of the hold for any reason, and you will not have her outside these walls after dark."

His tone was harsh, but Kira heard something else. She heard the sound of her father's voice when he scolded her for venturing too far from their cot. The voice that warned of danger, the voice that feared for her safety, the voice that wished to protect. It warmed her to know the holder felt that same way about his niece. "Yes, Holder Tem."

He started to leave, but his shoulders stiffened suddenly and he rounded on her. "And you will not take her out to hunt at any time!"

Kira started. Trad shimmied sideways with a high whinny, pulling her around and nearly tearing the reins from her hand. Kira stroked his mane, speaking quietly to him. When she turned back, the holder had gone.

CHAPTER TWENTY-THREE

Kira entered the hall and strode briskly to the table where Milvari waited. Her young student had paper and ink laid out on the table. Milvari glanced up at Kira's approach. Worry darkened her face.

"Good morn, Milvari," Kira said. "Is something wrong?"

Milvari dropped her head and let her hair fall forward. She reminded Kira of the frightened child she had been after the death of her parents. With a gentle touch, she raised the girl's head so she could see her face and gave her a reassuring smile. "Milvari, please go and let your uncle know that we will be going outside the hold for our lesson today."

Milvari's eyes grew round. "But—"

Milvari swallowed hard, but she didn't turn away from Kira. "What if he gets angry?"

Kira put her hand on Milvari's shoulder. She understood the girl's fear. But the holder had not acted out his anger in physical violence. "He was angry last night," she said softly, "and no one was harmed."

Milvari's eyes glistened. "But what if he sends us away from Tem Hold?" Her voice trembled.

Kira was caught off guard by the question. "Why would he do that?"

162

Milvari's lower lip quivered. "Because I'm not a proper lady and he won't be able to find me a husband and he doesn't want to have to take care of us forever," she blurted.

"Oh Milvari, I had no idea." She sat beside the girl and put an arm around her shoulders. "Did he really say that to you?"

"No," Milvari said. "He didn't say it. She did." She turned to Kira. "Do you think—?"

"She?"

"Mother. She's always telling me what a burden we are to him. How angry he is when I don't behave like a proper lady." Her dark eyes flashed. "It's not true, is it? He's not like that at all. Is he?"

Kira thought about the concern the holder had shown for his niece's safety. "No," she said. "I don't believe he is."

"Why does she say those things?"

Kira shrugged. "I cannot say."

"I hate her!" Milvari jumped up and ran from the room.

Kira wanted to go after the girl, but something told her that Milvari needed time. Betrayal by a loved one was a hard pain to bear, and Milvari felt betrayed by her own mother. Kira could not understand what would make someone lie and say such things to a child.

Kira wondered what would happen now. Her plan to teach Milvari more about plants today hadn't gone very well. She opened the book of animal drawings and turned the pages distractedly. The renderings were realistic, the accompanying descriptions penned in a neat hand. Each animal was depicted in its natural environment, its habits described in detail. It reminded her of the scrolls she had produced during her time with Heresta. She had worked hard to make her drawings as accurate as possible. She would go over them with her mentor and refine them until she knew the plants intimately. The person who had drawn the animals in this book knew them and understood them well.

"I had hoped Tratine would be interested enough to want to improve his skills in letters."

Kira jumped, letting the book fall shut.

Holder Tem moved from behind her. "I didn't mean to startle you," he said, picking up the book and leafing through it.

He stood a hand's breadth away. So near that the warmth of his body caressed her skin. She shifted in her chair.

"It was my field guide," he said. "My father had me make it when I was near to Tratine's age. He used it as a tool to interest me in my lessons."

So, the precise drawings were his. She waited to see if he would say more, but he was absorbed by the little book. His face was calm. The stern, angry holder was gone, and the caring man she had glimpsed the night before stood beside her. Kira was mystified. She felt her head tingle, realized she was staring, stood and walked to the window. The tingling was like the pull from Vaith or Kelmir when they wanted her attention, but with a subtle difference. There was no clear message. It was like a faint whisper drifting on a summer's breeze. A whisper so quiet it could not be understood.

Outside, gauzy clouds drifted across a pale blue sky. It would have been a perfect day to take Milvari out to gather herbs. Kira hesitated. Why should she fear to do what she had earlier suggested be done by Milvari? "Holder Tem," she began. His silence made her turn to face him. He was staring past her out the window at something distant.

"Holder Tem?"

He dropped his gaze. His face flushed. "Your pardon," he said. "I must have been daydreaming. Not appropriate behavior for a holder, I'm afraid." He handed the book to

Kira and his face settled back into its familiar severity. "What do you require, Hunter?"

"I've discovered that your niece has a keen interest in the lore of plants." Kira phrased her words with care and watched him closely. "I see that you understand the importance of inspiring young people to learn, and I would like your permission to foster her interest."

"And why should she be taught such lore?"

"Merely as a way to strengthen her interest in her other lessons, I assure you. To encourage her as you thought this might encourage Tratine." She held up the book.

"I see. And you feel that this is the best way for Milvari to learn?"

Kira looked him in the eye. "Yes."

He stared back at her. The strange tingle edged its way along her scalp. She ran her fingers through her hair and the sensation faded.

"All right," he said finally. "You may take her outside the hold for afternoon lessons as weather and time permit. But only until her mother returns. There are some battles not worth fighting."

Kira smiled in surprise at hearing one of Heresta's sayings on another's lips. "Thank you, Holder Tem. I know that Milvari will learn much."

The holder began to say more, but then he merely shrugged and walked away.

CHAPTER TWENTY-FOUR

Kira sat at the table in the little alcove off the kitchen. Across from her, Milvari busily jotted notes on a small bit of parchment. As Brilissa filled three large mugs with hot tea, Kira pulled a dark green, leafy plant with long thin tendrils out of the canvas pouch that hung at her side. "Most of the plants in the region are familiar to me, but this one I have never seen before. Do you know it?" she asked.

Brilissa settled into the chair beside Kira and examined the plant. "I'm not much for plants that aren't used for cooking, but this one I know." She promptly wiped her hands on her apron. "Demon's Claw, I've heard it called. You should destroy it."

Milvari stopped writing. "Why do we need to destroy it?"

"Eating it causes burning in the mouth and stomach, a heavy sickness of the bowels, headache and fever. Some describe it like being clutched by a demon, so I've heard. It will make a grazing animal sick to death for days."

Kira drizzled a spoonful of golden honey into her mug. "I thought it might be poisonous. The deer have left the grass surrounding it uncropped. It's a good thing I kept Trad away from the patch. Unlike wild deer, some grazing animals don't know any better."

"We ought to tell Harl," Milvari said. She took a sip from her mug.

Kira smiled. In the past fortnight, Milvari had grown confident enough to speak openly to both Brilissa and Kira. Perhaps she could be pushed a little further. "I agree. You should tell him as soon as you've finished your tea."

Milvari blanched. "Me?"

"You found it. Besides, I've work to do," Kira cast a glance at Brilissa.

"But I—" Milvari set her cup down. She tilted her head forward as if to let the hair fall over her eyes, but her long locks had been pulled back into a thick braid. "I wouldn't know what to say to him," she mumbled.

Kira pushed the leafy plant across the table. "You know where the patch is and you can take this with you, in case he's never seen it before."

Milvari stared at the plant as if it were a venomous reptile.

"Go on," Kira said. "Take it." She bit the insides of her cheeks to keep herself from smiling as Milvari continued to stare at the leafy stalk.

"I've got to get back to the kitchen before something boils over or catches fire," Brilissa said and bustled out of the room. As she passed by Kira on her way to the door, she covered her mouth to smother her amusement.

Milvari sat still for a long moment. "Couldn't you tell him when you go out to see to Trad?" she asked in a plaintive voice.

"Milvari, this is something you need to do. I've told you before that the knowledge you're gaining comes with a certain amount of responsibility. Someone needs to let people know of dangers like this. Sooner or later, you must be that someone. You know I won't be here at Tem Hold forever."

Milvari jerked her head up. "You always say that, but I thought you might change your mind. You like it here, don't you?" Her lower lip trembled, and her eyes glittered in the flickering candlelight.

Kira's mirth drained away. "I can't stay," she said with a wistful smile. "I wish that I could, but . . ." She reached over and gave Milvari's hand a squeeze. "You can do this."

Milvari pulled her hand away. "Fine," she said, grabbing the plant. "I will tell Harl about the danger." She turned and marched out of the room.

Kira sighed as the young girl's angry steps receded. Had she pushed Milvari too far? She stared down at the dark liquid cooling in her mug, but unlike Heresta she had no gift of dreams or foresight, and no answers swirled into view.

CHAPTER TWENTY-FIVE

Milvari paused inside the stable door, waiting as her eyes adjusted to the duskiness. The Demon's Claw felt sticky and heavy in her hand. She listened for a moment to the rustle and scratch of the hay rake before taking a hesitant step toward the sound. As she stood, willing herself to take another step, a gate opened and Harl backed out of a stall, pulling a full wheelbarrow. With an expert twist he swung the loaded cart around and started toward the stable door. Milvari stood frozen in place.

Harl stopped. "Your pardon, m'Lady."

Milvari realized she was staring and lowered her gaze. She kept her eyes on the ground and stuck out her hand, holding the plant up where he could see it.

"Do you want to feed that to the horses?" he asked.

Milvari frowned. "Why would I do that?"

"You used to—I mean—that is—"

Milvari's mouth popped open in surprise, and she let her hand fall to her side. He'd seen her feed the horses? She thought she'd been alone. She'd been so careful. Her eyes narrowed. "How do you know that?"

The wheelbarrow wobbled and he set it down on its supports. "I saw you." He wiped his hands on his breeches and shrugged.

Milvari peered at him. He seemed flushed. Had he been watching her, the way that she had watched him? She held up the plant once more. "I came to show you this."

He stepped forward and stared at the cutting. "What is it?"

Milvari's hand began to tremble as he drew closer. "It's a . . . poisonous plant . . . we . . . I found."

Harl reached for the plant, his rough fingers brushing hers as he took the leafy stem. Milvari drew back her hand. Her cheeks grew hot.

Harl seemed not to notice. He turned the cutting over in his hand and flattened out one of the dark leaves. "I've seen this before," he said. "You're right that it is bad for the animals, but I can't remember what it's called."

"Demon's Claw. It causes mouth and stomach pain, fever, headache, and—" Milvari stopped, embarrassed. Harl was watching her, a lopsided smile on his face.

"And other complications," he finished for her, his face contorted into a comical grimace.

Milvari giggled and covered her mouth to keep from laughing. "Yes," she said. "Other complications."

Harl chortled. Milvari tried to contain herself, but his mirth was contagious. Soon they were both laughing out loud.

"Harl!" the stable master called from the back stalls. "What are you doing, boy? These stalls won't clean themselves."

Harl gave Milvari a sly wink. "Yes, Master Jarrett. I was just conferring with Mistress Milvari about a patch of Demon's Claw she's discovered." He winked at her.

"Demon's Claw, you say?" The stable master's swift approach surprised Milvari. She had never before seen him move at such a rapid pace. He wore heavy boots and breeches of canvas, and his uneven gait seemed to slow him down most of the time. She had watched the stable master

170

from the shadows, but not as much as she had watched Harl, she realized with a warm rush.

Master Jarret's round face was ruddy with exertion. He held out a gloved hand and Harl placed the plant in it.

The stable master flattened the plant out, prodding it with his fingers. "Hmmmmm . . . long tendrils, yes . . . yes, dark green leaves with narrowing tips. It's Demon's Claw, all right." He looked up at Milvari. "Where did you say you found it?"

Milvari stared at him her eyes wide. He saw her. He was speaking to her.

Master Jarrett leaned forward. "Mistress Milvari?"

Her mouth opened and closed, but words refused to form.

Harl stood watching her. He nodded encouragement, but Milvari stood mute. Harl took a step back so the stable master wouldn't see him, pointed at the plant and grimaced. She had to purse her lips together to keep from laughing. She opened her mouth once more and the words rushed out of her. "North of the hold, about three leagues distance. On the western edge of the big meadow that lies inside a circle of frost berry trees."

The stable master squinted his face in thought. "Three leagues, yes . . . big meadow . . . circle of trees, yes, yes, yes. I know the place. Harl, we'll need to be sure to tell the herdsmen. They'll have to avoid the place. Yes . . . then we'll need to speak to the holder. He'll want to send someone out to destroy it. But not till winter. Maybe spring. It will have to be burned, and it's too dry to risk a fire now."

"It's a good thing Mistress Milvari found the patch, isn't it, Master Jarrett?" Harl grinned.

Master Jarrett's face smoothed out. "Yes, yes, it is. Very good," he said. He handed the plant back to Harl. "Make sure this is properly burned, my boy," he said. "Wouldn't want any of the animals getting a lip on it. Yes, indeed." He went back to his work, his gait slowed now by the dragging of his left leg. His foot twisted at an odd angle, swinging out with each step. Milvari had often wondered if he'd always had the limp, but had been afraid to ask anyone about it. She wanted to ask Harl now, but she didn't want Master Jarrett to overhear her. She wouldn't want to embarrass him.

She signaled frantically for Harl to follow her and turned to leave.

"Yes, of course, m'Lady," Harl said louder than necessary.

Milvari tried to shush him, but he only smiled and called out louder. "Of course, we'll take the plant and burn it right away." He followed her out of the stable.

Once outside he gave Milvari a conspiratorial look and she let out a relieved laugh. "I only wanted to ask about Master Jarret's leg," she said. "I've never heard him speak of it. Was it injured somehow?"

Harl gave her sidelong glance. "Has no one ever told you?"

"Told me what?"

Harl hesitated. "Perhaps they haven't," he said. "No one speaks of it much." He looked around. "Come on. We'll take this to the ash heap and burn it."

* * *

Harl stared straight ahead.

They stood before the mound of ash, watching the small pile of dried sticks catch fire. The leaves and tendrils of Demon's Claw curled and withered atop the burning twigs, emitting a bitter smoke that stung Milvari's nose and eyes.

"They say he nearly gave his own life trying to save Holder Kamar," Harl said in a low voice.

His eyes flicked toward Milvari. She focused on the burning plant and the thin wisp of smoke that rose into the pale blue sky.

"My mother never speaks of it," she whispered.

"You must miss your father very much." Harl snapped a twig into small pieces and fed them to the flames.

Milvari wrinkled her brow. "I was very young when it happened," she said. "But I do have a few recollections of him. Most of the time, in my memories, his arms are strong and warm, but his face seems hazy and distant."

"I'm sorry," he said.

"What about you?" she asked. "I've never seen your parents. Are they—?"

"Alive? Yes. Being so far from our own croft though, I rarely see them."

"Don't you miss them?"

"Sometimes." He sighed. "But there were far more of us then the croft could support. All boys, too." He picked up a stick and poked at the fire. Sparks jumped and rose with the acrid smoke. "Being the youngest, I'd have gotten the smallest share of land, if any share were left to have. I didn't really want to be a crofter, anyway. When Master Jarrett offered to take me as his apprentice, I made ready to go without another thought."

"Do you like being an apprentice?"

"I like working with the animals."

"I like animals, too." Milvari blushed as she remembered the feel of the comb as it slid through the horses' manes and they way they listened when she talked to them.

"Being apprenticed to a stable master is a good position and Master Jarrett is one of the finest. A person could do worse."

Milvari thought about that for a moment. "I should like to be an apprentice," she said.

Harl turned his gaze on her, his eyes opened wide. "But you're a lady! You're bound to marry a rich holder and go live in some far off region. Isn't that what all fine ladies dream about?" He added with disdain.

Milvari's face became fever hot. "Not all," she said harshly. She stared at the smoldering fire. "Besides, according to my mother, I'm not much of a lady."

"I think you're a fine Lady," Harl said, the scorn gone from his voice. "The horses think so, too."

Milvari glanced over to see if he was teasing her. He refused to look at her. His ears had turned deep scarlet.

They stood in silence and watched the fire dwindle.

CHAPTER TWENTY-SIX

Kira led Trad outside and eased the stable door shut. Frost twinkled under bright moonlight, breath rose in steamy clouds, and boots and hooves crunched on frozen ground. Shorter days allowed less time for hunting and outdoor lessons as Winter Turn approached, and each morning Kira set out earlier. But no matter the hour, Brilissa was in the kitchen before her, a bundle of provisions and a cup of hot tea at the ready. Kira was grateful for the tea and food, but she wondered if the woman ever slept.

The main gate stood open and a rider astride a black and white dappled horse waited in the predawn moonlight outside. Kira paused as a sensation washed over her. Not fear, something else. The gatekeeper stood outside the gatehouse, waiting to close the gate. He made no sign that anything was amiss. The tingling struck, trickled along her scalp and ran down the back of her neck.

The figure on the horse nodded. "I bid you good morn, Hunter." Though he spoke quietly, the holder's voice carried clear on the wintry air. "Although, it is still some while before the sun will wake the land with a new day."

Kira drew up her hood. "Good morn, Holder Tem." She stepped into the stirrup and casually pulled herself into the saddle. Trad ambled through the gate and Kira drew up beside the holder's horse. A bow and a quiver of arrows were slung on his back and a long blade hung from his waist. His presence at this hour surprised her and wariness folded itself over her as the heavy gate swung shut behind them.

"Are you traveling today, Holder?"

"A short distance, perhaps." He stared up at the night sky where silver stars winked against indigo. "As they will be wintering on my land, I think it is time I met your companions." He gestured in the direction of the forest.

Kira sat still. A small worry gnawed her. She wondered how he would react to the sight of Kelmir. Would he change his mind about allowing them to stay? She pushed the thought away. What was it Heresta would say? To worry about what may come is to throw away the moment. "As you will, Holder Tem. Do you know the small glade southwest of the ravine?"

"It is long since I spent much time in the woods." He shifted in his saddle. "I'm sure you know the way better than I."

Trad snorted, steam rising from his nostrils. Kira nudged him to a slow walk and the holder followed. They made their way across the wide swath of cleared land separating the hold from the forest.

When they reached the edge of the woods, Kira paused. With daybreak still some way off, darkness held the land and filled the spaces between the trees. She knew Kelmir waited not far inside the tree line, ready to lead the way deep into the heart of the forest where game was plentiful, but Kira was afraid his scent would frighten the holder's mount.

"Is there something amiss?" The holder sounded concerned.

"No, only that it would be better to skirt the woods until dawn," Kira said, turning Trad eastward. She sent out a quick thought. *Kel, meet us at the cave.*

Holder Tem reined his horse around to follow her lead. "I wondered how you meant to traverse the forest in the dark."

Kira pushed Trad to a faster walk, but held him from breaking into a trot. The holder, an adept rider, brought his horse up to keep pace beside her.

Milos Tem was a somber man, but he did not seem to be a threat. It had been a long time since she'd ridden with someone who wasn't a snarling guard. Kira found herself smiling as the two animals matched stride. She relaxed in the saddle and loosened her grip on the reins.

Ahead of them, the stars dimmed and the sky lightened, as if a doorway to a lit room swung slowly open. Kira gave Trad his head and he loped into a slow trot. The other horse kept pace.

The sun crested the mountains as they reached the eastern edge of the forest, and the holder slowed his mount. Kira pulled Trad to a halt and waited as the other horse and rider drew up even with her.

"The sunlight looks like liquid fire when it glances off the mountains," he said.

His beautiful words astonished her. Kira glanced over. His face was ruddy and she caught herself admiring the strong contour of cheek and jaw. She pulled her eyes away and turned Trad southward.

Within a league of the northern edge it was light enough to enter the forest. The cave was still some distance south, but they needed to cross the ravine where it wasn't too steep. Kira had just the place in mind. She paused at a narrow deer track that led into the woods.

"Holder Tem," she began, eyeing the sturdy-looking stallion with its black and white dappling, "how bold is your horse?"

"Zharik is a valiant animal," he said with certainty. "If you are concerned about him being alarmed at the first sign of the Moon Cat, you may rest your mind. He has been with me through worse than the scent or sight of a dangerous animal." He gave the horse's shoulder a firm pat and the animal raised its head and let out a short bluster. The holder smiled.

The warm sense of pride he exhibited toward the animal surprised Kira. She led the way into the woods and followed the winding animal track to the edge of the ravine, where they picked their way down the slope. The water streamed shallow, and they dismounted and let the horses drink their fill.

Kira pushed back her hood, then unrolled the oilcloth that held the day's provisions and passed it to the holder.

He tore off a hunk of bread and handed the rest of the food back to her. "Thank you, Hunter." While chewing the bread, he opened a worn saddlebag, polished with age, and pulled out a brandy flask and some fine white cheese, offering them to Kira.

She took a portion of cheese, but refused the flask. "Nay, Holder. My thanks, but I have game to hunt this morn."

He nodded and returned the flask to its place. "Wisdom is a welcome guide," he said, taking a drink from his water skin.

Kira heard Heresta in his words. "I know of at least one other who would agree with you," she said as she slid back into the saddle.

* * *

When they emerged from the trees, the glade was awash with flaxen light and Kelmir sat on his haunches in the midst of the clearing, his mottled fur reflecting the sun. Holder Tem held his mount steady. With slow movements, he slid down from the saddle, keeping a wary eye on the big cat.

Kel, please stay still. Kelmir's tail flicked almost imperceptibly.

Kira dismounted and dropped Trad's reins. "Holder Tem, this is Kelmir, my long-time companion."

They heard a loud screech and the holder's horse gave a nervous nicker.

"Easy, Zharik." The holder stroked the animal's neck.

Kira stepped away and extended her arm. A multicolored flutter flashed from above as Vaith swooped down and landed on her wrist. "This is Vaith. A prince among wyverns." Vaith flourished his wings before folding them.

"A dazzling display," Holder Tem said. He stood with his hand over his horse's nose to keep him calm.

"Yes." Kira smiled. "He does like to show his qualities."

"How long have they been with you?"

"Kelmir has been my friend for more than ten turns. Vaith I've known for only five, but he is the best of his kind." She ran a finger over Vaith's head and he arched his long neck moving gracefully against her touch.

"May I?" the holder asked.

"Of course. Shall I take Zharik's reins, or do you prefer to tie him?"

He watched Kelmir, who sat unmoving. "I think he'll do best tied," he said. He led the horse to a tree and looped the reins over a sturdy limb. He reached into his saddlebag, brought out a small apple and gave it to the horse. Trad raised his head at the crunching sound and gave a questioning blow. The holder extracted another apple, walked over to the grey and offered the treat on the flat of his palm. Trad lipped the apple into his mouth and bit into it with a small sigh.

When the horses were settled, the holder walked back toward Kira, arm extended and a youthful eagerness on his face.

Kira lifted her arm and Vaith leaped up, flew once around the glade, then landed on the man's forearm. Holder Tem held Vaith up and examined him. "When we were boys we tried everything to trap and tame a wyvern. How did you manage it?"

Kira hesitated. No one but her parents and Heresta had known about her abilities. Her secret was now hers alone. She was beginning to like this man, but she had no reason to trust him. She gave him the lie that wasn't a lie. "He was a gift."

The holder continued to inspect Vaith. "A handsome treasure to be sure." Finally, with some reluctance, he stretched his arm toward her. "But I am keeping you from your work, and I would still like to make better acquaintance with your cat."

Vaith, go and scout. Fowl or small game today. Kira made a low trilling sound and Vaith unfurled his wings and swept up and away.

The holder watched as Vaith launched himself out of the glade, a bright arrow of color that was gone in a moment. "Is it sound he responds to?"

"And some words. We manage to understand each other." Another partial truth.

Kira turned to Kelmir, who sat in the sunlight, still and patient. "As for Kel, we've been together so long he often seems to know my mind." Kira smiled as much at the double meaning of her words as her feelings toward Kelmir. She went over to where he sat and stroked his fur.

The holder moved a few paces nearer and halted, keeping a close eye on the cat.

"He's no threat to you as long as you're no threat to me," Kira said. Kelmir closed his eyes and pushed his head into her hand, and she scratched behind his ears.

Holder Tem stepped forward, arms down at his sides, clearly alert for any sudden movement. As he approached, Kelmir opened his eyes and turned his calm gaze on the man. "How well does he listen to you?" the holder asked.

"Kel, lie down," Kira said. With slow careful movements Kelmir stretched out his front legs and sank down onto his belly.

The holder shook his head. "I would not have believed it if I hadn't been witness to it. And they hunt for you?"

"We work together." Kira nodded. "Would you care to join us?" The words left her mouth before she realized she would have more half-truths to tell, but it was too late to take them back.

He replied without hesitation. "Yes."

In the past she and her companions had always hunted alone. Another person would have questions about their methods. So be it, she thought. "Trad is practiced in following Kelmir. He knows his scent," she told the holder.

He smiled at her, untied his horse, and stepped into the saddle.

She picked up Trad's reins and remounted. *Kel, Vaith is headed southwest. Let's make a short morning of it.* "Kelmir, find Vaith," she said aloud. Kelmir swept to his feet and loped out of the clearing.

* * *

The morning sun warmed the open spaces and the early frost that had clung to branch and limb had dissolved. They stood beside their horses at the edge of a large clearing. Six fat brush hens hung from Trad's pommel and a brace of rabbits were tied to the holder's saddle strings.

Kira was satisfied with the morning's catch, but Holder Tem was enthralled by the hunting tactics of Vaith and Kelmir. He sat motionless as Vaith soared overhead searching for more small game. "I still have no idea how you managed to train him to signal with a tilted wing, nor how the cat could possibly learn such a signal," he murmured.

Kira shrugged. She had chosen to spin a complicated story rather than expose her gift. "I merely used what came naturally to the wyvern," she lied. "I noticed the action each time he sighted just before he dove and struck, and I used it to my advantage. As long as he keeps to the air, the game stays still, frightened that movement will attract his attention. It distracts the prey so Kelmir can more easily sneak up."

Vaith spotted another rabbit and tugged her attention away. She let herself become a gateway between the two animals. A moment later, Kelmir emerged from the brush, a large rabbit in his jowls.

The holder gaped. "Do they ever miss?"

"Rarely," Kira said. She knelt and took the rabbit from Kelmir. The holder bowed his head as she held the animal out on the palms of her hands, moving it in a circular motion and giving thanks for its life. Then she tied a loop around its back legs and handed it up to the holder.

"I find myself captivated by their abilities," he said, tying the rabbit to his saddle.

"I need to call Vaith in to rest," Kira said. "And to eat. He's always hungry."

"As well they both should be after so much effort. I've grown hungry myself merely watching them work." He tied

Zharik to a sturdy branch, then opened his saddlebag and drew out two large rolled cloths and the flask he'd offered Kira earlier.

Kira whistled high and loud. *Vaith, Kelmir, come eat.* She drew off her cloak and spread it out on a dry patch of grass in the dappled sunlight at the edge of the trees. From her pouch she took out the rest of her morning rations and sat on the edge of her cloak, leaving room for the holder.

Holder Tem stood at the edge of the cloak in obvious embarrassment. "I should have spread out my cloak for you," he said. "It was unthinking of me not to be chivalrous."

Kira gave him a crooked smile. "Holder Tem, consideration is not for men alone to exercise." Vaith chose that moment to land between them. He furled his wings, squawked and gave Kira an expectant look. "Nor does it come naturally to wyverns." She laughed and held out a scrap of cooked fowl for Vaith.

The holder unrolled his parcels and spread out a small feast of breads, meats, cheeses, and fruit.

"You seem prepared for more than a morning of hunting," Kira said.

"Thank Brilissa. She feeds me as if every meal might be my last." He was silent for a moment, a frown drawing his face down.

Kira focused on tearing off another piece of meat. She held the morsel out to Vaith and caught the holder staring at her. Vaith took the fowl from her hand and shredded it into strips. One by one he plucked the pieces up and swallowed them. Kelmir padded out of the brush and sat beside Kira. She gave him a hunk of fowl.

The holder picked up a thick slice of meat and held it out toward Kelmir. "May I offer him this?"

"By all means," Kira said. Kelmir stepped around the edge of the cloak to stand beside the holder. Without taking his eyes from the holder's face, he leaned forward, sniffed, then tilted his head sideways and took the meat from the man's hand, each movement slow and deliberate. With the meat in his mouth, he glanced at Kira, then lay down a few feet away to enjoy his prize.

"It's odd," the holder said, watching Kelmir and Vaith eat. "After my brother's death, I thought I would never hunt in these woods again." He took in a deep breath before continuing. "Yet, today, with you and your companions . . ." He shrugged. "I was so taken with them, with the idea of them, I had no other thought. It was if I had forgotten . . ."

"I'm sorry, Holder Tem, I hadn't considered—"

"No." He held up his hand. "I'm glad of it. It has been a long time since I was able to forget, to think of something else for a time."

"That we think of the living doesn't mean we have forgotten those who have returned to the wheel," Kira quoted. She heard Heresta's voice echo her own as she spoke. "And sorrow must someday give way to hope."

He gave her a strange look, the corner of his mouth contracted into a half smile. "I once thought I would never be hopeful again. Kamar's death was more than the loss of a brother. It was the loss of freedom for me."

Kira found his words strange. She knew the loss of freedom, knew what it was to be caged, but what could a man of privilege know of such things? "I don't understand."

"My brother was firstborn, heir to Tem Hold by both tradition and law. When I was very young, I was jealous of his position, yet I admired him. My father tried to instill in both of us the roles and responsibilities of leadership. But as I grew older, I realized I was grateful that Kamar, not I, was Tem Hold's heir. It allowed me freedoms my brother never enjoyed."

He picked up a handful of dried berries and chewed them one by one, his eyes focused on some distant place or time. "Kamar was suited to be holder. I never was," he said finally.

"It seems to me you're a fine holder. Your hold is prosperous. And your people seem content." Kira nibbled at a piece of cheese.

"Content? Yes, they are that. But I would have them more than content."

Kira recalled her discussion with Brilissa. "You would have them rule themselves."

"Yes." His blue eyes filled with light. "I would give them the freedom to make their own choices, to decide their own fates."

"A noble ideal, but one that many will not share."

"I'm not concerned with what the other holders may think. They are blind to what the people desire. And I am not so selfless as my ideas might suggest. In offering my people freedom from one man's rule, I gain freedom for myself."

"But as a holder, you are free to do as you will."

His brow wrinkled. "Power is not freedom. I am yoked to my position just as any man or woman."

"You could choose to leave the hold to your nephew."

"Yes, I have choices, but I must also live with the consequences of those choices. If I chose to leave Tem Hold in the hands of my nephew, he might grow to rule, though how wisely I cannot yet tell." He paused, seemed lost in thought for a moment, then his brow furrowed and he continued. "There are also those who might see him as too young to keep a hold under his sway. In the southern regions, there are many second and third sons of holders who wish to rule but have no lands of their own. If they took Tem Hold from Tratine, I would always know that I was to blame. And if the people are treated badly by the next holder, be it Tratine or some other, would I not be responsible for their plight?"

Kira stopped eating as she considered his words. She understood a sense of responsibility. Heresta had thoroughly ingrained the idea in her. But the concept that rulers could be tied to their rank by a sense of accountability and not just their worship of power and position had not occurred to her. Choices bring consequences.

The holder smiled, his eyes filled with mirth, and she followed his gaze. Vaith had helped himself to a large hunk of meat. He stood in the grass a few steps away and watched her out of the corner of one green-yellow eye as he rapidly tore off large chunks and swallowed them whole.

"Vaith! My apologies, Holder Tem. As you can see I have not been able to teach him proper manners," Kira said with a shrug.

"Perhaps, his manners are proper for the company of wyverns and he merely honors us," the holder offered. "As for manners, I would have you call me Milos. I'm not overly fond of titles, especially between friends."

Kira paused. She had grown comfortable with her role and title of hunter. If he wished to forego his title, he would want her to do the same. To give him a name to call her by would require another lie. "Are you sure that would be proper? There are those in your hold who might find it unseemly."

"There are some privileges my position allows that I would take advantage of. Offering the use of my personal name to whom I choose is one of them." His deep blue eyes held hers and her scalp prickled. "Unless there is some reason that you would not give up the use of titles between us," he added.

Kira turned away. Something made her want to trust this man, but fear kept her in check. "You may call me Ardea," she said. What would be the harm in letting him call her by her mother's name?

"Thank you, Ardea." His smile was warm and open.

A thorn of guilt twisted through her. She studied the sky and realized the morning was gone. "We'll be missing the midday meal, Hold—Milos. And Milvari will be expecting me for her lessons." She began gathering up the remains of their meal.

Milos remained seated. "One late lesson will not harm her," he said. "I wish to know more about you, Ardea."

Kira tensed as she rolled bread and cheese up in one of the cloths, recalling how another man had once said much the same thing to her. How warm he had seemed. How charming. "What more would you know?" Her hands shook.

He took the roll of food from her, his fingers brushing hers. "I wish to know if you would consider staying on at Tem Hold after the winter storms have abated."

Fear and excitement stirred her blood. "Stay on?"

"Brilissa brags of your skills and my niece thrives under your tutelage," he said in a rush.

Kira's world shrunk. The trees seemed to lean toward her and the air collapsed against her. She shivered, felt as if a dark cloud had swept across the sun. "I cannot stay." Her voice seemed to come from someplace far outside herself.

She forced her hand to remain steady as she picked up the last of the meat and gave it to Kelmir. The big cat had been lying patiently in the grass, his head resting on his front paws. He sat up and took the meat. Kira wiped her fingers on the grass.

"Cannot? Or will not?" the holder asked. Disappointment was plain in his voice.

Kira turned to face him. His eyes had lost their light.

A mix of emotions tugged at her heart and mind. Tem Hold seemed a safe haven, a place she might come to call home. She had grown to care for Milvari, grown to appreciate Brilissa's warm heart and kitchen, grown to like this tall brooding man. All the more reason she couldn't stay. She would soon be a danger to them. "Holder Tem . . . Milos." Her voice dropped almost to a whisper. "There are things about me you do not know. Reasons I cannot stay."

He turned his eyes away. "Of course, you're free to do as you please, Hunter." He picked up the last of their things, shook out her cloak and handed it to her, keeping his face averted. He untied his horse, put his foot into the stirrup, and slid into the saddle. "We should return to the hold. After all, we each have our responsibilities to attend to."

They rode through the forest in silence, moving in and out of shadows as the sun passed high overhead. The holder led the way, his back and shoulders an insurmountable barricade.

Kelmir moved silently off to the left and Vaith flew ahead, flitting from tree to tree. Kira had closed her mind to them and they kept their distance, allowing her to sink into herself.

A loud hiss roused her from her thoughts with sudden alertness. Zharik screamed and reared back. Milos tried to bring the animal under control, but the horse's eyes were white with fear. Kira leaped out of the saddle and ran forward to grab Zharik's reins as the terrified horse reared again. Forelegs flailed and Kira ducked.

Another loud hiss erupted beside the trail. Kira kept her face averted. She dived away from the sound. A hoof caught her on the shoulder and she dropped to the ground. For an instant all she could see was a sharp yellow beak, a long black tongue below fiery eyes. A large basilisk arched its neck, preparing to strike.

Kira froze. The basilisk raised its head. A loud screech descended on them. The basilisk looked up. *No, Vaith!*

The brush beside the trail exploded into a dark shadow that sprang at the creature. Kelmir struck as the basilisk spewed its venom.

Liquid fire burst forth, burning through her shirt and searing her skin.

Kira screamed.

CHAPTER TWENTY-SEVEN

The chill wind ran icy fingers along Mayet's face and crept beneath her cloak as she stepped down from the carriage. She shuddered as the icy air swept aside the warmth from the fur blankets she had nested in for the better part of the day.

Her gaze passed over the faces of the few folk who had gathered to greet her. Household staff and servants. She scowled. Peasants all. Where was Milos? Where was the customary holder's welcome her station demanded? The redheaded she-dog was missing, too. If Milos and that wanton were together . . . No. It didn't matter. A burgeoning smile chased the scowl from her face. I hold the spokes now, she thought. The next turn of the wheel will move things in my favor.

Ignoring the servants, she picked up her skirts and strode into the main hall with her son by her side. "Tratine, see that my trunks are brought up and send someone to the kitchen for mulled wine. I'll be in my chambers. And find out where your uncle is, I would speak with him as soon as may be."

He opened his mouth to protest, but she silenced him with a look.

The hallway leading to her rooms was empty, and she slipped off the fur-lined gloves Lisana had given her when the weather turned harsh. At least her callow little cousin had the decency to ensure her guests were comfortable. Although, the gifting was probably more a matter of showing off her new wealth than actual concern for the comfort of others. What need did Lisana have to conciliate others? She was a wealthy holder's wife now. Very wealthy.

Mayet shoved open the door to her sitting room. A low fire crackled in the hearth. She shrugged off her heavy cloak into a heap on the floor and rolled her head to loosen the muscles of her neck. A hot bath would remove the knots, but first she had business to discuss with Lord Milos. A little matter of restoration. The hunter to her master, Tem Hold to its former rules.

Someone rapped at the door. Mayet smiled. Perhaps Milos had mistaken the time of her arrival and had come to apologize.

"Come in," Mayet cooed.

Alyn entered the room, a heavy goblet in one hand, and a steaming jug in the other. "Your wine, m'Lady."

Mayet's neck stiffened. She glared at the girl. "Set it on the table. Must I tell you how to do everything?"

The girl seemed startled. "No, m'Lady." She hurried to set down the wine and nearly tripped on the cloak heaped in the middle of the room.

"Then why is the fire dying?"

The girl flushed crimson. "It isn't my . . ."

Mayet spun around to face her. "What?"

"I beg your pardon, m'Lady, but I am assigned to the kitchen. The upkeep of your rooms is not among my duties."

Mayet's hands flew to her hips. "Your job is what I say it is. If you wish to retain your current position, you'll remember that."

The girl stared at her a moment, then lowered her eyes to the floor. She opened the grate and placed several small logs on the fire, poking the embers and the burning wood with a metal rod to encourage the flames. Soon, a bright blaze warmed the room.

As the girl stood up to leave, Mayet snapped her fingers. "My cloak."

Alyn picked up the cloak. She brushed the folds out with brusque strokes, then hung the garment on a peg near the door. Her face was blank when she turned back to Mayet. "Will there be anything else?"

Uppity disobedient girl, Mayet thought, she should be punished. But all in good time. She waved a hand at the door. "You may go, for now." She poured a glass of the spiced wine and inhaled the scent of sweet herbs as the door clicked shut behind the girl. Sasson Hold might claim a more obedient staff, but their kitchen was no match for Tem Hold's.

She let a small laugh bubble to the surface. It felt good to be home, to put the servants in their place. Sasson Hold's subservient staff had been a welcome reminder of the way things should be. Soon Tem Hold would be able to boast of the docility of its own staff. She sipped the warm brew as she went over her arguments once more. Until her visit at Sasson Hold, she hadn't realized just how far out of hand things had become at home. Milos would need strong persuading to return things to the way they should be.

She glanced down at the rumpled folds of her dress. Perhaps it would be better to bathe and dress appropriately before presenting her case.

CHAPTER TWENTY-EIGHT

Milvari headed toward the well, her basket sagging with its burden of winter roots. The fresh tubers were covered in dirt and needed to be scrubbed and cleaned before they were stored. As she struggled with the weight of the basket, Tratine intercepted her. He planted his feet, crossed his arms and stood before her, barring the way.

Milvari smiled. "Welcome back, Tratine."

"Welcome back! Is that all you can say?" Tratine's face was flushed and reddened by the winter wind and sun. "Mother looked for you when we arrived and you weren't there to greet her. Where were you?"

"I was out gathering roots," Milvari said in a small voice, nodding her head in the direction of the basket. She shifted the weight of the basket and attempted to take a step forward.

"Gathering roots?" Tratine refused to move.

Milvari lowered the heavy basket to the ground.

Tratine kicked at it, spilling the contents on the ground. Milvari stooped, picked up the tubers one by one, and placed them back into the container.

"Stop that!" her brother yelled. "That's a servant's job!"

Milvari's mouth flew open, but her throat tightened around her words. She finished gathering up the roots and stood.

Tratine glared at her. "What is wrong with you?" he asked. "Why can't you behave properly as Mother asks?"

Milvari bit the inside of her mouth to keep from crying. What was wrong with her? She looked down at herself and rubbed at the dirt on her hands.

"Mother is right," her brother derided her. "You'll never be a proper lady, and you'll never find a proper husband."

His words were meant to hurt, but Milvari's muscles suddenly turned to stone. Her head buzzed and small black dots swam before her, turning everything fuzzy and gray as confusion and anger roiled up in her. The past few weeks had been the first she'd known of freedom. Freedom to question. Freedom to learn. Freedom to be who she wanted to be, rather than who she was told she should be. Why did they insist that something had to be wrong with her just because she was different? "I can see you know all about it," she said. "My big brother has come back from seeing the world and will now tell me how to live." Her voice was high-pitched and coated with contempt.

Tratine jerked his head back, as if he'd been struck, and stared at his sister. A nervous giggle pushed its way up from Milvari's middle. She pursed her lips and feigned a frown.

"It's a good thing that hunter will be leaving soon," Tratine said. "Being around her has made you worse than ever."

"What do you mean, leaving?"

"Just what I said. Mother is going to see that peasant gone."

A chill ran cold fingers along Milvari's skin. "She can't!" she blurted. "She's injured."

"Injured?" Tratine sounded surprised.

"Yes, a basilisk. She's been ill for several days now. I—I'm caring for her." Milvari stuck out her chin.

"You? I suppose you think that you're some sort of healer, now."

Milvari stared at the ground. "No, I—I'm only making her teas and—and poultices," she murmured.

"Not that it matters. Mother is determined to be rid of her. And you know what happens when Mother sets her mind to something." Tratine gave Milvari a cold smile.

All of the confidence fled from Milvari. She felt small and weak. The way she used to feel. She wanted to hide, to be unseen. "Mother can't make her leave. Uncle Milos won't allow it." Her words were as much to reassure herself as to convince her brother, but they made her feel less afraid. She picked up her basket, stepped around her brother, and went to the well to finish her task. The voices in her head clamored at her to apologize, to tell Tratine he was right. No, don't listen, she told herself as she set the basket beneath the pump spout and worked the handle. Icy water spurted out of the pump and splashed over the basket of roots. She knew Tratine's eyes were fixed on her, knew his face was contorted into a fierce glower, but she refused to turn around.

She filled a bucket with water and scrubbed at the tubers, punishing the dirt from their thick hides. Tratine marched up beside her. "When I am the holder here, the servants will behave as servants. And the ladies will act like ladies," he grumbled.

Milvari tried to picture her brother as a grown man, running the hold, but all she could see was her father's hands reaching out to her to lift her into the air and carry her into the warm kitchen. Her mother's harsh, thin-lipped gaze suddenly appeared before her. She frowned. Tratine might have their father's hair and eyes, but he had their mother's mouth. And her hard, calculating nature.

She gazed past Tratine as Harl came out of the stable and headed toward the kitchen at the back of the main hall. Milvari smiled. Harl had become a good friend. With him she could be herself, just as she could with the hunter. Her eyes flicked back to Tratine. The two boys were close to the same age, but were utterly unalike. Decidedly, she preferred Harl.

Tratine stuck his fists on his hips. "What are you smiling about?" he snarled.

"Nothing." Milvari picked up another tuber.

Tratine glanced over his shoulder, but Harl had disappeared into the kitchen. Tratine rolled his eyes and stalked off.

Milvari stopped scrubbing and emptied the water bucket. She would need to speak to Uncle Milos about the hunter, to make certain he knew how ill she was. It was Milvari's responsibility to make sure the hunter healed properly. She picked up the basket of tubers and hauled them into the storage room.

CHAPTER TWENTY-NINE

Kira licked her dry cracked lips. Her tongue felt thick and furry. She was stiff all over and her arms burned. When she tried to open her eyes, the light cut into them like a knife. She inched open one lid, groaning as she lifted her hand as a shield against the brightness.

The light that had at first seemed so blinding slowly receded to a pale gloom, and she saw that she was lying in a large bed in a strange room. She tried to sit up, but fell back in agony, gritting her teeth against the burning pain. Pushing aside the coverlet, she peered down at herself.

Beneath the cotton sleeping-gown she wore, her arms and neck were covered with a thick salve. Ah, the basilisk, leaping at her without warning and releasing its poison. She knew that under the balm her skin wore a mess of blotches and dark blisters. More memories returned to her and she cried out. Vaith. Dear little Vaith. He had tried to protect her from his own worst enemy, a venomous basilisk. She saw again the fluttering of gilded wings, heard the screams of the terrified horses, relived the searing pain of the poison. Tears rolled down her cheeks. Foolish little creature, she thought, foolish and loyal and brave.

She leaned back into the pillows and covered her eyes with her hand, mouthing an oath as pain shot through her arms. Her mind reached out for Kelmir, seeking the comfort and reassurance of the connection. The big hunting cat paced beneath the trees just inside the forest southwest of the hold.

She sensed now that Kelmir had been with her and that he had struggled to stay linked to her semiconscious mind as Milos brought her back to the hold. He had watched as the holder lifted her, draping her across Trad's back, followed them back to the edge of the forest, and waited since without food or rest. Now, raw-edged hunger gnawed at him. *Go, my friend*, she told him. *Hunt. Eat. I will live.*

He hesitated. *Go*, she repeated. *I do not wish to lose you, too.* There was doubt in his mind, and something niggled at her brain.

Vaith?

No, it was wishful thinking and delirium. She had seen him attack the basilisk. She had heard his cries. The sensation pushed at her again and her wish became a certainty. *Oh, Vaith, it is you! I thought I had lost you.* His senses were weak and sluggish, but he was alive. New tears scalded her eyes.

Images flooded her mind in quick succession. The holder's horse rearing back. Her body thrown to the ground. The basilisk poised to strike. Vaith screeching and diving. The basilisk rising to the attack.

She recalled the scorching pain of venom burning into her flesh. Wherever her leather jerkin didn't cover, the venom had burned through her shirt, blistering the skin beneath. She remembered screaming as the poison blazed across arms and neck. Then darkness.

Kira thought the venom had exploded over Vaith, too. But Kelmir had finished off the basilisk, springing from behind to snap its neck. As Kelmir launched himself through the air, Vaith was knocked aside and tumbled into the brush. Hurt, not killed.

Kira closed her eyes. *Yes, my dear Kel. You did well to kill the beast swiftly. Now go. Hunt.*

The images drained away as he turned his thoughts to the hunt, instinct driving him. She stayed in his mind as he headed deep into the woods to sate his hunger. She allowed herself to sink into his senses, to feel his stride lengthen into a lope, to smell the moist odors of plants and soil as she drifted back to sleep.

* * *

It was night when she woke again. Stars glittered in the sky outside her window, and she saw the round hump of the waning moon as it rose over the eastern hills. A fire glowed in the hearth on the far side of the room and she wondered that she had slept through the tending of it. She sent out her thoughts, searching for Kelmir in the night, and sensed him in the distance, sated and sleepy. She left him and sought Vaith. He was half-asleep, but nearby. She didn't try to rouse him.

He is alive. He is hurt, but he lives.

She moved her arms in tentative motions, expecting the searing pain. But the sting had lessened. Her burns were healing. She exhaled in relief and coughed. Her throat was a scorched desert. Her mouth held a sour metallic taste. She must have breathed in some of the basilisk's poison. She picked up the drinking cup from the bedside table, sniffed at the contents and smelled chamomile and other soothing herbs. Ah, Milvari, you have learned well, she thought, taking small sips from the cup before placing it back onto the table. She tried to talk, rasping out a few whispery syllables. She would be hoarse for days.

She smiled. Heresta would have told her to take advantage of this opportunity to learn to think before she spoke. When she'd been a child, Heresta had cautioned her time and time again about her temper and flare for sharp words. *Words can be a knife. Capable of skinning the truth when need be, but liable to cut through the heart. And some wounds never heal,* she'd said.

Kira recalled the verbal wounds Toril had inflicted on her. They had gone deeper than the flesh he'd marred. Toril. His name caused a bitterness to rise in the back of her throat and her stomach tightened with sickness. Toril the Bold. The man she had met had been that. Bold as well as brave. The man she had fallen in love with, she reminded herself with another surge of bitterness. She had other names for him now. Toril the Brute. Toril the Beast!

Yes, he had been brave, but he had also been hungry. Hungry for power. Why did she still think of him? Why couldn't she make herself forget? But she knew the answer. He had been the first man, the only man she had ever been with. And she still remembered the time they had together before he had grown cruel and cold. She hadn't fallen in love with a warlord; she had fallen in love with a man. A man who could be tender and strong at the same time, a man she had believed had loved her in return.

Kira clenched her jaw, gritting her teeth as the bitterness in her throat turned to bile. Nausea washed over her. She leaned over the side of the bed, wincing at the pain, her hand seeking the chamber pot as the sickness burst from her. She wiped her face on a piece of linen, then lay back on the bed. Perhaps she should avoid thinking of Toril while the basilisk poison was still in her blood. The two things clearly didn't mix well. She closed her eyes and willed herself to drift back into healing sleep.

CHAPTER THIRTY

Milvari balanced the tray in her hands as she hurried toward the sickroom. As she passed her uncle's library, the sound of angry voices carried through the door. She paused just outside, setting her tray down onto a nearby table, pretending to adjust the items on it as she listened to her mother and uncle argue.

"I will not give her over to a bounty hunter simply on his word that she is an escaped indentured. She is wounded and in the care of Tem Hold. I will not hand over a wounded person to a man we know nothing of."

"But Milos, I gave him my word. She cannot be worth more than that."

"Have a care, Mayet. You forget your place. I am holder here, not you. Your word does not stand against mine."

"But he represents a powerful man. What do you expect me to tell him?"

"I expect you to have no further dealings with him, whoever he represents."

"If Kamar were alive, he would think of his people first."

"You mean he would defer to you. My brother was a good man, but in at least one thing he did not make the wisest choice."

"What do you mean by that?"

"You know well what I mean, Mayet. You have no concern for the people of this hold. Your motives are selfish, as they have ever been."

"How dare you? If it weren't for you, Kamar would be alive and I would still be lady of this poor excuse for a hold!"

There was a long pause. Milvari's hands stopped moving and she held her breath.

When her uncle spoke, his voice was a low growl, but his words pierced through the door like sharpened knives. "I am well aware of my role in my brother's death. Do you not think that I suffer every day with this knowledge? That he would be alive if I had not convinced him to go on the hunt with me that day."

"Then why do you dishonor his memory by running this hold into ruin?"

"I am tired of trying to keep the peace with you Mayet. If you dislike the way this hold is run, then I suggest you seek elsewhere for a place to dwell."

"You would drive us out? Over a disloyal peasant?"

"No. But neither will I keep you here against your will. As for the Hunter, she is under the protection of this hold, and by the laws of our land no one may remove her or send her away without my bidding. She is here at my sufferance and will so remain."

"You use the law as you would a herd beast, Milos Tem. You would give the people a say in hold business, but only when it is to your liking. You're no better than the holders you scorn. Worse. You say one thing and do another! Perhaps there is something more to your motives in protecting her."

There was no response from Uncle Milos. Angry footsteps moved toward the door.

Milvari gripped the tray in her hands and rushed down the hall, turning the corner at the same moment that the library door flew open. She hurried to the room at the end of the adjacent hallway and slipped inside. She shut the door quietly behind her and waited to catch her breath.

A wedge of late morning sunlight cut through the dark room and fell across the floor. Setting the tray on a table near the fireplace, Milvari went to the window and pulled at the heavy curtains to close the gap.

"Leave them," a voice croaked from the bed. "This is not a death room. A little light is welcome."

Milvari let go of the drapes and hurried across the room. "You're awake. How do you feel?" She stared expectantly at the young woman lying on the bed.

"Like a log that's been thrown onto the fire and dragged halfway out again." The hunter laughed with a whispery rasp. "Although, I am already healing, thanks to you."

Milvari's mind clouded with doubt. The voices inside chided her, listing her shortcomings. She frowned. "The herbs weren't ground fine enough and the salve was too thick. I'm afraid I might have torn the skin when I applied it—"

"Milvari, stop. The salve is fine. It's doing the work it was meant to do."

"I was so worried that I did everything all wrong."

"You've done well."

"Truly?"

"Truly."

A flush of pride warmed Milvari. "Brilissa helped with the tea," she said, wrinkling up her face as she recalled her first effort at concocting the healing draught. "It tasted horrible at first. She made it much better."

"There, you see? You took care to consider the taste of the medicine, and asked for help where you saw the need."

The last of the hunter's words were breathy and almost beyond hearing. "You should eat and rest," Milvari told her. "Brilissa made hot broth and fresh tea. Let me help you sit up." She arranged the cushions to allow the hunter to sit up, then retrieved the tray from the table. She waited as the hunter spooned some of the broth into her mouth and swallowed.

"You've added willow bark and valerian root to the broth?"

Milvari grimaced. "A small amount. I didn't think it was enough to be noticed."

"It probably wouldn't be to an untrained palate. But it will often help a patient rest." The hunter smiled, ate several mouthfuls of broth, then set the spoon down. She took a few sips of the fresh tea and leaned back into the cushions with a sigh. "How is your uncle?" she asked, her voice less raspy.

Milvari remembered the argument she'd overheard between her mother and uncle. Torn between loyalty to her mother and her desire to protect this woman she had grown to love, she decided to remain silent. The last thing she wanted was to upset the hunter while she was ill and needed to rest. "He wasn't hurt by the basilisk. He said you stepped between him and the creature when it attacked."

"That wasn't quite my intention. I was trying to get us both out of the way."

"Vaith is in the stable. Uncle Milos brought him back to the hold, as well," Milvari said. "I wasn't certain how to care for him, so Master Jarret and Harl have been tending him. He is hurt, but he is alive and his wounds are mending."

"Yes, I know," the hunter said sleepily.

How could she know? Milvari shook her head. The sleeping herbs must be making the hunter groggy and confused. She cleared away the tray and dishes, then set the mug of tea on the table near the bed and waited until the hunter fell asleep.

When she opened the door to leave, she found her uncle standing in the hallway outside. Milvari pulled the door shut behind her.

"How does she fare?" he asked.

"She has eaten a small amount of broth and she appears to be healing."

His face was grim. "Can she speak?"

Milvari did not move away from the door. She glanced at the floor, and then raised her eyes to his. "She's sleeping. And she should rest. I think the herbs have made her delirious," she mumbled. Being responsible was no easy charge.

He squinted at her, peering into her face, his forehead wrinkling. "It will keep, then. But not for too long." He stepped back to give her room to pass, and stood staring at the closed door behind her.

Milvari started to move toward the kitchen, then turned back. She drew in her breath. "Uncle. I heard what mother told you." He wrenched his gaze from the door, turning irate eyes on her, and she stopped. Gripping the tray to steady her shaking hands, she continued. "I know I should not have listened, but . . ." She forced herself to stand tall before him. "Mother said the hunter is a runaway bondservant. Is it true?"

"I don't know," he said. "But I intend to find out."

"If it is," Milvari said. "I know there must be a reason. She—the hunter—she has a good heart."

His fists clenched. "You have the innocence of youth, Milvari. You're too young to read the hearts of others."

She gave him a sad smile. "You may be right, Uncle. But I am learning."

CHAPTER THIRTY-ONE

Mayet tried to focus on what the messenger was saying, but the words ran together in a daze of sound. Tratine should be here. Her boy should be by her side, but the man before her claimed he was being held until an exchange could be arranged. A cry escaped her and she covered her face with her hands.

Milos! It was all his fault. If only he had sent that harlot to the bounty hunter, Tratine would be here now. But he had refused. Refused! Mayet had had no option but to send Tratine to tell Lagos of her failure to convince the holder to hand over the woman. There was no one else she could trust. No one else to send.

The man cleared his throat and Mayet looked up.

"Lagos requires an answer," he said. His beady eyes, sunk deep in a bloated face, darted nervously about the room.

"I am only a holder's widow. I have no power here."

"Lagos gave you the opportunity to turn over the woman, as you agreed. Yet, now you say that you have no power." The man sneered.

"What you are doing goes against the land law. These actions will condemn you," Mayet blurted.

"Lagos made the effort to abide by your petty local customs, but you have refused to fulfill your side of the bargain." He spat upon the floor and wiped his bulgy lips on his sleeve.

Mayet cringed. "What does he expect of me?"

"He expects you to arrange a simple trade. He'll even give you the better value. An heir for a lowly peasant." He scowled. "You wouldn't want anything to happen to your precious boy, would you?"

Mayet's throat constricted and she shuddered. "No."

The messenger smirked at her, obviously enjoying her fear. The bastard! A writhing anger rose up and she pulled it close, shielding herself from the terror that scrabbled inside. But anger would not serve her now, nor would fear. "Very well," she said, donning a mask of haughty annoyance. Her mind whirled. She needed a new plan, but nothing came to her. "I will need some time to make the arrangements."

"You have one day. There is a copse of trees three leagues northwest of here bordering a large meadow. Bring the woman there at dusk tomorrow. If you are late, we'll leave the boy for you." He let out a gruff chuckle. "But not all in one place." He bowed mockingly and left the room.

Mayet sank into a chair, her knees too weak to hold her. Milos would be furious, but he couldn't possibly refuse her now. Not when the life of Tem Hold's heir, his own nephew, was at stake.

CHAPTER THIRTY-TWO

Breathless, Milvari ran beside her uncle, attempting to keep pace with his long strides. "At least let me prepare her—"

"Just make certain she is awake." He glared at the heavy wooden door that barred the way into the room.

Milvari's hand shook as she turned the handle. She slipped inside the room and quickly shut the door behind her. The bed lay empty. The heavy curtains were pulled back and the hunter stood at the window, staring out at the dull morning where dark clouds lowered in an overcast sky. Wintry light cast the room in muted grays, and in the wrinkled sleeping gown her pale figure was nearly invisible against the soft whiteness outside.

"You should be resting," Milvari said.

"I have rested enough," the hunter responded in a hoarse voice. "I need to move and to stretch."

"My uncle wishes to speak with you."

The tall woman looked down at herself and held up the folds of white cotton that draped her body. "I cannot see him like this."

Milvari nodded. "He will not wait. You could get back into bed."

The hunter hesitated. "No. I need clothes, a fresh shirt."

"In the wardrobe." Milvari pointed to a heavy oak cupboard on the far side of the room. "Please, hurry. His mood is dark. He will not be patient for long." She spoke quietly, but tried to convey a sense of urgency with her tone.

The hunter threw open the cupboard doors and took out a stack of fresh clothes. "These aren't mine," she said, holding up a new shirt, leather jerkin and breeches.

"Your clothes were ruined. Brilissa sent those for you."

Wincing, the hunter shrugged off the gown and pulled on the fresh shirt and new breeches. Before she had time to slip on the vest, there was a loud pounding the door.

Milvari rushed to open it. Her uncle brushed past her. He stood by the table and stared at the hunter, his fists clenching and unclenching.

"Who are you?" he demanded.

The hunter's eyes grew wide, then her face went blank. Milvari quietly swung the door shut and stood with her back to it, apparently forgotten. She waited in silence, hoping to learn what angered him so.

The hunter tensed. She seemed poised to flee. "My name is Kira."

"And who is Ardea?" His voice was gruff.

"Ardea is—was—my mother's name."

Kira? Ardea? Why was Uncle Milos asking these questions? Milvari watched the two intently, her uncle glaring at the woman before him, the hunter with her eyes on his face. Milvari held her breath.

"Why did you lie about your name?" he asked finally.

"I was afraid." Green eyes flashed in the pale light.

He raised his hands in a questioning gesture. "Afraid of what? What about your service frightens you? Fulfilling your contract or keeping your bargain?"

The hunter stiffened. She appeared confused. Her eyes followed Uncle Milos' movements, but she remained completely still. "I have always fulfilled my bargains," she said quietly.

"Truly? Then why does a bounty hunter hold my nephew in exchange for your return?"

Milvari gasped and her uncle fixed his eyes on her. "Wait outside," he commanded.

"But—"

"Now!"

"Yes, Uncle." Milvari slid shaky hands across the wood of the door and clutched the handle.

His bellowed words chased after her. "And do not listen at the door!"

CHAPTER THIRTY-THREE

Tratine held by a bounty hunter? Kira's mind raced as the information settled. The boy must be terrified. The people of this hold had been kind to her and she had brought this evil upon them. Kira was filled with alarm for the boy's safety. She must find a way to free him, but at what cost?

Her chest constricted with fresh fear. Too soon. It was too soon! Winter still held the seaports closed. There would be no escape by ship. There was nowhere left for her to run. Whether Toril's men, or a bounty hunter, it didn't matter. They had caught up with her.

"I await your answer." Milos Tem crossed his arms and stared at her.

"Are you certain it is a bounty hunter who holds Tratine?"

"I know that my nephew is missing and that a messenger came to his mother demanding an exchange," he said hotly. "Tell me why."

"I am sorry," Kira said. Fear and guilt struck her as hard as any fist ever had. The blood pounded through her in waves, making it difficult to speak. "I didn't expect them to find me so soon. I have put your people in danger. Forgive me."

"Them? Who is it you are running from?"

Kira sat on the rumpled bed. Her throat constricted. "Warlord Toril."

"You're indentured to the Warlord?"

"Indentured?" Kira was taken by surprise. "No," she said. "I have no contracts except the bargain I made with you."

"Then why does he hunt you?"

"Because I was his . . . his mated woman." The words hissed out of her.

The holder started.

Kira searched his face. "I wanted to tell you, but I was afraid. If I go back . . ." The shame overwhelmed her. She couldn't bring herself to say the words, to admit to this man what had been done to her at another's hands. "I was not content there."

The holder's jaw fell open and he snapped it shut. "My nephew's life is threatened because you were discontented?" he said through his teeth.

Kira stared out the window at the slate colored sky. Her insides matched the black clouds that held back the sun. It was inevitable. She would return to her imprisonment with Toril. The holder would have no choice but to exchange her for Tratine.

As much as she feared the wrath of Toril, she would have it no other way. Tratine did not deserve to be punished for her choices, her actions, her mistakes.

A single shaft of light pierced the clouds and she thought about her time with her companions, thought about Milvari and the others at the hold. It almost made her smile. Though tinged with fear and watchfulness, these past few moons of freedom had held an ease and joy she had almost forgotten could exist.

The ray of light disappeared as suddenly as it had come.

There was only one course open to her. "I am sorry," she said, rising and picking up the new leather jerkin. "I will see that Tratine is returned to you unharmed." She stuck her arms through the garment, grimaced, then tied the laces.

The holder watched in silence as she strapped on her belt and pulled on her worn boots. "What do you plan to do?" he asked.

Kira picked up her knife and stuck it in her boot. She pulled her leather pouch from the cupboard, reached inside and took out her mother's medallion. She squeezed it in her fist as her eyes met his. "I am going to put things aright."

"No." He stood before the door and planted his feet. "This is my hold. And Tratine is my responsibility. It is I who will put things aright."

CHAPTER THIRTY-FOUR

They rode in silence through softly falling snow. Large glistening flakes caught in the horses' manes and tails. Milos rode ahead, gripping Trad's lead. Kira sat up straight, her hands laced to the pommel with thick leather cords.

She scanned the tree line ahead, her eyes searching the tall grasses that still lingered into the winter season. How many men would be with the bounty hunter?

She was restless and uneasy. This sort of ploy was not like Toril. There was no show of power in an exchange of this kind. Toril would more likely bring his war band to bear on Tem Hold in a display of strength, crashing down on the quiet farmers and cot holders if they refused his demands. If this were truly the work of a bounty hunter, Toril and his men might still be some distance off. There might still be a chance to deflect his anger from Tem Hold and its people.

Kelmir had prowled ahead, out of sight, and now his thoughts broke into hers. He had found the men's encampment. Through him, Kira counted five horses tied near the campsite. It was possible that others on horseback lurked nearby, but without Vaith to scout from overhead, it was difficult to know more. Kel, see if you can find any of the men. They may be hiding in the trees.

214

Milos slowed the horses and swept the scene with furtive glances. Shaped in a half-circle, the copse lay just ahead, bordering an open meadow filled with dried stalks and mounds of snow. Kira recognized the place. Not far off lay the meadow where she and Milvari had discovered the demon's claw barely a fortnight ago. She focused her attention on the trees, searching for men hidden in the shadows.

A burly man stepped out from behind one of the nearer trees. "That's far enough," he called. "Halt the horses and drop your weapons."

"Not before I see that my nephew is unharmed," Milos called back.

"You're in no position to call for terms." The man spat and wiped at his mouth with his sleeve.

A thin man stepped out into the meadow. "Now, Lemm, is that any way to treat a landed holder?" His words carried across the open field. His dark tunic glittered with silver embroidery and his black cape stood out against the snow-covered ground. "Good day, Lord Holder. I am Lagos Surrat." He gave Milos a curt bow, but Kira felt his gaze linger unpleasantly on her.

"I did not come to exchange pleasantries with you," Milos growled.

"True, true," the man said. "But as my friend has informed you, you are here on our terms." His malicious smile showed long crooked teeth.

Kira followed the conversation while staying connected to Kelmir, which made it difficult for her to sense clearly what he saw, but she somehow managed to remain aware of both his senses and the goings-on around her.

Milos stiffened and gestured to where Kira sat behind him. "I have brought the woman. Where is my nephew?"

"Ah, yes, do let us get on with our business." Lagos waved his arm. A short distance away, a thin blond man stepped out of the trees. He held a large knife in one hand and gripped Tratine's upper arm with the other.

The boy's wrists were tied together in front of him and dirt smeared his face. Kira's throat tightened at the sight of him. Tratine had never been friendly, but he was only a boy. He did not deserve to be treated this way.

Kelmir crept past a large gnarled tree and crouched. Before him, a man stood beside a tree facing the meadow. He had an arrow nocked in the bow he held, the string pulled taut, ready for release. *Good job, Kel. Keep an eye on him.* Four men accounted for. The fifth horse would be Tratine's. Kira once more wondered if there were others, and how many.

"As you can see, the boy is fine. For the moment," Lagos said. "Now, put down your weapon and we will conclude our business here."

Milos slowly drew his broadsword and dropped it onto the frozen ground with a loud clang. Then he held open his cloak to show he had no other weapons.

"Good," the bounty hunter said. He nodded to the burly man, who walked out to the center of the field. "Now," said Lagos, "you will bring the woman to the center of the meadow while Jolon walks the boy out. You will hand the horse's lead to Lemm and Jolon will release the boy to you. Then you can be on your way."

Milos nodded and glanced back at Kira. She blinked once and they started forward. Across the field, the blond man, Jolon, walked toward them, pulling Tratine with him. As they came closer, Kira recognized the man. He had been among her escort the day she escaped. She had thought he'd been uncomfortable because of her bruised and broken appearance. She had apparently been wrong. He was just another mercenary soldier. Worse now, a kidnapper of children. She gritted her teeth in anger.

They reached the center of the field. Lemm leered at her, spat on the ground, and reached out to take Trad's reins from Milos. Kira kept her eyes on the big man as, with a surreptitious movement, she slid her hands out of the loose ropes.

Now, Kel!

A snarl erupted from the trees followed by a horrible scream. The men instinctively turned toward the blood-curdling sound. Milos leaped from the saddle. He pulled a short blade from the sheath hidden at his back and lunged at Jolon. Jolon shoved Tratine aside and dodged the thrust.

Lemm grabbed for Trad's reins. Kira aimed a kick at his bulky head. Her booted foot connected low, catching him in his pudgy throat. He stumbled back from her and Kelmir was on him before he could recover. She turned to see Jolon dodge Milos' blade, let the knife fall from his hand, and retreat from the holder.

"What are you waiting for? Kill them!" Lagos shrieked.

From the edge of the field an arrow sliced through the air, speeding toward the holder's unprotected back. Kira watched in stunned silence as Jolon ducked beneath Milos' next stroke and shoved the holder aside. The arrow sunk into the blond man's chest with a sucking sound and he dropped to his knees.

Kira leaped from the saddle as another arrow arced across the open space. Narrowly missing Milos, the shaft grazed Zharik's neck. The horse screamed and reared.

Kelmir shot across the meadow like a streak of night. The next arrow flew wide. Noise erupted from the trees as the archer fled from the big cat. Kelmir pounced and the man shrieked out his last breath.

Lagos ran toward the encampment and Kira sprang onto Trad's back to give chase. Before she could catch up with him an arrow struck the bounty hunter between the shoulders. He toppled forward and lay still. Milos had retrieved the archer's bow.

Kira dropped out of the saddle, leaned down, and rolled the bounty hunter over. His eyes glittered with malice as his arm flew up. The dagger in his hand carved through her soft leather jerkin, slicing into her shoulder. She threw herself back and away from him and pulled the knife from her boot. She leaned in and held the knife up under his chin. Her hand shook and she hesitated. As a healer she had sworn to save lives, not take them. As she wavered, the dagger fell from his hands. His nose twitched, blood bubbled out of his mouth with a gurgle, and the light faded from his eyes.

CHAPTER THIRTY-FIVE

The man, Jolon, swayed on his knees. The arrow in his chest moved up and down with his breathing.

The rest of the men were dead. When they'd set out from the hold, Kira had known that their desperate plan would likely end in killing. She shook her head. These men were cruel, willing to harm a child for personal gain. They deserved to die. But Lemm's vacant face hovered before her. She had never killed anyone before.

Milos untied Tratine. The boy's wrists were red and chafed and his pale hands shook from the cold. Milos rubbed his fingers to warm them.

Kira walked over to where Jolon knelt in the snow. She peered at the man's wound. The arrow had hit high, away from his organs. It looked painful, but there was little blood.

Milos dropped the piece of rope he was holding. "You're hurt."

Dark crimson stained her sleeve as blood ran from her wound and dripped from her fingers. Dark red dots that froze in the pale snow. She flexed her arm. "The cut is long, but not deep."

Gripping her sleeve, she tore it the rest of the way from the shirt. She wrapped the fabric over her shoulder and around her arm, holding it tight to stop the bleeding. Milos helped her tie the linen in place.

She faced Jolon. "I know you. You're one of Toril's men. Why are you here?"

The warrior looked up. His young eyes pleaded with her. "Forgive me," he panted. "I had hoped to find some way to warn you."

Kira frowned. She had seen Jolon push Milos aside and take the arrow intended for the holder, but perhaps he had merely chosen to change sides when the fight turned against the bounty hunter and his men. "Why should I believe you?"

He closed his eyes and shook his head. "Don't. I would not. But you should know that the warlord and his army, what remains of it, is no more than a fortnight off."

"What do you mean, what remains of it?" Kira repeated.

"Many have deserted. There were those who already questioned his actions. But his obsession with you has driven them and others away." Jolon panted with the exertion of talking. Blood oozed from where shaft of the arrow rose out of his shoulder. "Only those most loyal, or most cruel, remain with him. But though they are few, they are hardened men and remain a formidable force."

Kira sneered at him. "I don't believe you. Toril would never let his army fall apart like that."

Jolon grunted. "There have been . . . attempts to . . . dissuade the deserters," he said. "But still they find the means to leave. And he no longer sends men out after them. For the past fortnight, his thoughts have been turned toward you. He blames you for his every trouble. "

"Why are you telling us this?" Milos asked.

The young man winced as he turned toward the holder. "Because, from that first day, I have been tormented by what he did to her." Jolon's face contorted in pain and he sat back on his heels with a groan.

220

Milos gave Kira a sharp look. "What does he mean?"

Kira was silent. She couldn't tell him about Toril. Not now. Not because she was ashamed, but because she couldn't let him stop her from turning herself over to Toril. She had let Milos Tem talk her into the risky rescue plan to save Tratine, but unlike Lagos and his men, the warlord's men were not a small band of opportunists. They were battle-hardened warriors. There was only one way left to save Tem Hold and its people. "It is nothing."

Milos looked from Jolon to Kira. His eyes narrowed. He looked as if he would speak, but he said nothing.

She turned away. "If what he says is true, there is still time for me to stop Toril. If I go to him now, he will have no reason to attack Tem Hold."

Jolon tried to rise. His face twisted in pain, and his eyes filled with tears. "No! You can't go back. No one should be treated that way. Above all, not you. Please. I know you can't know what is in my heart. I wanted to tell you. That's why I volunteered to escort you." He shuddered.

Kira gave Jolon a compassionate look. Was he saying that he cared for her? Could it be true? Or was it an attempt to play on her emotions? She could find no words for the young man. Too many times she had been told one thing and shown another by a man she thought she could trust.

She directed her attention to Milos. Only one thing could save Tem Hold and its people. "I must go to Toril. There is no other way."

Milos gently placed a hand on her uninjured arm. "Yes, there is."

221

CHAPTER THIRTY-SIX

Milvari held the blade of the knife in the fire as Kira had directed her. She had never before seen anyone shot by an arrow. There was so much blood. She glanced back at the wounded man, amazed that he still lived.

Jolon sat on the bed. Sweat beaded on his forehead, and pain wracked his young face. Master Jarret stood on one side of him, Uncle Milos on the other. Blood from the wound trickled down the young man's bare chest.

Kira looked into Jolon's brown eyes and raised the cup to his lips once more. "It will be painful, even with this," she told him as he swallowed the last of the pain-numbing draught Milvari had prepared.

Jolon's eyes held fear, but he nodded in understanding.

"Lie down," Kira instructed him.

The men helped him lean back, gripping his arms to hold him steady.

"Bite down on this." Kira put a leather-wrapped stick in the young man's mouth. "Milvari, bring me the knife."

The knife made a hissing sound as the hunter doused the blade in a bowl of cool clear water. Milvari winced, but forced herself to watch. With a steady hand, Kira cut into the bloody flesh at the edge of the arrow's shaft. Jolon groaned though the leather, jerking back against the bed, but other men held him tight. It took all their combined strength, but they kept his upper body still.

Kira used two small wedges of wine soaked wood to hold the wound open. Jolon's eyes squeezed shut and he moaned as bit by bit she drew the arrow out. She held the arrow up and examined the tip. "It's intact," she said, handing the bloody quarrel to Milvari. "If it had not been, we would have had to search the wound for the pieces."

Milvari shuddered and realized there were tears in her eyes. Her uncle glanced at her, concern on his face. She wiped her eyes and inspected the arrow. How strange that such a small bit of iron could cause such pain and damage. She had wanted to help, had demanded to be allowed to stay. She was learning more than she had anticipated.

Kira removed the wedges from the open wound, then poured a small amount of wine directly into it. Jolon yelped and lay still.

Master Jarrett put his hand near the young man's face. "He's unconscious."

"It is for the best," Kira said, wiping away the blood and wine. "Milvari, bring me the needle and silk thread."

Milvari watched closely as the hunter sewed the wound shut with quick, deft movements. "Your arm is bleeding again," she said as Kira tied off the final stitch. "Won't you let me tend to it?"

"No, Milvari," the hunter told her in a tired voice. "I can see to it, if you will bandage Jolon's wound. Put the poultice you prepared between two layers of linen, then wrap it in place. Master Jarrett, will you help?"

"Yes, yes. Of course, I will. Are you sure you'll be all right?"

"I will be fine." She picked up some linen bandages, the bottle of wine, and a pot of herbs. "I will be in the room at the end of the hall if you need me."

CHAPTER THIRTY-SEVEN

The room was dark except for the red glow of embers on the hearth and the faint light from stars that twinkled in the night sky outside the window. Kira set the wine and bandages down onto the table and lit a taper. A yellow flame fluttered from the wick as she placed the candle in its holder.

A metal pot hung from a hook on one side of the fireplace. She stirred the embers and tossed on a small piece of wood. The urn on the bedside table was almost empty, but there was enough water for her purpose. She poured the water into the pot and added a handful of herbs, then sank into a chair. She poured a small amount of the wine into a cup and drank it down while she waited for the water to boil.

She pulled her arms out of her vest and tossed it onto the table. It was too bad about the damage. The leather was thick and supple. She let out a small laugh. Why was she so worried about a garment?

Steam rose from the kettle and she inhaled the aroma of healing herbs. The familiar scent calmed her. The escape had been difficult, but Tratine was safe, Kelmir was well and her wound was minimal. It remained to be seen if Jolon would heal as well, and whether or not what he had told them of himself and of Toril's army was true.

She dipped out some of the herbal brew and dropped a piece of clean linen into it. Her hand shook with weariness as she untied the end of the linen shirtsleeve and began to unwrap her wound.

There was a gentle knock at the door. Could they need her so soon? Perhaps there was some complication with Jolon. She paused at her task. "Yes?" she called.

The door opened and Milos stepped inside. "I thought you could use some help," he said as he crossed the room. "And I brought you this." He held up a clean shirt.

Kira nodded toward the shirt. "That's very kind. I'm afraid I have been a bit rough with my new clothes." She gave him a wry smile. "How is Jolon?"

"Milvari is caring for him. I seemed to be in her way."

"She learns quickly." Kira continued to remove the linen from her shoulder. She winced as the last of the cloth peeled stiffly away and a small trickle of blood ran down her arm.

"She is much like her father. He seemed to know things almost before he was shown." Milos draped the clean shirt over the back of a chair. "Let me help you."

There was concern in his eyes.

"I can tend a minor wound," he said, gently moving her hand away from her arm to examine the cut. He drew the candle closer and Kira heard his sharp intake of breath.

She jerked her head around to see. The cut extended from her upper arm, across her shoulder and ended at the back of her neck. The bounty hunter had tried for her throat. If Troka hadn't called him, if his life force had not already faded when she'd leaned over him, Kira would now be dead.

"It's really not so bad," she said. "It still bleeds because it hasn't been properly cleaned and bound." She removed the cloth from the bowl and squeezed most of the liquid from it before handing it to him.

She tensed, trying not to jerk away from him as he dabbed at the wound with the cloth. He stopped. "I'm sorry," he whispered.

"It needs to be done," she said. "It will help if you wring some of the liquid onto the wound before wiping it. I have added something to help diminish the pain."

He was gentle, but the wine stung like nettles inside her shoulder. It was difficult not to pull away from his ministrations, but she held still. He dropped the bloody rag on the table and Kira handed him a freshly soaked cloth. At last the numbing herb began to work. The pain faded into a faint tingle, spreading from the wound into the surrounding tissue. She closed her eyes and relaxed.

"Kira." Milos spoke her name quietly as he continued to wipe at the blood on her arm and shoulder.

"Yes?"

"Will you tell me now?

She opened her eyes. "Tell you what?"

"About your past. About him. What he did—to you." There was cold anger in his voice.

"There is little worth telling, little more worth hearing." Kira sighed. She had put this man and everything he had, everyone he cared for, in danger. He deserved to know the truth. "He was a man whose strength and power made him attractive to a young girl who wanted to feel safe in an uncertain and dangerous world. It was an illusion. The danger he swore to fight against is the danger he became. And the safety that he offered came at a brutal price."

"Did you love him?"

The question caused her to recoil. Milos' fingers slipped and the linen dug into her wound. She gasped and he jerked the cloth away from her back. "I am sorry," he said.

"No. I am the one who is sorry. Part of me knows that Toril would have come here, either soon or late. He would not pass by such a rich region once he was aware of it. But it is because of me that he is coming now, and this hold and its people will become a target for his ire. I need to leave and soon."

Milos put down the cloth and reached for another length of linen. "Most of the bleeding has stopped, but I know the cut must be wrapped. You will have to slip the shirt off this shoulder."

Kira reached across with her right hand and untied the lacing. Her left shoulder burned and a trickle of blood ran down her arm as she slipped the shirt down. "It has opened again, hasn't it?"

"Yes."

She handed him her knife. "It will be better to cut the fabric."

He took the blade in his hand. It glinted in the firelight as he slid it up under the gusset of her shirt. Cold steel grazed her shoulder as he sliced up through the collar, careful not to knick her with the sharp edge of the blade.

Kira held the front of the shirt to her chest. His eyes fell on the skin beneath her throat still dark and discolored from the basilisk's poison. "You're still burned."

"It is not as bad as it looks," she said. "The salve Milvari made has helped. The marks will fade with time."

Milos wiped away the blood that had run down her back.

"You will need to make a poultice from the herbs in the bowl," Kira told him.

"Placed between sheets of linen," he finished.

"It seems that you also learn quickly." She gave him a weak smile.

He placed the prepared bandages against her skin and she held them in place as he bandaged her arm and shoulder. Afterward, he helped her to slip her right arm out of the remaining sleeve and pull the fresh shirt over her head.

He turned his attention to cleaning up the bloodied rags as she finished dressing. The garment was too large for her and billowed out when she dropped the last of the old torn fabric and cautiously put her arms into the sleeves.

"Thank you for helping to rescue Tratine," he said.

Kira pulled the front lacings of the shirt tight and tied them. Tratine's rescue had been foolhardy and they were lucky to be alive. "It would have been safer to turn me over to them. I should not have let you talk me into such a risky plan."

"They might have killed him anyway," he said. "Without your help and that of your companions we might all have been lost. I told you before that I never wished to be a holder, but it is my responsibility to protect those in my charge. I count you among them."

"I should have kept moving." Kira stared into the fire. "I should not have tarried here."

Milos tossed the last of the herb mixture onto the fire. It sizzled and steamed, filling the room with an aromatic scent. "I am glad you had to stop for aid. And I am glad you chose Tem Hold."

Kira ran her fingers through her hair. "I am both glad and saddened that I came to Tem Hold."

Milos took her hand between both of his. "You have given much to the hold. To Milvari. To me. And we will need your help to prepare for the Warlord's coming."

"You are right. I know enough of his tactics to be of aid to you. I will stay long enough to help you prepare. But then it will be best if I leave." With reluctance, Kira pulled her hand away. "Better for everyone."

"No," his voice was gruff. "It will be better for me if you stay."

Kira studied his face, unsure of what she read there. Did he feel as she did? Did his breath tremble inside his chest as hers did? Like a moth fluttering near a lantern?

He touched her cheek, tracing the curve of her chin with his fingers. Lightning raced along her skin.

"When you first came to Tem Hold, I felt afresh the anger and guilt of my brother's death. I was jealous of your freedom, frustrated that you could go where you willed, ride and hunt when I could not. But there were other emotions, as well."

What was he saying? Kira gazed at him. His eyes shone bright, the way they had when they'd supped in the woods and he'd told her of his views and his wishes for his people. Was this who he truly was? A man of passion, hiding beneath the grim visage of the stern and reliable holder?

"Like you, I no longer wish to be shackled." He searched her face, as if he would find some deep secret hidden there.

His hand fell away from her face and a crushing need rose in her at the loss of his touch. She shuddered. This feeling. It was too akin to what she'd felt when she realized Toril would leave her once his wounds were healed. She closed her eyes, struggled away from the memory. Would she be misled again? Was this yet another mistake?

"But you have taken action, where I have remained my own jailer," Milos said.

Kira opened her eyes. There was sadness in his face and a longing to match her own. No, Milos was different. He did not lust after power as Toril had. As Toril still did.

"We have both been imprisoned because of the choices we made. Choices made for the wrong reasons." She took his hand, closed her eyes, and brushed the back of his fingers against her cheek. "But no more."

"Yes," he said. "No more." He leaned forward and kissed her gently, his warm lips pressing against hers.

The tingle rose in her scalp, flashed along her skin, and washed inside her, like the coursing of hot wine through her blood. Kira pulled back unsteadily, searching his face. His eyes were filled with a soft light. A desire unlike anything she'd ever felt before spread through her, making her limbs tremble. Not the excitement of lust, but something quiet that filled her with warmth. A feeling of homecoming.

He held his ground and extended his hands, offering her the intimacy of his embrace.

CHAPTER THIRTY-EIGHT

Mayet watched with a mix of anger and terror while the hold prepared for battle. Milos had sent messengers to the outlying farms and cots throughout the region, and droves of able-bodied men arrived daily to prepare for the defense of the hold. All her plans had come to naught. The hold she longed to possess, the only place where she had held any position, the only place where she had any future, was now threatened.

Had she known it was the warlord who sought the red-haired harlot, Mayet would never have dealt with Lagos. Why bargain with an underling, when you know where the real power lies? She paced before the blazing fire, twisting and grasping her hands together.

Amidst the chaos that seemed to fill the hold from dawn to dusk and deep into the night, Mayet found herself accorded fewer considerations than ever before. Even Tratine was caught up in the unrest and spent little time with her. Her frustration and horror at this new turn of events was increased by the knowledge that Milos had gone to the hunter's bed.

They tried to hide it, but Mayet recognized the signs, the overt looks, the soft words, the way they brushed against each other at odd moments. When he was younger, Milos had been less than circumspect about the women he wooed. Many of them had been completely unsuitable, but this! It grated against her the way a rasp ground into rotten wood.

She spent most of her time in her rooms, trying to think of some way to stop this madness. Milos would not even grant her a short audience, and Tratine no longer brought her information as he had. She was closed off and alone.

She stopped pacing and stared into the fire. Perchance there was still a way to keep Milos from destroying Tem Hold, a way to save her son's inheritance, and secure her own position for good.

CHAPTER THIRTY-NINE

Outside the library Harl and Milvari sat on a low wooden bench, watching as people went in and out of the room. A murmur of voices floated out into the hallway each time the door swung open.

"Do you think we should bother them?" Harl whispered to her. "They seem very busy."

"Not too busy for this," Milvari assured him. "It's a brilliant plan."

"But it was only a joke. You know." Harl made a face.

Milvari laughed. "Yes, but it's still a brilliant idea. I wish I had thought of it." She patted his arm and he blushed.

"Well, you did. I mean you took my joke and saw how to make it useful."

"It was still your idea."

The door opened and a group of men and women left. Brilissa gave Milvari and Harl a wave and a nod as she walked by, deep in conversation with a tall thin man Milvari recognized as the miller who ground much of the hold's grain and supplied them with flour.

Kira stuck her head out into the hallway. "The meeting has adjourned," she said with a tired smile. "Your uncle will see you now."

Milvari and Harl leaped up and glanced at one another, then followed the hunter into the library.

Her uncle sat at the end of several wide wooden planks that had been set up on blocks as a meeting table, staring at a large map. A collection of chairs lined each side of the plank. Uncle Milos' blue eyes were pale and his clothes were rumpled, as if he had slept in them, but he sat up tall as they approached.

Kira ushered them forward and took a seat beside him. The hunter's hands rested on the table. Milvari watched wide-eyed as her uncle slid a hand across the table to cover one of Kira's.

"I understand you have something important to tell us." He gave them a questioning look.

Milvari jerked her head up and froze. It had seemed like the perfect plan, but now she worried that her uncle and the hunter would think the idea childish. They had probably already thought of it and discarded it as impractical. She swallowed hard. "I—that is—we were thinking—" she turned to Harl for help, but he nervously drummed his fingers against the sides of his legs.

Uncle Milos pushed the map aside and leaned across the table, folding his hands before him. "Milvari, if there is something you feel we must know, please tell us what it is."

"Demon's Claw," she blurted.

Uncle Milos seemed confused, but Kira jumped up, a smile spreading across her face. "That's a splendid idea, Milvari. I don't know why I didn't think of it."

"I didn't think of it either," Milvari said. "It was Harl. He reminded me that of the patch we found and asked what I thought would happen if Warlord Toril's horses ate it—"

Harl blushed. "It was supposed to be a joke," he mumbled.

Uncle Milos looked from one to the other of them. "What are you talking about? This is no time for jokes."

"It is no joke, Milos, but an excellent tactic." Kira rose from her chair, eyes gleaming. "And exactly what we need to reduce Toril's numbers and turn the wheel in our favor. But not by afflicting the horses." She glanced at Milvari and Harl, and then pointed to a place on the map. "Three leagues north, near the place the bounty hunters held Tratine, there is a large patch of Demon's Claw. According to Brilissa, it's a hardy plant and most of it will probably have survived the snowfall we've seen this winter."

"That's why Master Jarrett wanted to have it burned," Milvari added.

Kira nodded. "If we harvest it and find a way to add it into the army's food or water, it will be enough to make a large number of men too ill to fight."

Uncle Milos stared at the map. "Getting to the army's food supplies will be no easy task," he said as if speaking to himself. He raised his eyes to Kira. "How much of this plant would it take to make them ill?"

Kira shrugged. "It would take a great deal to make the entire army too sick to bear arms. And they would probably taste it in their water. We have to get it into their food."

Milvari remembered the miller. "But if we harvest and dry it, it could be ground into powder and mixed with their grain or flour," she suggested.

Kira nodded in agreement. "By all accounts, a few small sacks might contain enough at least to cut their numbers."

Milos rested his chin on his hand. "Then it only remains to find a way to smuggle three or four sacks of Demon's Claw powder into the Warlord's camp and mix it into the food without getting caught."

"Oh," Milvari said, feeling the excitement drain out of her. "I didn't think about that."

"I did not say it could not be accomplished," Milos said. "Your idea is a sound tactic. We only need to figure out how and if it can be put into service."

"Jolon!" Kira said.

"What?"

"Jolon. His wound is healing well, is it not?"

Milvari thought about the progress her patient was making. "Yes. He has been walking in his room and he grows restless to do more."

"He should be well enough to ride in a few days and the Demon's Claw should fit into his saddlebags. Toril already believes Jolon to be his man."

"What if he still is?" Milos asked.

"The reports we've received in the past few days have confirmed what he told us about Toril's troops."

"And if he betrays us?"

Kira sat beside him and put her hand on his arm. He seemed to ripple with excitement when she touched him. Milvari nearly blushed. She had never seen her uncle so affected by a woman. The sound of the hunter's voice pulled Milvari's attention back to the conversation.

"I, too, hesitate to trust him, but he knows nothing of our defense strategy," Kira said. "If he betrays our plans for the Demon's Claw, we are no worse off than before."

CHAPTER FORTY

Mayet donned the worn cape and eyed herself in the mirror. With most of her face covered and the tattered skirts draped over her shift she could almost pass as one of the peasants. She scowled. It was the result she sought, but all too easily achieved. She examined her smooth hands. They told the tale of who she really was, a proper lady. She would have to keep them covered.

She went out through her sitting room, careful not to make a sound. The banked fire cast a dim red glow through the murky gloom. Her skirt caught on a chair and, startled, she pulled up short. Her fingers tugged and twisted the fabric as she disentangled it from the arm of the chair. The layers of torn skirts hissed as she moved, mixing with the murmurs of her conscience. She hushed her misgivings with reasoning. Tratine would understand in time. Once he learned the responsibility of being a holder, he would know that she had done what she had to, that she did it for him.

Keeping to the shadows, she paused to listen every few steps. It would not do to be caught dressed this way. There was no explanation she could think of that Milos would believe.

She waited in the darkness near a little used side door for what seemed like hours. Her skin crawled with nervous energy. Just when it seemed the sun would refuse to appear, the stars began to fade against the black curtain of night. She slowly opened the door, just far enough to slip outside and closed it with a hushed click.

There were already a number of people congregating at the gate, waiting to be let through. A gathering crowd of people moved in and out daily, bringing in supplies and going out to work on the defense structures, ditches and pike lines, that Milos and his men had designed and ordered installed around the hold. Mayet joined their ranks. A few people spoke in low murmurs, as if afraid to break the quiet of the day's pale dawn. She stood silent among them, her hands tucked inside her ragged cloak and her head down in a posture of weariness, and prayed no one would speak to her.

The gate opened and the crowd moved forward, flowing out of the hold to go to their respective tasks. Mayet followed a few paces behind a small group of women headed toward the forest. They dragged a small sled meant for firewood. When they reached the edge of the forest Mayet quickly headed off through the trees toward the north road. She skirted along the tree line, staying in the shadows. She would follow the road and meet up with Toril's army.

It would then be a simple matter to convince the warlord of the value of keeping Tem Hold intact. And perhaps he would see her value as an ally, a potential partner, or even something more.

Mayet pursed her lips. A man as powerful as Warlord Toril would be more of a match for her than any landholder. Surely, a man as great as he would appreciate the virtues of a true lady. He certainly wouldn't want that redheaded witch back once Mayet informed him of the harlot's liaisons with Milos.

* * *

She walked until midmorning, staying along the edge of the road and watching for other travelers. The cold chill of winter still clung to the land and small piles of snow gleamed white in the hollows and shady spots beneath the trees. At the sound of approaching riders, she slipped off the road and into a nearby thicket where her feet sank into cold slush. She shivered as three men rode by, heading south in a hurry. Whether they were Warlord Toril's soldiers or men from the region heading to Tem Hold, she couldn't tell. She waited in the brush for a long while after they passed before stepping back onto the road.

Her feet complained in painful throbs, her wet shoes chafing the already sore places. She'd not realized before how difficult it was to walk a great distance. Yet, the horseless peasants seemed to manage it easily enough. Her stomach rumbled hollowly and the small piles of dirty snow she passed made her realize how thirsty she was.

Damn Milos and that woman! This was all their fault. They were the cause of all her sorrows. First Kamar's death and her loss of position, the state of Tem Hold and the degradation of its holder, the threat to her son's inheritance.

And now here she was, subjected to taking this brutal path in order to put things to rights.

CHAPTER FORTY-ONE

Kira stared out the window. The hazy blue sky belied the storm that she knew approached from the north. With Toril's army a scant few days away, the hold's inhabitants labored anxiously to complete the necessary defenses in time.

Vaith snoozed in Kira's lap. The little wyvern was no longer in need of healing, but took advantage of every opportunity to be close to her. Kelmir lay curled in the corner beside the fire. He appeared to be sleeping, but Kira sensed that he was alert to the goings on around him.

When Milos had suggested his design to rescue Tratine, Kira realized they would need Kelmir's help for the plan to be successful and had decided to explain to Milos about her method of communicating with her companions. It had taken some time to convince him, but after illustrating the point through a series of exercises, he had stared at her in surprise. After the rescue, Milos had insisted the cat be brought into the hold so that the people would grow accustomed to his presence before the battle. No one else knew her secret, knew of her bond with Kelmir and Vaith, but the people of Tem Hold trusted their holder and accepted his assurances of their safety with Kira's companions.

Milos sat at the table deep in conversation with several grizzled looking farmers and cot holders, men who had served in battle before settling in Tem's region and would now act as Tem Hold's captains for the coming battle.

Jolon had left the hold two days earlier. Although his wound was still stiff and painful, he had readily agreed to help with their plan. Milos had worried that he seemed too eager, but Kira hoped they could trust the young man to do his part.

Brilissa and her staff had worked tirelessly to speed up the drying and preparing of the harvested Demon's Claw. Unable to use the mill for fear of contaminating the hold's flour stores, they had ground the dried plants by hand. The job was well done and the resulting fine powder would be easy to mix into the army's food.

There was an insistent knock at the door. The men turned their attention to the interruption as a young man stepped inside without waiting. "Holder Tem," he said. "There is an urgent matter that needs your attention."

Kira tensed. Could Toril have sent advancements?

"What is it?" Milos asked, his eyes alert.

"There is an envoy at the gate, requesting an audience with the Lord Holder."

"Is the Warlord with them?"

"No, Lord Milos. There are no soldiers among them. They all appear to be gnomes. They claim they have come to aid Tem Hold and the healer who has taken refuge here."

Confused, Kira looked to Milos and then back at the messenger. "Did any of them give you a name?" she asked.

"One of them said to tell the healer that Ryospar bids her greetings and his brother Ragnar, King of Uldastwer, sends his thanks for the healing of his only daughter, Talya."

* * *

241

In the yard outside the main hall, a small group of gnomes stood in a semicircle behind their king. Each wore a stiff suit of lacquered leather armor and each held a sturdy axe. Their sharp blades glinted in the sunlight.

Ryospar stood beside his brother and smiled up at Kira. She remembered the gnome's gentle ways with the young goat. In his polished armor, Ryospar appeared much more imposing than he had when Kira had first met him in the woods.

Kira and Milos bowed politely to the group of gnomes.

Ryospar bent his thick waist, giving them a curt bow. "Afore ye stands King Ragnar, Lord and Ruler of Uldastwer."

The king of the gnomes stood a half head taller than the other gnomes assembled around him. His armor was inlaid with a blue colored metal that shimmered in rainbow colors. Long black hair, twined with colored thread, spilled out from beneath his burnished helm. His pupils were black as wells, but the edges of his eyes crinkled as his face split into a wide grin. He bowed low. "'Tis an honor to meet the healer who brought my dear daughter back to the livin'."

Kira was taken aback. She wasn't really a healer, she had never completed her training, but she decided now was not the time to raise issue with the title the gnome king had chosen to infer on her. "The child is well, then?" she asked.

"Aye that she is, thanks to you. And we are in yer debt." He put his hand on his chest and bowed his head.

"I am pleased that Talya has regained her health, but your thanks is payment enough," Kira said.

The smile faded from the gnome king's face. He raised one eyebrow and cast her a dark look. Ryospar coughed and stepped forward. "As yer know, the Uldast are well regarded as traders. We take pride in our bargainin' skills and seek always to land on the best side of an agreement, but we hold our children dear. The Uldast deem no pact higher than that of a life debt. We have come to yer today to honor such a debt, and to make recompense for a precious life saved."

Kira held out her hands, palms up, in a gesture of entreaty. "I apologize, King Ragnar, I did not mean to offend you or your ways. I am honored you have come, but may I ask how you came to find me here?"

The king nodded and the darkness slipped away as a smile lit his face. "Unlike the kingdoms of men, the kingdom of Uldastwer is not a place. It is everywhere our people dwell. Our network is great and we are able to communicate rapidly over great distances."

Kira realized she had been wrong about Ryospar. He had known about her not because he had been in contact with Toril's men, but because of the gnomes' ability to pass messages quickly and efficiently among their people.

"We knew where ye were because our people have watched for ye," the king continued. He hefted his axe and leaned toward her. "We fight the same enemy."

Ryospar nodded in agreement. "'Tis true. Ye see, our people have suffered from the warlord's depredations. Many a time have our folk been displaced and misused by his soldiers."

"Once my brother told me the woman who saved wee Talya and left with naught for payment was also the enemy of our own enemy, I knew the best way to repay yer kindness and get the best side of the bargain as well." The king winked at her.

"Aye," Ryospar added. "'Tis why we've sought ye out. We and our kin will fight alongside ye and yers."

CHAPTER FORTY-TWO

Mayet felt sorely used. The canvas tent offered no comfort from the cold night. She shivered in the darkness and rubbed at her wrists where men's rough hands had bruised the tender flesh. The harsh voices of the mercenaries outside carried on the cold night air as they argued. "No lady dresses in rags," one man said. "She's only trying to save her scrawny hide by claiming to be high born."

"Give 'er to me," said another. "I'll show you what to do with a woman."

"When have you ever had a woman?" another snorted amidst a roar of laughter and heavy backslapping.

"What if she's telling the truth? What if she knows something worth hearing? D'you want to be the one to answer to *him*?"

There was silence and then a disgusting sound as one man spat. "Ah, she's not worth the trouble. Too scrawny to be any real sport."

Mayet cringed as heavy steps approached and the tent flap was yanked aside. A burly figure was silhouetted against the opening. She huddled in her cloak, her arms wrapped tight around her.

"Come on," the big man growled.

"Where are you taking me?" Mayet demanded. She gasped when he gripped her arm and squeezed it till she thought the bone might snap.

"You wanted to see Lord Toril, said you had information for him, didn't you? Not that he'll be any too pleased at the sight of you."

He led her through the group of men gathered outside the tent. They leered at her, grinning maliciously. Mayet tried to remain aloof, but her feet were covered in sores and the man beside her moved rapidly. He half-dragged her toward the center of the encampment.

They arrived at a large well-lit pavilion, surrounded by guards. The man who held her spoke to one of the guards, who abruptly disappeared inside. He returned in a few moments and stood aside, holding the tent flap open. "Enter."

Mayet stepped up to the opening and the soldier pushed her ahead of him into the tent.

Bright lanterns hung at intervals around a well-appointed space filled with colorful banners and tapestries. At the center of the pavilion, an ornately carved chair stood atop a heavy dais. A broad-shouldered man sat lazily in the chair, his blond hair and beard reflecting the lamplight.

His dark eyes roved over Mayet, taking in her appearance, then he turned to the man beside her and smirked. "I have already enjoyed my evening entertainment," he said, taking a drink from the heavy gold goblet in his hand.

"Lord Toril," the man beside Mayet went down on one knee and bowed his head. "This woman claims to be a—a lady of Tem Hold. She says she has news of your woman." He grabbed Mayet's arm and pulled her down beside him and her hood fell back. She caught a sudden movement out of the corner of her eye. The man, Jolon, the one who had turned sides in the fight to rescue Tratine, sat on a low wooden bench to one side.

Toril set his cup down with a loud bang and her attention was drawn back to the dais. He leaned forward and his eyes glinted like knives. "What is it you think you know?"

"I know the woman you seek. I know where she is hiding," she said.

"Is that all?" Toril waved a dismissive hand. "That is old news, is it not, Jolon?"

The traitor, Jolon, stared directly at her, his face pale in the bright lamplight. Traitor? Her mind whirred.

"My Lord Toril," she said, holding her hands out in appeal. "I also have news of a traitor in your camp." She did not trouble herself about the young man's fate. Traitors deserved the destiny the wheel would bring them.

Toril gave her a menacing glare. His fists opened and closed and the muscles of his arms rippled. "There are none among my men who would dare try me." He swung his head on his thick neck, and surveyed the room.

The Warlord's voice was quiet, but Mayet heard the danger that lurked behind the calm. The man beside her flinched as Toril's gaze raked over him. Her father had held such a swaying power. She recalled how, as a child, she had thought his look might crush her into dust. He had wielded his power like a club, but he had also rewarded his allies handsomely. Finally, here before her was a man she understood.

Mayet gave him her most flattering smile. "I see that you are right, Lord. Your strength and power are formidable and none might come at you openly. But the rat that chews at the mightiest oaken pillar may in time weaken it from below."

Toril leaned forward, his eyes boring into her. "And who is the rat in my hall?"

CHAPTER FORTY-THREE

Wrapped in her heavy wool cloak, Kira gazed out from the top of the wall, waiting for Kelmir to return from his evening hunt. She was restless anyway, and pretending to watch for Kelmir kept her from having to explain to anyone who might be curious how she always knew the time of his return.

A light gleamed in the distance, then another. Campfires. They flared up one by one to become a huge cluster of red and yellow stars that spread out across the land just beyond the river north of the hold. A watch called out and a messenger sped into the main building to carry word to Milos and his captains. Toril's army had arrived.

Memories of torn and bruised flesh lay cold fingers on her and she shivered. A small fluttering cry tried to release itself from inside, but she choked it down. Probing the forest south of the hold, she moved into Kelmir's feline thoughts.

Be watchful, Kel. He paused at his meal and sniffed the air. The wind carried the scent of fire and men upon it and he growled low in his throat.

The forest hummed with the sounds of stealthy industry as Ragnar's people toiled in the dark making their final preparations for the impending battle.

Kira groaned. Why had it come to this? Why must there be more violence and death? Had the people of this land not suffered enough at the hands of the off-land marauders? Guilt and shame whipped around her. She gripped the top of the wall. It wasn't her fault, she told herself. Toril was a deep dark well that could never be illuminated. He took what was given him, sank it to the bottom of his empty heart, and came back wanting more.

* * *

Dawn spread its light across the land and a swift breeze sent tattered clouds scudding across a pale sky. Few of Tem Hold's residents had slept once word had reached them of the army encamped on the northern fields.

Kira stood atop the wall, girded in leather and light chain mail. She hefted the weight of the short sword Ragnar had gifted her. Her years as a healer's apprentice had not prepared her for war or taking of another's life. Her time with Toril had done nothing to dissuade her that killing was wrong. Yet, here she was, preparing to join her friends on the battlefield. To defend their lives. And her own.

Milos pursed his lips. "I don't want you in the battle."

Kira sheathed her sword. She wanted no part in killing, but she would not remain behind while others protected her. She would fight for her freedom. "You will need Vaith's eyes, and for that you will need me beside you on the field."

"Against a small group and with your companions you are a formidable force, but a battlefield is different."

Kira crossed her arms and frowned, repressing the comment that crouched on the tip of her tongue. She knew that Milos wanted to protect her. As much as she loathed the idea of killing, she needed him to understand she did

248

not want his protection. Not if it meant that others must fight in her stead. "I have the chain mail Master Jarrett provided and the shield and short sword from Ragnar. Just because I do not always carry a warrior's weapon, does not mean I have never learned to wield one." She pushed aside the painful remembrance of those hard lessons at Toril's hands. "And Kelmir will be beside me."

"We will also have need of your healing skills."

"Milvari will take charge of the wounded with Master Jarrett's assistance, and Brilissa and her staff are prepared to do their part."

"Kira, please."

Milos reached out for her and she backed away. "I will not stay behind with the women and children. This is my fight, even more than it is yours."

A horn sounded in the distance and they both turned toward the blaring. Across the flat expanse of frozen ground, a lone horse galloped toward the hold. There appeared to be no rider, but the archers who stood at intervals along the walls threw back their cloaks and reached into their quivers to nock arrows in preparation for an assault.

The horse slowed as it came closer. Something lay slung over the saddle like a sack of grain. The steed stopped and began to graze, cropping the short dry stalks just outside the line of pikes and barriers that now surrounded the hold.

Milos grew pale.

"What is it?" Kira squinted, trying to focus on the distant animal in the early morning light.

"Not what." His voice was gruff. "Who." He climbed down the ladder and headed toward the main gate.

As he strode toward the gate, Milos gave orders to the archers on the wall to stand ready and called for Harl to bring his horse. "I need two men to accompany me," he said.

A short muscular man with gray hair and a grizzled beard approached. "Holder Tem," the man said urgently. "It might be a trap. Allow me to go in your stead. My brothers and I will bring in the horse and its burden."

Milos began to protest, but before he could speak two mounted riders arrived leading a saddled horse. The man mounted his horse without waiting for the holder's response. He gave Milos a crooked smile. "It has been some time since this farmer went to war, but I have not forgotten how to swing a blade."

"Ride in Troka's light," Milos told him before directing the gate to be opened.

The men galloped out of the hold, and the gate swung shut behind them. Kira stayed on the wall, watching the riders leave. They skirted the pikes and spread out in a line. The gray-haired man sidled slowly up to the grazing horse and took hold of the reins that dangled from its neck as the other two men kept watch. He raised the covering from the horse's burden and dropped it again before leading the animal back to the hold.

No riders attacked from Toril's encampment, no arrows flew, and the men returned without incident. Kira held her breath when the gates opened to allow them back inside. With a shake of his head, the gray haired man dismounted and handed the horse's reins to Milos. Kira hurried down the ladder.

Milos lifted the cloak and dropped his head. Jolon hung limp over the saddle, his shirt covered in dark blood. In death, his blond face seemed even younger than his years.

"It seems you were right about trusting him," Milos said. "He is no longer Toril's man."

Kira's throat tightened at the sight of Jolon's broken body. She reproached herself for asking him to go. He had been too eager. Now, one more death was charged to her. She lowered her head and made the sign of the circle. "May Troka gather and keep him."

"Take him to Master Jarrett and Brilissa." Milos laid the cloak back over Jolon and gave the reins to Harl. "Tell them the rites will have to wait until we are finished with this day's sorry work."

Kira watched Harl lead the horse carrying Jolon's body toward the stables and hope waned. "Jolon must have been discovered with the Demon's Claw. It appears we face the full strength of Toril's army."

"It does, indeed," Milos said.

"Then let me go to him," Kira hissed.

"No. This was a clear message. Even if you were to go to him now, he would not be merciful."

Kira opened her mouth to argue, then clamped it shut. Milos was right. Any hope she had harbored that Toril could become the man she had once thought him to be, died when she saw what he had done to Jolon. Mercy was not one of Toril's qualities. Power his only advisor. The flame of anger the only light in the darkness of his heart.

CHAPTER FORTY-FOUR

Mayet sat at the heavily laden table, trying to look alluring despite the dirty rags she wore. Bright pennants fluttered in the brisk morning wind outside the open tent flaps. She had spent a hungry night in a cold cheerless tent and had been brought to the warlord's pavilion this morning without explanation. Her guard pushed her into a chair at the end of the table and stepped back. Hunger scratched at her insides, but she had been offered no food or drink, so she sat in silence.

Across from her, the warlord ate heartily, breaking his fast with mounds of freshly cooked venison, fresh fruits, and dark ale. Mayet's mouth filled with saliva and her nostrils flared wide at the scent of seasoned meat, but she kept herself in check, breathing in a natural way as the muscular man ate his fill, his handsome bearded jaw moving as he chewed.

He glanced up at her, stabbed his knife into the table, and licked his fingers. "You must be hungry."

Mayet tilted her head. "A bit, my Lord."

"Please feel free to partake." He waved his hand over the table. "I would not want you faint on such an important day." His lip curled in a half-smile.

"My thanks to you." Mayet surreptitiously wiped her hands on her skirt before reaching for a plate of meat. She was starved, but she moved casually, doing her best to maintain the manners of a proper lady. There were no utensils set at her place, so she picked up the meat and held it daintily between her fingers. Her stomach urged her to stuff the food quickly into her mouth, but she resisted, taking tiny ladylike bites and chewing them well. No other food, not one delicacy she could recall, had tasted as good as this plain roasted meat now did.

She finished the first piece and reached for another, but the guard stepped from behind and grabbed her by the wrist. Toril's icy blue eyes locked on hers.

"Tell me once more about the hold's defenses," he said quietly.

The guard tightened his grip and Mayet whimpered. "As I told you, they have had little time to prepare. Only what time it took to build the barriers, and not all of those are complete."

"Yes, my spies have told me of the weakness at the southern walls. Strange, one would think that the holder has no knowledge of fighting tactics. Why is that?"

The guard squeezed again. "Ow! Why are you hurting me? I have told you all I know."

"How many men defend the hold and what weapons do they carry?"

"I'm not certain of their number," Mayet gasped. "But they have only bows and swords. Tem Hold has no catapults or other machines of war."

"Tell me again why you sought me out."

Mayet whimpered. "I wish to be your ally. I ask only that you consider allowing my son to take control of Tem Hold and the region surrounding it."

"Yes, but think of my position. You come to me in rags and tell me you are the rightful holder's widow, Lady K'Tem.

You offer me information that I have already gleaned from my spies, and you ask a favor of me in return." Toril stared into her eyes. He sneered at her and held up a fist.

The man dug his fingers deeper into her flesh and Mayet sank down in her chair. There were tears in her eyes. "But what about the traitor? That man Jolon? I warned you about him."

Toril opened his hand. The guard loosened his grip, but his fingers remained wrapped about her wrist.

"Ah, that is true. You did warn me of the rat in my midst." The warlord picked up his knife and toyed with it. The cruel blade glinted as he turned it this way and that, admiring his reflection in the shiny metal surface. "We must remember to show our appreciation to those who aid us, must we not?"

Mayet heard running footsteps outside the tent and a soldier rushed inside. The man knelt quickly and bowed his head. His words came out between panted breaths. "Lord Toril, please forgive the interruption, but I have urgent news."

Toril grasped the knife tightly in his hand and glowered at the man. "What is it?"

"The camp steward sent me. The men, my Lord. They are ill."

"What men? How many?"

The panting man seemed to shrink lower, cringing into himself. "I know not yet how many, Lord. More than a hundred, so far."

Toril stood. His hand moved with the speed of a striking snake and the knife stuck in the ground at scant distance from where the messenger knelt. "Go back and find out how many are ill and from what cause," he roared. "And send me my generals."

"Yes, Lord." The messenger leaped up. Eyes focused on the floor, he backed rapidly out of the tent and disappeared.

Toril whirled about and Mayet felt his eyes burn into her. "What do you know of this?"

Mayet shook her head, but remained silent.

Toril snapped his fingers and the guard who held her slapped her hard across the face. Tears filled her eyes. Her cheek stung and she tasted blood.

"I asked you a question," Toril snarled.

Mayet's lower lip trembled and she swallowed hard. "I—I know nothing of any illness, Lord Toril. I swear it." Her voice was high and squeaky.

"We shall see." He scowled at her, then turned to the guard. "Take her from my sight, but keep a close watch on her. We may need a key to pry open the hold gates."

The guard loosened his grip. "But, Lord," he said. "If she has come here to betray them, of what use will she be?"

He ogled her meaningfully and his lip curled. "Never underestimate the value a man may place on even the lowest of women."

CHAPTER FORTY-FIVE

Archers manned the walls as foot soldiers filed out of the hold to take up positions behind the barriers. Kira had told Milos that Toril would wait until nearly midmorning to assemble his men. He enjoyed the anticipation before the battle, the air of tension that it brought. And he believed that waiting put his enemies on edge.

Tem Hold's riders stood at the ready inside the narrow back gate that faced the forest to the south. Kira stood atop the north wall beside Milos, gazing out over the plain. Vaith perched on her shoulder, his tail wrapped behind her neck. Kelmir sat on his haunches beside them, carefully cleaning his face. Milos had finally given in. When the time came, they would ride out together with the mounted troops.

A shout carried across the yard, relayed by the men on the wall. Toril's men were on the march. Kira stroked the little wyvern's head. *Vaith, it's time. I need to see from above. But stay near. And safe.* Vaith flicked his tail and stepped off her shoulder. He winged his way overhead, circling the hold, his eyes sighting clearly on the wall of riders that galloped toward Tem Hold.

Through Vaith's keen sight Kira watched the soldiers spread out across the horizon like a growing swarm of stinging insects. They stopped just out of bowshot, their horses stamping and throwing their heads about excitedly. Even their mounts seemed impatient for battle.

A lone rider separated himself from the troops. He raised his hand to indicate that he wished to speak, and rode forward at a slow pace. He stopped his horse before the barriers and called out. "Lord Holder, a word."

Milos called down to the man. "I am Holder Tem. To whom do I speak?"

"I am Lord Toril's messenger. He bids you to come to his camp and confer with him."

Milos looked over his shoulder toward Kira. Toril did not negotiate, not when his men heavily outnumbered their enemies. She shook her head. Milos turned his attention back to the man. "I have nothing to say to a man who condones the kidnapping of children and the mistreatment of women."

As he spoke, Vaith continued to circle high above the hold, and Kira tried to count the numbers of opposing men. Their ranks were spread wide, but shallow and she estimated their numbers to be less than half what Jolon and the hold scouts had stated. What did it mean? Hope and fear struggled within her. Had Jolon succeeded in tainting the army's food after all? Or was Toril merely baiting them?

"This will not end well for you," the man shouted. "Why not make a bargain and save your people and your lands? Lord Toril may yet be generous and merciful."

"I have not heard those attributes assigned to the warlord before. Nor do I wish to be beholden to your master. Tell him we are prepared to face him and his army on the field."

"A single woman is not worth all of this," the messenger's voice rose in frustration.

"Does your master know your thoughts?" Milos retorted.

The man shifted uneasily in his saddle. "Have you looked to your own, Lord Holder? There are those of your household that do not agree with you!"

The messenger turned his horse and rode back through the assembled ranks and Kira did not have time to wonder about the meaning of his words. With a thundering of hooves, the mounted troops at each end of the line broke away from the main body and circled around the hold toward the southern wall. Kira stiffened.

The battle had begun.

Kira followed Milos down the ladder to where Trad and Zharik stood waiting. She heard the thud of arrows striking the outer walls and the cries of men wounded or dying. Voices called out atop the walls and the hold's archers let fly their bolts in a whizzing flurry.

Milos leaped onto his horse's back. Vaith circled above the hold. "What do you see?" he asked Kira.

"Less than half of Toril's warriors are on the field. No foot soldiers, but nearly five hundred horsemen. More than two to each of us. I could not see the rest of them."

"We need to find out where they are."

"I can send Vaith, but won't we need him to watch the southern grounds?"

"Send him. I think we'll know when our trap is sprung." Milos gripped his reins and turned to face the riders.

Vaith, I need to see the camp. But stay high and out of danger. I don't want you harmed!

Vaith headed north in a bright flash of sunlight reflecting off glittering scales.

The hold's riders waited restlessly. The thunder of hooves grew louder as Toril's troops closed in, encircling the hold. The staccato galloping grew faster and louder as the soldiers headed toward the weakest point on the hold's defenses, the southern barriers.

258

The ground shuddered and horses screamed in terror. "Now," Milos yelled. "Stay close to the wall till you pass the yellow flags." The narrow gate was thrown open. They made a mad dash out of the portal. Kira rode beside Milos with Kelmir on her flank.

Between the barriers and the forest, a wide chasm had opened in the earth, the bottom lined with wooden spikes. The air filled with yelling and confusion. Toril's men had been drawn into the trap.

Seeking to take advantage of the apparent weakness in the barriers, they had ridden directly across the path of the Uldast gnomes' tunneling. Men and horses writhed in agony or lay twisted and broken in the pit.

The first wave dropped hard onto the spikes. Unable to pull up, the men who rode behind had tumbled over their comrades. Dozens of gnomes came pouring out of the woods bearing axes and staves. They swarmed among the remaining mounted soldiers, tripping horses and pulling men from their saddles. Amidst the chaos and disorder, the hold's riders attacked.

Kira held her shield and sword at the ready, as skirmishes erupted around them. A snarling man charged at her. His horse's eyes went white with pain and fear as Kelmir raked his claws down the animal's shoulder. The horse screamed, skittering sideways. The man's blade swung wide and Kira ducked. Her sword sank into something soft as the man twisted aside. Kelmir leaped and the man was ripped screaming from the saddle.

Milos traded blows with a beefy soldier wearing heavy chain mail. The holder aimed a lunge at the man's chest. His sword glanced off the soldier's mail and Milos lost his balance. He teetered in the saddle and the man raised his sword with a gleeful smirk. But before the soldier could strike, an arrow plunged into his neck, and he fell from the saddle.

The way before them was open and Kira followed Milos past the flags that marked the edge of the gnomes' trap and away from the walls. She tried to keep alert, seeking to stay cognizant of two places, as her mind flitted to where Vaith soared over Toril's encampment. Far below, men lay thrashing on the ground, clutching at their bellies. The Demon's Claw gripped them tight.

Vaith tilted on the wind and circled. At the southern edge of the camp, a group of riders sat watching the battle. In their midst a bronze helm gleamed in the sunlight, a bright red plume jutting from the top. Toril.

The din of battle faded away and, for a moment, Kira heard only the sound of fists hitting flesh. Her jaw tightened and she clenched her teeth as a thousand hurts came welling back. Toril.

Beside Toril's horse a dark-haired woman in a tattered dress struggled between two men. The messenger's words floated back to Kira. "There are those of your household that do not agree with you."

An arrow whizzed past her ear and Kira was wrenched back, fully alert to the fighting around her once more. A bloody hand gripped her leg and tried to pull her from the saddle. A single downward slash severed the man's hand from his arm. He howled in pain and slammed his body against Trad. Kira clutched tight as her horse leaped to the side. She leaned forward and squeezed her knees in hard. Trad whirled about and kicked. Hooves struck flesh and bone and the man went down.

Dried blood stuck to Kira's hands and neck. Bodies littered the ground, men and gnomes and horses. Still, the fighting continued. Kira needed to tell Milos what she had seen. "Milos!"

"Here!" he called from behind her. She turned in time to see the holder pull his sword from a soldier's chest and the man topple from his mount. The horse dashed away from its rider's ruined body.

"Milos." Kira rode up next to him. His face was covered in sweat and blood. His shield arm hung limp at his side. "Are you hurt?"

"My shield was shattered by a heavy blow," he said. "But the bones appear unbroken." He raised his arm and grimaced. There were ugly splinters sticking out of the back of his bloodied hand.

"Vaith has spotted Toril. The rest of his men are still in the encampment. They seem to be ill. Jolon must have managed to slip the Demon's Claw into the food stores before Toril butchered him."

"Good." Milos gave her a hard smile. "At least he did not die in vain."

"There's something else." Kira hesitated.

"Kira, this is a battle. I cannot fight it blind. I need to know everything you saw."

"I think Mayet is with him."

His face paled beneath the spattered blood and he tensed. "How could she—Are you certain?"

"I was distracted by the fighting, but I saw her."

A blaring horn resounded from Toril's encampment. The remaining soldiers whirled their horses around pulled back from the fighting.

"They're retreating," Kira said.

"It will give us time to regroup."

"We have to move quickly. We evened our odds with the gnomes' trap, but if Toril decides to wait until the rest of his men are recovered from the Demon's Claw . . ."

"We will meet him before that comes to pass." Milos called out orders and men and gnomes began to search the field for the wounded and carry them into the hold.

* * *

The bright afternoon turned chill as the late winter wind turned eastward. The hold's remaining horsemen, archers, and footmen assembled in the yard, men and gnomes together. Kira spied Tratine among them. His face was drawn, his cheeks bright red from the bitter wind, but he sat tall and erect in his saddle, his bow at the ready and a full quiver of arrows on his back.

She wanted to ask Milos to make Tratine stay behind, to remain in the hold where he might be safe, but she knew full well that on this day Tratine was no longer a child. With his mother in danger, this was also his fight. She knew as well, that all the hold's able-bodied fighters were preparing to meet the remainder of Toril's army. And if they failed, those who stayed behind would be left to face the Warlord's terrible cruelty. She shivered at the thought.

"Hunter! Kira!" Milvari ran toward her. Her hair had come partly undone from her braids and wisped about her worried face and her skirts were stained with blood.

"What is it, Milvari? How goes the healing?"

"We are doing what we can," Milvari replied breathlessly. Her young face was tight with fear. "Master Jarrett is a great help, as is Brilissa. But we need more hands. I sent Alyn to ask if mother would come and help, but she wasn't in her rooms—"

Milvari's words confirmed what Kira already knew to be true. It was Mayet she had seen with Toril. Pangs of loss from her own mother's death tore at Kira afresh. How much should she say? "Milvari, your uncle and I will find your mother. For now, we need your skills in tending the wounded. You're responsible for them, now."

Milvari's cheeks were white and her eyes glittered with unshed tears.

Kira turned away from the girl as the gates swung open and Tem Hold's small force surged forward. Some of the hold's men wore armor that had been stripped from the bodies of Toril's dead warriors. Blood still caked the leather and steel, dulling the polished surfaces.

Kelmir padded beside Kira. His fur was sprinkled with blood and he shone black-red in the sunlight. Vaith perched on Trad's pommel, resting. Kira had called him back when the retreat had sounded, but now she needed his eyes again. *One more flight, my little princeling,* she coaxed. He tilted his head to one side and eyed her with his yellow orbs, then launched into the wind.

The man who rode on the other side of Kelmir flashed Kira a smile. "He'll be safer in the air," he said, reassuringly. Kira smiled back at him. He believed Vaith to be no more than an unusual pet. There was no point in telling him otherwise.

They halted just beyond the reach of the enemy archers. Milos galloped down the line and she rode to meet him. He had a new shield strapped to his arm, the edge of it resting solidly against his thigh. Kira worried whether or not he would be able heft the heavy circle of wood and iron well enough to protect himself from a quick blade.

Milos followed her gaze. "I will manage," he told her. "Now, let us not give our foe another moment to prepare."

* * *

Arrows flew on both sides. Metal tips thunked deep into wooden shields and sliced through leather armor. Archers aimed high over the heads of their own horsemen, their missiles arcing in the air far above the ground before plummeting down among their enemies.

Riders raced forward, a rumble of thunder beating against the solid ground. The clash of weapons rang in her ears as the two lines met. With Kelmir between them, Kira slashed left and Milos wielded his sword to the right. Guided by Vaith they fought side-by-side, cutting a path through the midst of the battle. Not far ahead, a bright red plume fluttering atop a polished helm marked their goal.

Toril had joined the battle, surrounded by his strongest men. He swung his heavy broadsword with powerful strokes, felling each man touched by his blade. Kira recoiled as Dagger's leering grin loomed suddenly before her. His old scar stood out white against his blood caked face and a new one ran across his other cheek. He sneered at her. "I will end this," he shouted. "By ending you!"

Dagger's blade sliced down and Kira barely had her shield up in time to catch the blow. He expelled his breath in a hiss of rage and swung again. Shards splintered from the shield. He struck again and again. The power of his angry blows sent a blazing pain up her arm. She used her sword arm to help brace the shield against his attack.

Kira gritted her teeth. Her arm was a burning leaden mass. Tears formed in the corners of her eyes. She wondered how long she could stand up against this barrage. Wondered how long her shield would hold. Which would give out first?

Abruptly, the malevolent pounding stopped. Dagger's horse screamed and reared back. The scarred man flailed his arms, trying not to fall as Kelmir swiped again at the horse's hindquarters. Kira backed Trad away from the other animal's thrashing hooves. Dagger lost his grip and flew out of the saddle. His horse reared and, mad with terror and pain, trampled its own rider.

Kira's stomach churned with a mixture of hate and disgust. Shield arm burning, she turned her attention back to the fighting. Around her the last of Toril's main guard fell at the hands of Tem Hold's men. Before her Rasten held three men at bay as Toril turned and galloped back toward camp, his red plume wavering atop his now-dented helm.

She pulled on Trad's reins, pressing in with her knees to urge him after Toril. Milos was immediately at her side. Kelmir loped behind them as they followed the Warlord into the camp. "Where is he heading?" Milos called over the din of clashing swords.

"I don't know," Kira answered. "But I don't think it's a trap. Vaith hasn't seen much movement in the camp since this last affray started."

Kira and Milos raced past rows of tents and the forms of sick men, following close behind the fleeing warlord. Toril yanked his horse to a halt and jumped down. He crashed through the dark opening of a dirty canvas tent. Kira and Milos pulled the horses up outside the tent and dismounted warily, weapons at the ready.

Milos signaled to Kira to move around to the other side of the doorway. She nodded, but before she could move Toril burst through the opening, dragging Mayet with him.

He forced Mayet before him, one arm around her waist and a knife at her throat. "Stay back," he barked.

Mayet struggled against her captor but her hands were bound. She was worn and exhausted, but when her red-rimmed eyes spied Kira, her face turned angry. She tried to lunge at Kira. "Filthy harlot!" she screamed. "This is all your doing!"

Toril pulled her back roughly and she whimpered. "I see you know a kindred spirit when you see her." A tight sneer drew back his lips. A thin red stream trickled down Mayet's neck where the tip of his knife had cut into her flesh.

"Let her go," Milos told him.

Toril sidestepped toward his horse, dragging Mayet with him, his eyes flicked back and forth, finally settling on Kira. "Come home, Kira, my sweet. Come to me and I will let this worthless ragged woman go."

His smile was charming and his voice held the promise of pleasure. Kira knew it was a lie, but Mayet must be saved. Kira took a step forward.

"No," Milos said quietly, stopping Kira. "Let her go and I will grant you safe passage from these lands."

"These lands are mine. I saved them from the marauders." Toril's fingers dug into Mayet's flesh. She let out a small yelp. "I am Lord Toril. I need no favors from a lowly holder." Tears trailed down Mayet's dirty face.

"Toril," Kira said. His eyes slid back to her. "Have you forgotten who you were? What you promised? You were the people's hero. You were my hero." She tried to keep the tremor from her voice. How was it she could have ever felt that way? Bitterness and sorrow shivered inside her.

His expression twisted into a snarl. "It is the people who have forgotten what I did for them." He spat the words at her. "And you. I took you from that hovel. I gave you everything a woman could desire, and you gave me bitterness in return." He yanked his captive closer.

He kept one arm wrapped around Mayet's shoulders, and held the knife blade firmly at her throat. He put his mouth beside her ear. "And this for the rat in my hall." With a swift motion, he pulled the blade across Mayet's throat and shoved her at Milos.

Milos reached out to catch his kinswoman as her body collapsed against him. Toril ripped his sword from its sheath and bore down on Milos. His blade sliced through the air to strike the encumbered holder. Kira thrust outward and caught the blow on her sword. The force of the strike wrenched her arm and seared into her already suffering shoulder. But pain from this man was nothing new to her. She had borne up under seasons of abuse, learned to endure, to hide the hurt. Her blade arm held.

Toril's eyes locked on hers. There was fire in them. Fire filled with destruction. The fire from her dreams.

Toril smiled. Heaving his sword up, he pushed her away. She staggered back. Cold prickles of fear crawled over her. Before her stood the man who had punished her again and again merely to satisfy his own lust for power and control. Behind her, the man she cared for tried to staunch the wound of his kinswoman. The sound of rapid shallow breathing told Kira that Mayet would soon die if her wound was not tended. She stood her ground to keep herself between them and Toril. The icy prickling turned to angry daggers and she squared her shoulders.

Flexing powerful arms, Toril swung his sword. Sunlight glinted on the brutal blade as it arced over Kira. She raised her blade to block the blow. A clatter of hooves sounded behind her as something whizzed past her head.

Toril's eyes went wide as the arrow plunged into his shoulder, and he swayed backward. Then, just as quickly, he regained his balance and raised his sword to strike.

With all her strength Kira thrust her sword into his chest. The blade cut through his leather armor and slid into his flesh as cleanly and easily as butchering a hare.

The twisted fury on his face turned to surprise. He gasped as he fell to his knees. His gaze followed the length of the sword, traveled up her arms and rested on her face. He reached for her and Kira took a step back. He grimaced, slid from her blade, and toppled over. Blood seeped from the wound and flowed across his chest. He coughed, expelling flecks of blood. His fingers trembled, loosening their grip on the sword hilt. The shaft of the arrow quivered in his shoulder, then stilled.

A moment of triumph and relief rose up in Kira, and then rapidly dissolved. Stunned by what she had done, she stood in silence, horrified by how readily she had turned from healer to killer. The sounds of battle swirled and faltered around her. A tremor shook her and she let the bloody sword fall from her hand.

"Mother!" Tratine jumped from his horse, casting aside his bow, and rushed to Mayet's side. He dropped to the ground, kneeling beside her. "Mother!" He pulled her away from Milos and cradled her head to his chest.

The boy's anguished cry brought Kira's head around. Blood from Mayet's neck spilled over Tratine's hands. Her eyes were open, but unable to focus on the boy who held her.

"It was for you," Mayet rasped. "Everything I did."

Kira knelt beside Mayet. She tried to press a hand on the woman's wound, though she could see from Mayet's pallor and the clouding of the dying woman's eyes that it was too late.

With the last of her strength, Mayet pushed Kira's hand away.

CHAPTER FORTY-SIX

Milvari watched as Tratine touched the torch to the pyre. The gnomes had done her great honor. The sturdy scaffold they had built as a bier held her body aloft over the heads of the tallest men in the hold. The dried kindling caught quickly and the flames rose high into the night sky, dimming the stars above. Milvari cried openly. Her mother had rarely given her a kind word, but in her own way Mayet had loved her children. Harl moved closer to Milvari and wrapped his fingers about hers. She grasped his hand in return.

When Uncle Milos told her of his plans to divide a portion of the holding between her and Tratine, Milvari had worried about how she would manage. But Harl had promised to help her and Master Jarrett said he was too old to start a place of his own and would stay on at the main hold with them. "You will want to raise horses and other livestock," he'd said.

"And you'll need a good Stable Master," Harl had put in.

Through the billowing smoke and flame, Tratine gave them a sour look. Milvari remembered her shock when he'd returned from the battle covered in blood. She'd rushed to his side, thinking he'd been hurt, but he brushed her aside and stormed off. Later, he'd accepted their uncle's announcement that the hold should be divided, but he'd done so grudgingly, and he'd made it clear that he disapproved of the growing relationship between his sister and Harl. "That's Mother's intolerance," Milvari had told him. "Now, we must make our lives anew. I will follow my heart and be who I was meant to be."

Tratine had scowled and stalked away.

Milvari stared past the flames at her brother and shook her head. No one could convince him that their mother's death was not the hunter's fault, that Mayet had gone willingly to the warlord in an effort to betray Uncle Milos and the people of Tem Hold.

A log crumbled and fell, sending sparks spiraling into the cold night sky. Milvari shivered and Harl squeezed her hand. She turned to him with a smile, but her eyes returned to her brother. How long would he hold onto his anger?

CHAPTER FORTY-SEVEN

A full moon blushed against the indigo sky as wisps of clouds scudded past. An early spring shower had drizzled throughout the day, leaving the cool night clean and crisp.

Standing at the top of the wall, Kira inhaled the freshness of the night air. It tasted of green buds and the new herbs that grew in the patch of dark soil below. The scent of Milvari's garden reminded Kira of Heresta and the little plot the old healer had tended so carefully.

So much had changed, Kira thought as she stared over the wall at the fields awash in silver light. Across the way, the river rippled the moon's reflection up toward the star-littered sky. Kelmir hunted in the woods while Vaith slept nestled in the pillows on Kira's bed. He'd hardly noticed as she'd left the room, one eye slitting open just far enough to watch her don her cloak.

She shivered in the cool dampness and Milos moved closer. He stood behind her, wrapped his arms about her, and placed his head beside hers, the warmth of his body radiating through her light cloak.

"Kira." His breath warmed her ear as he whispered her name and she turned in his arms. Her lips sought his and a tingling surge fired through her as they kissed. When they separated, she saw the question in his eyes. "Stay with me, with us." His voice was husky with longing.

Kira gently pulled away from him. "Milos—"

He put a finger to her lips. "You don't have to run anymore. You don't have to hide. You can live here at the hold and hunt the woods with Vaith and Kelmir."

Kira searched his face. There was honesty there, and yearning in his eyes. Her body tingled with passion. But was this love? Her time with Toril had taught Kira to mistrust her own heart. She remained silent.

"Does the time we have spent together mean nothing to you?" he asked. His voice rose toward anger.

"It has meant so much. You mean so much to me."

Kira wanted to move away, to put a safe distance between them, so that she wouldn't be tempted by his closeness, drawn to his strength. The wall at her back was cold and unyielding.

"Prove it. Say you will stay."

She stiffened.

He raised his hand to reach for her and she pushed back, flattening herself against the wall. Milos dropped his arm. He shut his eyes and his jaw tightened. "I am not the one you fear."

Kira struggled to keep her pain and longing at bay. Why must he make this so hard? Why couldn't he understand? It wasn't that she wouldn't stay. She couldn't. She had already given up all that she was for a man and had nearly lost all that she might one day be.

He opened his eyes and watched her, his gaze intent as she touched the medallion that now hung from a thin chain around her neck. "I—" she began. She wanted to say yes, to fall into his arms. She wanted to let him be strong for her and protect her. But fear gripped her. No! Not again. She had thought Toril would keep her safe, but he couldn't protect her from himself. She stared up at the stars, her eyes burning. "I'm sorry, Milos. Truly."

"Can you not see that I love you? That I would never hurt you the way that he did?"

Strong emotions tore at her, buffeting her back and forth. It took all her strength not to fall into his arms. But her path lay elsewhere. "You don't understand. As much as I wish for it, as much as I would that it were otherwise, I cannot stay."

"Cannot or will not?"

"I must know who I am," Kira said.

"I can tell you that. You are Kira. Hunter, healer, and the woman who holds my heart." The yearning in his voice was a caressing wind, but Kira still stung with guilt and sorrow.

"I'm sorry," she whispered, "but—"

"But you will not stay." He spat the words as if they tasted of bitterroot.

"I need to know who my mother's people are. Why she never told me about them."

"And then?" he asked, a hopeful timbre in his words.

"And then . . ." Kira paused. There was nothing she would not promise him, if only she knew she could keep her word. But she did not have Heresta's gift of sight, and she had no idea what the future held. "I don't know," she said finally.

Milos turned away from her. He looked out over the fields, his gaze locked on something far away. Suddenly he rounded on her. "Then go, if you must," he said, his voice deep and harsh. "The sooner, the better," he added before storming off.

Kira watched him march away, his shoulders rigid. Then he climbed down the ladder and disappeared from view. She waited as he reappeared and strode across the yard, his boots beating against the ground. As he vanished into the hold, she clutched at the medallion, squeezing it in her fist, as if she could wring the sorrow out of it. She had a powerful urge to rip it from its chain and heave it into the gloom. But she held on, leaning against the wall and letting the sadness drain out of her in aching billows.

By the time she felt the familiar pull of Kelmir's mind, she was spent. The gate watch had grown used to opening the gate for her and allowing Kelmir to enter the hold after his nightly forays into the woods. The watch usually greeted Kira and spoke with her for a few moments, but tonight he watched in silence as the big cat stepped lightly in through the gate. Kira was grateful. She knew the man must have heard her argument with Milos, but he acted as if he had heard nothing.

Kelmir's mind nudged hers, seeking to understand her mood. Kira placed a hand on the big cat's head and rubbed his ears. She searched for thoughts that could convey the nature of her uncertainty and pain to him. If she could find a way to communicate her feelings to Kelmir, she might come to understand them herself. But she could find no words to explain the confusion of whirling emotions that swept across her heart.

CHAPTER FORTY-EIGHT

The kitchen door hung open to let in the cool spring breeze and with it the chattering of birdsong. Kira sat at the table as Brilissa fussed. "I don't know why you have to leave so soon," Brilissa told her, as she selected and wrapped a large quantity of food. "I could use a good hunter this spring. What with all the changes and everyone going off to make their own way, it will be quite lonely here. The only time I'll get to see them all is at the meetings here in the main holding." Brilissa wiped her hands on her apron.

Kira smiled up at the cook. "You know I never intended to stay. Now that the seas are calm, I'll be crossing the Faersent Sea to the western lands." She rubbed her medallion between thumb and forefinger. "Besides, you have Tratine," she said, unable to keep the sadness from her voice. "It seems he spends all of his waking time in the woods now. And he is a fair hunter. He'll keep the kitchen well-supplied." Kira couldn't help but think that Tratine's endless hours of hunting were in part a way to avoid her.

"Oh, that poor boy," Brilissa said. "I just wish he could find some comfort. Seeing his mother murdered by that devil. May Troka's wheel crush him endlessly."

Guilt and anger warred within Kira. Her hands twitched with the urge to make the sign of the circle for Toril's departed spirit. But what blessing could she give him? Toril's death was on her hands. She knew without doubt that he would not have gone away peacefully, that he would have haunted her steps, hunted her down. Had Tratine's arrow not distracted him, Toril, a veteran swordsman, would have bested her in short order. And then he would have made them all suffer. But Kira could not escape from the thought that she had struck him down at that instant of distraction, and in that moment had killed him as much out of hatred as fear.

Kira raised her eyes and Brilissa put a hand to her mouth. "I'm sorry. I did not mean to upset you. It's only that the poor boy is so lost without his mother, such that she was."

"It's all right, Brilissa." Sadness welled up in Kira when she thought about Tratine. She understood his pain and anger. He had lost his mother horribly, and he'd wrapped himself inside his resentment, blaming Kira and Milos for Mayet's death. In the months that had passed since the battle, he had been even more unfriendly than before, blaming her and avoiding her as much as possible. Kira couldn't help feeling that he was right. It was she who had brought Toril's wrath down upon Tem Hold and its people.

"I'm sure Tratine will find his way. Such a deep pain can take a long time to heal," Kira found herself quoting Heresta once more. She hoped her words would help convince herself.

She hugged Brilissa and hefted the heavily laden pack and grunted. "I think you've packed the entire kitchen's stores in here."

Brilissa blushed bright crimson. "It's my job to—"

"Ensure the hold is well-fed." Kira smiled again. "Thank you, Brilissa. I'll miss our morning tea."

Brilissa clutched her apron as Kira left the kitchen.

Trad stood in the yard, patiently nibbling at a shoots of early grass. Kelmir lay nearby, sleeping in the sun, his eyes closed to mere slits.

As Kira heaved the pack onto Trad's back, Vaith flapped his gilded wings and landed on the saddle. He tilted his head to one side and trilled softly.

Harl and Milvari emerged from the stable, deep in conversation. "I quite agree," Milvari said. "And the new stable will have to be large enough to contain a proper drying room for herbs, as well."

They came up beside Kira as she tied the pack down with strong leather laces. "I wish you weren't leaving," Milvari told her. "There's so much more for me to learn."

Kira smiled. Milvari had grown so much in the past few months. She would miss the girl's bright eagerness and quick ability with plants. She hugged her tightly. "You'll have to find other teachers, Milvari. I have taught you all I can."

Harl held out his hand to Kira. In his palm lay a shiny black sliver. "It's the Troll's claw," he said. "I kept it, but I thought you might like it back now."

Kira pressed her lips together. Tears forced themselves into her eyes and she blinked to keep them at bay. "Hold onto it," she told him, her voice thick. "You may find it useful one day."

Harl closed his hand around the shard, a brilliant smile on his face. She gave him a quick hug and looked around. Milos was nowhere in sight. He was clearly still angry with her. Last night she had warred with herself. Part of her wanting to stay with him, the other part knowing she couldn't. She doubted herself, but could not choose otherwise. Her path lay westward, on a journey to find her mother's people, to discover the secret of her lineage.

Kira placed her foot in the stirrup and pulled herself into the saddle. She needed to be off. Ragnar's dwelling lay many hours away, and she had promised to spend the night with the gnomes before traveling on to the coast harbor where she would board a ship and sail across the sea to the land of her mother's kin.

Kelmir yawned and stood, stretching his legs. She clicked her tongue and gave Trad a gentle nudge and the big horse set off across the yard. At the main gate she paused to look back. The midmorning sun shone brightly on the rooftops, casting the place in a warm glow. She would miss Tem Hold and its people.

When she turned back toward the gate, a black and white dappled horse stepped into view. "I bid you good morn, Hunter," Milos said.

Kira sat up straight. Her scalp tingled as she eyed him with suspicion. Zharik was laden with heavy saddlebags and the holder carried a full array of weapons. He was prepared for a lengthy journey.

"Are you traveling today, Holder?" she asked.

"A short distance, perhaps." He gave her a questioning nod.

Kira sat still, considering the tall man before her. She knew he longed to be free of the burden of ruling Tem Hold, knew also that he had been setting things in place for the time when he could pass his duties and responsibilities on to others. But could he truly be willing to leave his home to go with her? Or would he one day change his mind? Change the way that Toril had?

No. Milos was a very different man from what Toril had been. And, she realized with a start, she too had changed. She had been drawn to Toril by her need to feel safe and had stayed with him out of fear. What had grown between her and Milos was something else. It was the drawing together of two people with similar hearts and minds. But would it last?

Another of Heresta's sayings came to her unbidden, and she heard the old healer's voice as the words rose in her mind. *Each and every path in life has its own risks and rewards, but to refuse to make a choice brings nothing but regret.*

Kira nodded once and urged Trad out through the open gate. Milos reined Zharik in beside her. The wind freshened, blowing from the west, as the rest of Heresta's words played out.

And some risks are well worth taking.